Rhode Island

Acts and Laws of His Majesties Colony of Rhode-Island

and Providence-Plantations in America

Rhode Island

Acts and Laws of His Majesties Colony of Rhode-Island
and Providence-Plantations in America

ISBN/EAN: 9783337381400

Printed in Europe, USA, Canada, Australia, Japan

Cover: Foto ©Andreas Hilbeck / pixelio.de

More available books at **www.hansebooks.com**

THE
CHARTER

Granted by His Majesty

King CHARLES
The Second,

TO THE

COLONY

OF

Rhode-Island,

AND

𝕻𝖗𝖔𝖛𝖎𝖉𝖊𝖓𝖈𝖊=𝕻𝖑𝖆𝖓𝖙𝖆𝖙𝖎𝖔𝖓𝖘

In *A M E R I C A.*

B O S T O N, in *N E W-E N G L A N D:*

Printed by *John Allen,* for *Nicholas Boone,* at the Sign of the
B I B L E in *Cornhill.* 1719.

The CHARTER granted by His Majesty KING CHARLES the Second, &c.

CHARLES THE SECOND, By the Grace of GOD, King of *England*, *Scotland*, *France*, and *Ireland*, Defender of the Faith *&c.* TO ALL to whom these Presents shall come, Greeting. Whereas We have been informed by the Humble Petition of our Trusty and well- *The Peti-* beloved Subject, *John Clarke*, on the Behalf of *Benjamin Arnold*, *tioners.* *William Brenton*, *William Coddrington*, *Nicholas Easton*, *William Bolston*, *John Porter*, *John Smith*, *Samuel Gorton*, *John Wicks*, *Roger Williams*, *Thomas Olney*, *Gregory Dexter*, *John Coggeshall*, *Joseph Clarke*, *Randell Holden*, *John Green*, *John Roome*, *Samuel Wilbore*, *William Field*, *James Barker*, *Richard The Petition Tew*, *Thomas Harris*, and *William Dyre*, and the Rest of the Purchasers, and *and Grounds* Free Inhabitants, of our Island-called *RHODE-ISLAND*, and the rest of the *of the Grant.* Colony of *Providence-Plantations*, in the Narrogansett Bay in *New-England* in *America*. That they pursuing with Peaceable and Loyal Minds, their Sober, Serious and Religious intentions, of Godly edifying themselves, and one another in the Holy Christian Faith and Worship, as they were perswaded : together with the gaining over, and Conversion of the poor Ignorant *Indian* Natives in those parts of *America*, to the sincere Profession, and Obedience, of the same Faith and Worship ; did not only by the Consent and good Encouragement, of our Royal Progenators, Transport themselves out of this Kingdom of *England* into *America*. But also since their arrival there, after their first Settlement amongst other our Subjects in those parts, for the avoiding of Discord, and those many Evils which were likely to ensue upon some of those our Subjects, not being able to bear, in those Remote parts, their different Apprehensions in Religious concernments. And in the pursuance of the above-said Ends ; *Did once again*, *Leave* their desirable Stations, and Habitations, and with Excessive Labour and Travel, Hazard and Charge, did Transplant themselves into the midst of the *Indian* Natives. Who as We are informed, are the most Potent Princes, and People of all that Country, *Where by the Good Providence of GOD*, from whom the Plantations hath taken their Name. Upon their Labours, and Industry ; have not only been preserved to Admiration, but have Increased and Prospered, and are Seized, and are Possessed by Purchase, and Consent of the said Natives to their full content, of such *Lands*, *Islands*, *Rivers*, *Harbours*, and *Roads*, as are very convenient, both for Plantations, and also for Building of *Ships*, supply of *Pipe staves*, and other Merchandize, and which lyes very commodious, in many respects for Commerce, and to accommodate our Southern Plantations, & may much Advance the Trade of this our *Realm* ; And greatly enlarge the Territories thereof, They having by near Neighbourhood to, and Friendly Society with the Great Body of the Narrogansett *Indians*, given them Encouragement of their own accord, to Subject themselves, their People and Land unto Us : *Whereby* as is Hoped there may in Time by the Blessing of GOD, upon their Endeavours, be Laid a Sure Foundation of Happiness to all *America*. AND Whereas in their Humble Address, They have Freely Declared, that it is much on their Heart, if they may be permitted to Hold forth a Lively Experiment, That a most Flourishing Civil State, may stand and best be Maintained, and that amongst our English Subjects, With a full Liberty in Religious Concernments ; And that true Piety, Rightly Grounded upon Gospel Principles, will Give the Best and Greatest Security to Soveraignty ; And will lay in the Hearts of Men the Strongest Obligations to true Loyalty. NOW KNOW YEE, That we being Willing to Encourage the Hopeful Undertakings of our said Loyal and Loving Subjects, And to Secure them in the Free Exercise and Enjoyment of all their Civil and Religious Rights Appertaining to them, as our Loving Subjects ; And to Preserve unto them that Liberty in the true Christian Faith and Worship of GOD, Which They have fought with so much Travel, And with Peaceable Minds and Loyal Subjection to Our Royal Progenitors and Our Selves to Enjoy. AND because some of the People and Inhabitants of the same *Colony*, cannot in their private Opinions, Conform to the Publick Exercise of Religion, according to the Liturgy, Forms and Ceremonies of the *Church of England*, or take or Subscribe the

Oathes

Orthes and Articles made and Eftablifhed in that behalf. AND for that the fame by reaſon of the Remote Diſtances of thoſe Places will (as we Hope) be ſto Breach of the Unity and Uniformity Eſtablifhed in this Nation. HAVE THERE- FORE Thought fit, AND DO HEREBY Publifh, Grant, Ordain, and Declare. That Our Royal Will and Pleaſure is, That no Perſon within the ſaid Colony, at any Time hereafter, ſhall be any ways Moleſted, Puniſhed, Diſquieted, or called

The Grant for Liberty of Conſcience. in Queſtion for any Differences in Opinion, in matters of Religion, And do not Actually diſturb the Civil Peace of Our ſaid Colony. But that all and Every Perſon and Perſons, may from time to time, and at all times hereafter, Freely, and Fully, Have and Enjoy, His and Their own Judgments, and Conſcience in matters of Religious Concernments Throughout the Tract of Land hereafter Mentioned ; They Behaving themſelves Peaceably and Quietly, And not Uſing This Liberty to Licentiouſneſs and Prophaneſs ; nor to the Civil Injury, or outward Diſturbance of others. Any Law, Statute, or Clauſe, therein contained, or to be Contained ; Any Uſage or Cuſtome of this Realm to the Contrary thereof in any wiſe notwithſtanding. And that they may be in the betterCapacity toDefend themſelves in their Juſt Rights and liberties, againſt all the Enemys of the Chriſtian Faith, and others in all Reſpects. WEE Have further thought Fit, And at the Humble Petition of the Perſons aforeſaid, Are Graciouſly pleaſed to Declare, That they ſhall Have, and Enjoy, the Benefit of Our Late Act of Indemnity, and Free Perſon, as the reſt of our Subjects in other Our Dominions and Territorys have. AND TO CREATE, And make Them a Body Politick and Corporate, with the Powers, and Priviledges herein after-mentioned. AND accordingly Our Will and Pleaſure is, AND of Our Eſpecial Grace, Certain Knowledge, and meer Motion, WEE Have Ordained, Conſtituted, Declared, and by theſe Preſents, for Us, Our Heirs, and Succeſſors DO Ordain, Conſtitue, and De- clare, That they the ſaid *William Brenton, William Coddrington, Nicholas Eaſton,*

Patentees. *Benadict Arnold, William Rolſton, John Porter, Samuel Gorton, John Smith, John Wicks, Roger Williams, Thomas Olney, Gregory Dexter, John Coggeſhall Joſeph Clarke, Randal Holden, John Green, John Roome, William Dyre, Samuel Wilbore, Richard Tew, William Field, Thomas Harris, James Barker, Rainsborough Williams,* and *John Nixſon.* And all ſuch others as now are, or hereafter ſhall be admitted, and made Free of the Company, and Society, of Our Colony, of *Providence-Planta- tions,* in the *Narroganſett Bay* in *New-England.* Shall be from time to time, and for ever hereafter, Be A BODY CORPORATE and POLITICK in Fact and Name ; By the Name of the GOVERNOUR and Company of the *Engliſh Colony* of RHODE-ISLAND, and *Providence-Plantations,* in *New-England* in *America.* AND that by the ſame Name, They and their Succeſſors, ſhall and may have Perpetual Succeſſion. And ſhall and may be Perſons able and capable in the Law, to Sue and be Sued, to Plead, and be Impleaded ; to Anſwer, and to be An- ſwered unto, to defend, and to be defended, in all and Singular Suits, Cauſes, Quarre's, Matters, Actions and things, of what Kind or Nature ſoever. AND ALSO TO HAVE, Take, Poſſeſs, Acquire, and Purchaſe Lands, Tenaments or Hereditraments, or any Goods or Chattels ; and the ſame to Leaſe, Grant, Demiſe, Aliene, Bargain, Sell and diſpoſe of, at their own will and Pleaſures, as other our Leige People of this Our Realm of *England,* or any Corporation, or

Power to make Common Seal. Body Politick within the ſame may Lawfully do. AND FURTHER That they the ſaid Governour and Company, and their Succeſſors, ſhall and may for ever hereafter have a common Seal to ſerve and uſe for all Matters,Cauſes and Things and Affairs whatſoever, of them and their Succeſſors: And the ſame Seal to Alter, Change, Break and Make New, from time to time at their Will and Pleaſure, as they ſhall think fit. AND FURTHER, We Will and Ordain, And by theſe Preſents, for Us, Our Heirs and Succeſſors. Do Declare and Appoint, that for the Better Ordering and Managing of the Affairs and Bhſineſs of the ſaid Company and their Succeſſors, there ſhall be One GOVERNOUR, One DEPUTY GOVERNOUR, and TEN ASSISTANTS, to be from time to time Conſtituted, Elected and Choſen out of the Free-men of ſaid Company, for the

The Number of Magiſtrates, and their Duties. time being, in ſuch Manner and Form as is here-after in theſe Preſents Ex- preſſed ; Which ſaid Officers, ſhall apply themſelves, to take care for the Beſt diſpoſing and ordering of the General Buſineſs and Affairs of and concerning the Lands and Hereditraments herein after-mentioned ; to be Granted, and the Plantation thereof, And the Government of the People there : AND for the better Execution of Our Royal Pleaſure herein, WE DO, for Us, Our Heirs and

Succeſſors,

Affign, Name, Conftitute and Appoint the aforefaid BENADICT ARNOLD to *N'1 mes of the*
be the firft and Prefent GOVERNOUR of the faid Company, and the faid *juft Magi-*
WILLIAM BRENTON to be the Deputy GOVERNOUR, and the faid *fir ates.*
William Bolfton, *John* Porter, *Roger Williams, Thomas* Olney, *John* Smith, *John*
Green, *John* Coggefhall, *James Barker, William* Field, and *Jofeph Clarke,* to be the
Ten prefent Affiftants of faid Company; to continue in the faid feveral Offices,
Refpectively, until the firft *Wedn fday,* which fhall be in the Month of *May*
now next coming : AND FURTHER, We Will, and by thefe prefents, for Us,
Our Heirs and Succeffors, Do ordain and grant, that the Governour of the faid
Company for the time being, or in his abfence, by occafion of Sicknefs, or other-
wife by the Leave and Permiffion, The Deputy Governour for the time being,
Shall and may from time to time upon all occafions, Give order for the Affem-
bling of the faid Company, and Calling them together, to confult and advife of
the Bufinefs and Affairs of the faid Company. AND THAT FOR EVER here-
after,twice in every year, *That is to fay,* on every firft *Wednefday* in the Month of *Affemblies*
May, and on every laft *Wednefday* in *October,* or oftener, in cafe it fhall be
Requifite, the Affiftants and fuch of the Freemen of the faid Company, not exceeding Six Perfons for *Newport,* four perfons for each of the refpective
Towns of *Providence, Portfmouth,* and *Warwick,* and two perfons, for each other
place, Town or City, who fhall be from time to time thereunto Elected or Deputed by the Major part of the Freemen of the Refpective Towns and places for
which they fhall be fo Elected or Deputed, fhall have a general Meeting or
Affembly, then and there to Confult, Advife and Determine in and about the
affairs and Bufinefs of the faid Company and Plantations. AND FURTHER,
We Do of Our Efpecial Grace, Certain Knowledge, and meer motion,Give and
Grant to the faid Governour and Company, of the *Englifh Colony* of *Rhode-Ifland,*
and *Providence Plantations* in *New-England* in *America,* and their Succeffors ; that
the Governour, or in his abfence, or by His permiffion, the Deputy Governour of
the faid Company for the time being, the Affiftants and fuch of the Freemen of
the faid Company, as fhall be fo as aforefaid Elected or Deputed, or fo many of
them as fhall be prefent at fuch Meeting or Affembly as aforefaid, fhall be called
the General Affembly ; and that they or the greater part of them then prefent,
whereof the Governour, Deputy Governour, and Six of the Affiftants, at leaft   *Number*
to be Seven. Shall Have, and Have hereby Given and Granted unto them, FULL   *Perfons are*
POWER AND AUTHORITY from time to time, and at all times hereafter,   *quifite to be at*
to appoint, alter, and change, fuch Days, Times, and Places of Meeting, and   *an Affembly,*
General Affemblies,as they fhall think fit. And to Choofe, Nominate,and Appoint   *and their*
fuch & fo many other perfons as they fhall think fit,and fhall be willing to accept   *Power.*
the fame, to be free of the faid Company and Body Politick, and them into the
fame to Admit ; AND to Elect, and Conftitute, fuch Officer, and Officers. And
to Grant needful Commiffions as they fhall think fit & requifite for the Ordering,
Managing and Difpatching of the affairs of the faid Governour, and Company, and
their Succeffors. AND from time to time to Make, Ordain, Conftitute or
Repeal fuch Laws, Statutes, Orders and Ordinances, Forms and Ceremonies of
Government and Magiftracy, as to them fhall feem meet for the Good and
Welfare of the faid Company ; and for the Government and Ordering of the
Lands and Hereditraments therein after mentioned to be Granted, and of the
People that Do, or at any time Hereafter fhall Inhabit ; or be within the
fame ; So as fuch Laws, Ordinances and Conftitutions fo made be not contrary
and Repugnant unto, But as near as may, agreeable to the Laws of this Our
Realm of *England,* confidering the Nature and Conftitution of the Place and
People there. AND ALSO to Appoint, Order and Direct, Erect and fettle fuch
Places and Courts of Jurifdiction, for the Hearing and Determining of all Actions,
Cafes, Matters and Things happening within the faid *Colony* and *Plantation,* and
which fhall be in difpute & depending there as they fhall think fit.AND ALSO, to
Diftinguifh and fet forth the feveral Names and Titles, Duties, Powers, and
Limits of each Court, Office, and Officer, Superiour and Inferiour. AND
ALSO, to Contrive and appoint fuch forms of Oaths and Atteftations, nor
Repugnant,but as near as may be agreeable as aforefaid, to the Laws and Statutes
of this Our Realm, as are convenient and requifite ; with Refpect of the Due Ad-
miniftration of Juftice,and Due Execution and Difcharge of all Offices & places of
Truft, by the Perfons that fhall be therein concerned. AND ALSO, to Regulate,   *Laws how*
and order the way and manner of Elections to Offices and Places of Truft, and to   *near the Laws*
B   Prefcribe   *of England.*

Power of the Assemblies to Order Elections. Precribe Limits, and Distinguish the Numbers, and Bounds of all Places, Towns, or Cities within the Limits and Bounds herein after mentioned and not herein particularly Named, Who have or shall have the Power of Electing and Sending of Free-men to the said General Assembly. AND ALSO to Order, Direct and Authorize the Imposing of Lawful and Reasonable Fines, Mulcts, Imprisonments, and Executing other Punishments Pecunary and Corporal upon Offenders and Delinquents, according to the course of other Corporations within this Our Kingdom of *England.*

Power of the Assembly to Pardon and Remit. AND AGAIN to Alter, Revoke, Anull or Pardon, Under their Common Seal, or otherwise, such Fines, Mulcts, Imprisonments, Sentences, Judgements and Condemnations as shall be thought fit; and to Direct, Rule, Order and Dispose of as all other Matters and Things, and particularly that which Relates to the making Purchases of the Native Indians, as to them shall seem meet. WHEREBY our said People and Inhabitants in the said Plantations, may be so Religiously, Peaceably and Civilly Governed, as that by their good Lives and orderly Conversations, they may win and Invite the Native Indians of the Country, to the Knowledge and Obedience of the only true GOD, and Saviour of Man-Kind,

Laws to be Published under the Colony Seal. WILLING, COMMANDING, AND REQUIRING, and by these Presents, for Us, Our Heirs and Successors, Ordaining and Appointing, that all such Laws, Statutes, Orders and Ordinances, Instructions, Impositions and Directions, as shall be so made by the Governour, Deputy Governour, Assistants and Freemen; or such Number of them as aforesaid and published in Writing, under their common Seal; Shall be Carefully and Duly Observed, Kept, Performed and put in Execution, according to the true Intent and Meaning of the same: And these Our Letters Patents, or the Duplicate or Eximplification thereof, Shall be to all and every such Officer, Superiour or Inferiour, from time to time, for the putting of the same Orders, Laws, Statutes, Ordinances, Instructions and Directions, in Due Execution against Us, Our Heirs and Successors, a Sufficient Warrant and Discharge. AND FURTHER, our Will and Pleasure is, and We do hereby for Us, Our Heirs and Successors, Establish and Ordain, that Yearly once in the Year for Ever hereafter; Namely the aforesaid *Wednesday* in *May,* and at the Town of *Newport*; or else-where, if urgent occasion do Require the Governour, Deputy Governour, and Assistants of the said Company, and other Officers of the said Company; or such of them, as the General Assembly shall think fit, shall be in the said General Court or Assembly, to be held from that Day or time, Newly Chosen for the Year Ensuing, by such Greater part of the said Company for the time being, as shall be then and there present: And if it shall happen, that the present Governour, Deputy Governour, and Assistants by these presents appointed, or any such as shall hereafter be Newly Chosen into their Rooms, or any of them, or any other of the Officers of the said Company, shall Dye or be Removed from his or their several Offices or Places before the said General Day of Election, whom We do hereby Declare for any Mislemeanour or Fault, to be Removeable, by the Governour, Assistants and Company, or such greater part of them in any of the said publickCourts to be Assembled as aforesaid.

Provision in case the Governour Die, or be Removed. THAT THEN and in every such Case, it shall and may be Lawful, to and for the said Governour, Deputy Governour, Assistants and Company as aforesaid, or such greater part of them so to be Assembled, as is aforesaid in any of their Assemblies, to proceed to a New Election of one or more of their Company, in the Rooms or Places of such Officer, or Officers so Dying, or Removed, according to their Discretions. AND IMMEDIATELY Upon, and after such Election or Elections made of such Governour, Deputy Governour, Assistant or Assistants, or any other Officer of the said Company in Manner and Form aforesaid THE AUTHORITY, Office and Powers before Given to the former Governour, Deputy Governour, and other Officer and Officers so Removed, in whose Stead and Place New shall be Chosen, shall as to him and them, and every of them Respectively Ceafe and Determine. PROVIDED ALLWAYS, and our Will and Pleasure is, that as well such as are by these Presents Appointed to be the present Governour, Deputy Governour, and Assistants, of the said Company, or those that shall Succeed them, and all other Officers to be appointed and Chosen as aforesaid, shall before the undertaking the Execution of the said Offices and Places Respectively give their Solemn ENGAGEMENTS by Oath, or otherwise, for the due and faithful Performance of their Duties in their several Offices & Places, before such Person or Persons as are by these hereafter appointed to take and receive the same (that is to say) the said *Benadict Arnold,* who is herein

before

before Nominated and appointed, the Present Governour of the said Company, *Who shall give and take the Engagement,* shall give the aforesaid Engagement before *William Brenton,* or any two of the said Assistants of the said Company, unto whom We do by these Presents Give full Power, and Authority, to Require and Receive the same: AND the said *William Brenton,* who is hereby before Nominated and Appointed the Present Deputy Governour of the said Company; shall give the aforesaid Engagement before the said *Benadict Arnold,* or any two of the Assistants of the said Company, unto whom We do by these Presents, give full Power and Authority to Require and Receive the same; AND the said *William Bolston,* *John Porter,* *Roger Williams,* *Thomas Olney,* *John Smith,* *John Green,* *John Coggeshall,* *James Barker,* *William Field,* and *Joseph Clark,* who are herein before Nominated and Appointed the Present Assistants of the said Company; shall give the said Engagement to their Offices, and Places Respectively belonging, before the said *Benadict Arnold,* and *William Brenton,* or one of them : to whom Respectively We do hereby give full Power and Authority to Require and Administer or Receive the same : AND FURTHER, Our Will and Pleasure is, That all & every other future Governour, or Deputy Governour to be Elected & Chosen by virtue of these Presents, shall give the said Engagement before two or more of the said Assistants of the said Company for the time being, unto whom We do by these Presents, give full Power and Authority to Require, Administer or Receive the same. AND the said Assistants, and every of them, and every other Officer or Officers to be hereafter Elected and Chosen by virtue of these Presents, from time to time, shall give the Like Engagement to their Offices and Places Respectively Belonging, before the Governour, or Deputy Governour for the time being; unto which said Governour, or Deputy Governour, We do by these Presents give full Power and Authority to Require, Administer or Receive the same accordingly : AND WE do Likewise for Us, Our Heirs and Successors, give and Grant unto the said Governour and Company, and their Successors by these Presents, that for the more peaceable and orderly Government of the said Plantations, it shall and may be Lawful for the Governour, Deputy Governour, Assistants, and all other Officers and Ministers of the said Company, in the Administration of Justice, and Exercise of Government in the said Plantations, to Use Exercise and Put in Execution such Methods, Rules Orders and Directions, not being Contrary or Repugnant to the Laws and Statutes of this our Realm, as have been heretofore Given, Used and Accustomed in such Cases respectivly, to be put in Practice, until at the next or some other General Assembly, special provision shall be made, and ordained in the case aforesaid : AND WE do further, for Us Our Heirs and Successors, Give and Grant unto the said Governour and Company, & their Successors by these Presents: THAT IT it shall and may be Lawful to and for the said Governour, or in his Absence, *Power of the Governour and Council to appoint Commission Officers for the Militia.* the Deputy Governour, and Major part of the said Assistants, for the time being, at any time when the said General Assembly is not Sitting to Nominate, Appoint & Constitute such and so many Commanders, Governours, and Millitary Officers as to them shall seem Requisite for the Leading, Conducting and Training up the Inhabitants of said Plantations in Martial Affairs; & for the Defence and Safeguard of the said Plantations : AND that it shall and may be Lawful, to and for all and every such Commander, Governour and Millitary Officers that shall be So as aforesaid, or by the Governour, or in his Absence the Deputy Governour, and Six of the said Assistants, and Major part of the Freemen of the said Company present at any General Assembly; Nominated, and Appointed and Constituted according to the Tenor of his and their Respective Commissions, and Directions ; To Assemble, *Power as to making War;* Exercise in Arms, Martial Array, and put in Warlike Posture the Inhabitants of said Colony for their Special Defence and Safety ; AND to Lead and Conduct the said Inhabitants, and to Encounter, Expulse, Expel and Resist by force of Arms, as well by Sea as by Land ; and also to Kill, Slay and Destroy by all fitting ways, Enterprizes and means whatsoever, all and Every such Person and Persons, as shall at any time hereafter Attempt or Enterprize the Destruction, Invasion, Detriment or Annoyance of the said Inhabitants or Plantations; AND to Use and Exercise the Law Martial in such Cases only as Occasion shall Necessarily Require: AND to take or Surprize by all ways and means whatsoever, all and every such Person or Persons, with their Ship or Ships, Armour, Ammuniton or other Goods of such Persons as shall in Hostile manner Invade or Attempt the Defeating of the said Plantations, or the Hurt of said Company and Inhabitants ; AND upon Just Causes to Invade and Destroy the Native Indians, or other Enemies of said Colony. *Liberty to destroy the Indians.*

NE-

NEVERTHELESS Our Will and Pleafure is, and We do hereby Declare to the Reft of our Colonies in *New-England*, that it fhall not be Lawful for this our faid Colony of *Rhode-Ifland* and *Providence-Plantations* in *America* in *New England*, to Invade the Natives Inhabiting within the Bounds and Limits of their faid Colonies, without the Knowledge and Confent of the faid other Colonies.

Not to Invade the Indians of another Colony, nor another Colonies to Invade the Indians of this Colony. AND IT IS HEREBY DECLARED, that it fhall not be Lawful to or for the reft of the Colonies, to Invade or Moleft the Native Indians, or any other Inhabitant, Inhabiting within the Bounds and Limits hereafter mentioned ; they having Subjected themfelves unto Us, and being by Us Taken into Our Special Protection, without the Knowledge and Confent of the Governour, and Company of Our Colony of *Rhode-Ifland* and *Providence-Plantations*. ALSO OUR WILL and Pleafure is, and We do hereby Declare unto all Chriftian Kings, Princes, and States, that if any perfon which fhall hereafter be of the faid Company or Plantations, or any other by Appointment of the faid Governour and Company for the time being, fhall at any time, or times hereafter Rob or Spoil by Sea or Land, or Do any Hurt or Unlawful Hoftility to any of the Subjects of Us Our Heirs or Succeffors ; or any of the Subjects of any Prince or State being then in League with Us, Our Heirs or Succeffors ; upon Complaint of fuch Injury done to any fuch Prince or State, or their Subjects : We, Our Heirs or Succeffors will make open Proclamation within any part of our Realm of *England*, fit for that purpofe, the Perfon or Perfons committing any fuch Robbery or Spoil, fhall within the time Limited by fuch Proclamation, make full Reftitution or Satisfaction of all fuch Injuries done or Committed, fo as the faid Prince or others fo Complaining, may be fully Satisfyed and Contented , AND if the faid perfon or perfons who fhall Commit any fuch Robbery or Spoil, fhall not make Satisfaction accordingly, within fuch time fo to be Limited, that then We our Heirs and Succeffors, will put fuch perfon or perfons out of our Allegiance and Protection ; and that then it fhall and may be lawful and free for all Princes or others, to Profecute with Hoftility fuch offenders, and every of them, their and every of their Procurers, Aiders, Abettors and Counfellers in that behalf. PROVIDED ALLSO, and our Exprefs Will and Pleafure is, and We do by thefe Prefents for Us Our Heirs and Succeffors, Ordain and Appoint, that thefe Prefents fhall not in any manner, hinder any of our Loving Subjects whatfoever from Ufing and Exercifing the Trade of Fifhing upon the Coaft of *New-England* in *America* ; But that they, and

Liberty of Fifhing. every, or any of them fhall have full and free power and liberty to Continue and Ufe the Trade of Fifhing upon the faid Coafts in any of the Seas thereunto Adjoining, or any Armes of the Seas, or Salt Water, Rivers and Creeks where they have been accuftomed to Fifh ; and to Build and Set upon the Waft-Land belonging to the faid Colony & Plantations, fuch Wharfs Stages and Work-Houfes as fhall be neceffary for the Salting, Drying and Keeping of their Fifh to be taken or gotten upon that Coaft : AND FURTHER, for the Encouragement of the Inhabitants of our faid Colony of *Providence-Plantations* to Sett upon the Bufinefs of takeing Whales ; it fhall be Lawful for them, or any of them, having Struck a Whale, Dubertus, or other great Fifh, it or them to Purfue into any part of that Coaft, or into any Bay upon the faid Coaft, or in the faid Bay, River, Cove, Creek or Shoar belonging thereunto, and it or them to Kill and order for the beft Advantage, without Moleftation, they making no wilful wafte or fpoil of any thing in thefe prefents contained, or any other matter or thing to the contrary notwith-ftanding ; AND FURTHER ALSO We are gracioufly pleafed, and Do Hereby

Liberty as to Wines. declare, that if any of the Inhabitants of our faid Colony, do lett upon the Planting of Vineyards, the Soil and Climate both feeming Naturally to concurr to the Production of Wines, or be induftrious in the Difcovery of Fifhing Banks in or about the faid Colony, We will from time to time give and allow all due and fittnig Encouragement therein, as to others in cafes of like Nature. AND FURTHER, OF OUR MORE AMPLE GRACE, Certain Knowledge and meer Motion, We have Given and Granted, and by thefe Prefents, for Us Our Heirs and Succeffors, do Give and Grant unto the faid Governour and Company of the *Englifh* Colony of *Rhode-Ifland* and *Providence-Plantatons* in the Narra-ganfet Bay in *New-England* in *America* ; and to every Inhabitant there, and to

Liberty to Tranfport Perfons. every, Perfon and Perfons Trading thither, and to every fuch Perfon or Perfons as are, or fhall be free of the faid Colony, full Power and Authority from time to time, and at all times hereafter to take Ship, Tranfport and carry away,

away out of any of Our Realms and Dominions, for and towards the Plantation and Defence of the said Colony, such and so many of our Loving Subjects, and Strangers, as shall and will willingly accompany them in, and to their said Colony and Plantation; except such Person or Persons, as are, or shall be therein Restrained by Us, Our Heirs and Successors, or any Law or Statute of this Realm. AND ALSO to Ship and Transport all, and all manner of Goods, Chattels, Merchandizes, and other things whatsoever, that are, or shall be useful or necessary for the said Plantations, and Defence thereof, and usually Transported, and not Prohibited by any Law or Statute of this our Realm; yielding and paying unto Us, Our Heirs and Successors, such the Duties, Customs and Subsidies, as are, and ought to be paid, or payable for the same: AND FURTHER, OUR WILL AND PLEASURE IS, and We do for Us, our Heirs and Successors, Ordain, Declare and Grant unto the said Governour and Company, and their Successors, that all and every the Subjects of our Heirs and Successors, which are already Planted and Settled within our said Colony of *Providence-Plantations*; or which shall hereafter go to Inhabit within the said Colony, and all and every of their Children which have been Born there, or which happen hereafter to be Born there, or on the Sea going thither, or returning from thence, shall have and enjoy all Liberties and Immunities of free and natural Subjects, within any the Dominions of Us, our Heirs or Successors, to all Intents; Constructions and Purposes whatsoever, as if they, and every of them were Born within the Realm of *England.* AND FURTHER KNOW YE, that We of our more abundant Grace, certain Knowledge, and meer Motion, have given, granted, and confirmed; and by these Presents, for us, our Heirs and Successors, do give, grant and confirm unto the said Governour and Company, and their Successors, ALL THAT PART OF OUR DOMINIONS in *New-England,* in *America*; Containing the *Nahantick* and *Nauhygaufett,* alias, *Narraganfet-Bay,* and Countries and Ports adjacent; Bounded on the West, or Westerly to the middle or Channel of a River, there commonly called, and known by the name of *Patatncke,* alias, *Pawcamtuck* River, and so along the said River, as the greater or middle Stream thereof reacheth, or lies up into the *North* Country, Northward unto the head thereof, and from thence by a Strait Line, drawn due, *North,* until it meet with the South Line of the *Maffachufetts-Colony*: AND on the North or Northerly, by the aforesaid *South* or *Southerly* Line of the *Maffachufetts-Colony,* or Plantation, and Extending toward the East, or Easterly, three *Englifh* Miles to the East North-East, of the moft Eaftern and Northern parts of the aforesaid *Narraganfet Bay,* as the faid Bay lieth or extendeth it felf from the Ocean, on the South or Southerly, unto the mouth of the River which runneth towards the Town of *Providence,* and from thence along the Eafterly fide or Bank of the faid River higher, called by the name of *Seconk* River, up to the Falls, called *Patruckett* Falls, being the moft Wefterly Line of *Plimonth* Colony, and fo from the faid Falls in a ftraight Line due North, until it meet with the aforefaid Line of the *Maffachufetts-Colony*; and bounded on the South by the Ocean, and in particular the lands belonging to the Towns of *Providence, Pawtuxket, Warwick, Mfquomicuck,* alias, *Pawcatuck,* and the reft upon the Mainland, in the Tract aforefaid; together with *Rhode-Ifland, Block Ifland,* and all the reft of the Iflands and Banks in the *Narraganfet-Bay,* and bordering upon the Coaft of the Tract aforefaid; (*Fifhers-Ifland* only excepted) Together with all firm Lands, Soils, Grounds, Havens, Ports, Rivers, Waters, Fifhings, Mines Royal, and all other Mines, Minerals, Precious Stones, Quarries, Woods, Wood Grounds, Rocks, Slates, and all and fingular other Commodities, Jurifdictions, Royalties, Privileges, Erranchifes, Preheminencies, and Hereditaments whatfoever, within the faid Tract, Bounds, Lands and Iflands aforefaid; or to them, or any of them belonging, or in any wife appertaining: To have and to hold the fame unto the faid Governour and Company, and their Succeffors, for ever upon truft, for the ufe and benefit of themfelves, and their Affociates, Freemen of the faid Colony, and their Heirs and Affigns: To be holden of us, our Heirs and Succeffors, as of the manner of *Eaft Greenwich* in our County of *Kent,* in free and common Soccage, and not in *Capite,* nor by Knights Service, yielding and paying therefore unto us, our Heirs and Succeffors, only the fifth part of all the Oir of Gold and Silver, which from time to time, and at all times hereafter fhall be there gotten, had or obtained, in lieu and fatisfaction of all Services, Duties, Fines,

Liberty to Tranfport Goods,

Claufe of Denization.

Bounds of the Colony.

Weftern Bounds.

Eafterly Bounds.

Northern Bounds.

General Grant of all the Commodities, and Minerals, &c.

To have and to hold.

Forfeitures;

Forfeitures made, or to be made, Claims, Demands whatfoever, to be to us, our Heirs or Succeffors; therefore or there out rendered, made or paid: ANY GRANT or Claufe in a late Grant to the Governour, and Company of *Connecticut* Colony in *America*, to the contrary thereof, in any wife notwithftanding: The aforefaid *Pawcatuck* River having been yielded after much debate, for the fixed and certain Bounds between thefe our faid Colonies, by the Agents thereof;

The Narraganfet River ftated. who have alfo agreed, that the faid *Pawcatuck* River fhall be alfo called *alias Narraganfet* River; and to prevent future Difputes that otherwife might arife for ever hereafter, fhall be Conftrued, Deemed and Taken to be the *Narraganfet* River, in our late Grant to *Connecticut* Colony mentioned as the Eafterly bounds of that Colony. AND FURTHER, Our Will and Pleafure is, that in all Matters of Publick Controverfie which may fall out between our Colony of *Providence Plantations*, and the reft of our Colonies in *New-England*; It fhall and may be lawful, to and for the Governour and Company of the faid Colony of *Provi-*

Power of Appeals. *dence-Plantations*, to make their Appeals therein, to us, our Heirs and Succ. ffors, for Redrefs in fuch Cafes, within this our Realm of *England*. AND that it fhall be lawful, to and for the Inhabitants of the faid Colony of *Providence-Plantations*, without Lett or Moleftation, to Pafs and Repafs with freedom into and through the reft of the *Englifh* Colonies, upon their lawful and civil Occafions;

Free Trade with other Colonies. and to Converfe and hold Commerce and Trade with fuch of the Inhabitants of our other *Englifh* Colonies, as fhall be willing to admit them thereunto; they behaving themfelves peaceably among them: Any Act, Claufe or Sentence in any of the faid Colonies provided, or that fhall be provided to the contrary in any wife notwithftanding. AND Laftly, We do, for Us, Our Heirs and Succeffors, Ordain and Grant unto the faid Governour and Company, and their Succeffors by thefe Prefents, That thefe our Letters, Pattents, fhall be firm, good, effectual, and available in all things in the Law, to all Intents, Conftructions and Purpofes whatfoever, according to our true intent and meaning herein before Declared; And fhall be conftrued, reputed and adjudged in all cafes moft favourable on the behalf, and for the beft benefit and behoof of the faid Governour and Company, and their Succeffors; although exprefs mention of the true yearly Value, or certainty of the Premifes, or of any of them, or of any other Gifts or Grants by us, or by any of our Progenitors or Predeceffors heretofore made to the faid Governour and Company of the *Englifh* Colony of *Rhode-Ifland* and *Providence-Plantations* in the *Narraganfett-Bay* in *New-England*, in *America*, in thefe Prefents is not made, or any Statute, Act, Ordinance, Proclamation or Reftriction heretofore Had, Made, Enacted, Ordained or Provided, or any other Matter, Claufe or Thing whatfoever to the contrary thereof in any wife notwithftanding. In Witnefs whereof, we have caufed thefe our Letters to be made Pattents. WITNESS Our Self at *Weftminfter*, the Eighth Day of *July*, in the Fifteenth Year of Our Reign.

By the King,

Howard.

ACTS
AND
LAWS,
Of His Majesties
COLONY
OF
Rhode-Island,
AND
𝔓𝔯𝔬𝔳𝔦𝔡𝔢𝔫𝔠𝔢=𝔓𝔩𝔞𝔫𝔱𝔞𝔱𝔦𝔬𝔫𝔰
IN
AMERICA.

BOSTON, in *NEW ENGLAND:*
Printed by *John Allen*, for *Nicholas Boone*, at the Sign of the
BIBLE in *Cornhill*. 1719.

LAWS

Made and Past by the General Affembly of His Majefties Colony of *Rhode-Ifland.* and *Providence-Plantations* in *New-England.* Begun and Held at *Newport,* the firft day of *March* 1663.

AN ACT Regulating the Election of General Officers.

BE IT ENACTED, *by the General Affembly of this Colony, and by the Authority of the fame, and it is hereby Enacted,* That all perfons what- *Who fhall Vote at General* foever, that are Inhabitants within this Colony, and Admitted Free- *Elections.* men of the fame, fhall and may have liberty to Vote for the Electing of all the *The time when* General Officers in this Colony, either in Perfon, or by Proxy, upon the firft *Elected.* Wednefday of *May* Annually, as is Exprefs'd in our Charter.

AND, *Be it further Enacted by the Authority aforefaid,* That on the firft Wednefday of *May* Annually, there fhall be Chofen and Elected, one General Recorder, who fhall be Secretary of the Colony, one Sherift, who fhall have *General Re-* the Care and Cuftody of His Majefties Goal in *Newport,* one General Attorney, *corder, Sheriff,* and one General Treafurer ; for the better regulating and managing the *Attorney-Ge-* Affairs of the Government, and fhall be Chofen in manner as aforefaid. *neral. & General Treafu-*

AND that each and every Perfon that fhall vote by Proxy, fhall on the *rer appointed.* Town-Meeting Day next preceeding the General Election, openly in faid *Proxy Votes* Meeting, deliver in his Votes to the Town Clerk of the Town wherein he *how taken.* dwells,with his name written at length on the backfide or the bottom thereof; which Votes fo taken, fhall be immediately fealed up by the Town Clerk, *And return'd* and by him delivered either to an Affiftant, Juftice, Warden or Deputy of *to the Affem-* faid Town, as fhall be by the faid Town Meeting appointed for the fame ; by *bly.* him to be delivered to the Governour, or Deputy Governour in Open Court, before the Election proceed.

AND, *Be it further Enacted by the Authority aforefaid,* That all General *General Of-* Officers fhall take the following Engagement, before they fhall Act in *ficers to be En-gaged.* their refpective Offices.

YOU A. B. are by the free Vote of the Free-men of this Colony of Rhode- *The Form of* Ifland, and Providence-Plantations, Elected unto the Place of *the Engage-* in this faid Colony, AND Do folemnly Engage true Allegiance unto His Majefty, *ment.* His Heirs and Succeffors to bear, and in your faid Office, Equal Juftice to do, unto all Perfons, Poor and Rich within this Jurifdiction, to the utmoft of your Skill and Ability; without Partiality, according to the Laws Eftablifhed; or that fhall be Eftablifhed according to our Charter, as well in Matters Millitary as Civil. And this Engagement You make and give upon the Peril of the Penalty of Perjury.

The Reciprocal Engagement.

I Do in the Name and behalf of this Colony, Reingage to ftand by YOU and to fupport you by all due affiftance and Encouragement in your Perjormance and Execution of your aforefaid Office, according to your Engagement.

AND be it further Enacted by the Authoriy aforefaid, That no Perfon fhall be

D   Elected

None but Free-men and Free-holders to be Deputies.

Elected to the Place of a Deputy to fit in the General Affembly of this Colony, but thofe that are Free-holders therein, and Free-men of the fame ; And that each refpective Town in this Colony, fhall Chufe and Elect their Number of Deputies as Stated in the Charter, at their refpective Town Meetings next preceeding fuch Court of Affembly, for the which they fhall be Elected. And that the Town Clerk of each refpective Town fhall grant forth his Warrant to the Town Sergeant or Conftable of faid Town, to warn fuch Deputies as fhall from time to time be Chofen in each refpective Town,

What time the Deputy fhall be Elected. And how returned to the Affembly.

to attend the Affemblies for which they are Chofen ; and alfo the Town Clerk fhall make return of fuch Deputy Chofen as aforefaid to the General Recorder for the time being, on the firft opening of the Affembly ; who is hereby appointed Clerk of the fame.

On Urgent Occafion the Governour, or Deputy-Governour to Call the Affembly.

And be it Enacted by the Authority aforefaid, That when and fo often as any Emergent occafions fhall rquire an Affembly to be called at any other times then is Exprefly mentioned in the Charter, that then and in fuch Cafes, the Governour, and in his abfence the Deputy Governour, fhall, and they are hereby fully Authorized and Impowered, to Grant forth a Warrant to the Sheriff, to warn and require the Free-men of each refpective Town in the Colony, to Chufe and Elect their Refpective Number of Deputies as aforefaid, to fuch Court as by the Governour, or Deputy Governours Warrapt fhall be Directed ; their Notification and Return to be in manner as aforefaid.

Deputies paid Three Shillings per Diem.

And be it Enacted by the Authority aforefaid, That Each refpective Town fhall Pay unto their Deputies, three Shillings *per Diem* each, during their attendauce on the Court of Affembly.

Deputies fined for neglect of Attending the Affembly, Six Shillings per Diem.

And be it Enacted by the Authority aforefaid, That whofoever fhall be Chofen a Deputy for any Town, to ferve in the General Affembly, and being Legally warn'd to attend the fame ; fhall neglect or refufe to give his attendance during the Seffion thereof, fhall pay as a Fine, Six Shillings *per Diem* for each and every Days neglect, into the Town Treafury of fuch Town, to and for the Ufe of faid Town. And if the Perfon fo Offending, fhall neglect or refufe to pay the fame as aforefaid : Then any one of the Affiftants, Juftices of the Peace, or Wardens of fuch Town fhall Grant forth a Warrant to a Conftable of faid Town, to diftrain fo much ot the Perfonal Eftate of fuch Offender, as will pay the aforefaid Fine, and all reafonable Charges accruing thereon ; and the Fine fo taken, to be difpofed of as afore-

How recovered and difpofed of.

faid, and the Clerk of the Affembly fhall return to each refpective Town a Lift of all fuch as fhall be Delinquent as aforefaid.

And be it further Enacted by the Authority aforefaid, That every Perfon, that fhall be Elected to the place of a Deputy fhall take the following Engagement before he fhall act therein.

Form of Deputies Engagement.

YOU A. B. *Being Chofen to the place of Deputy, to fit in the General Affembly,* [Do *as in the Prefence of GOD*] *folemnly Engage true Allegiance to His Majefty His Heirs and Succeffors to bear, as alfo Fidelity to this His Majefties Colony of* Rhode-Ifland, *and* Providence-Plantations, *and the Authority therein Eftablifhed according to our Charter ;* AND YOU *do further Engage Equal Right and Juftice to do to all Perfons as fhall Appeal unto YOU for your Judgement in their refpective Cafes. And this Engagement YOU make and Give upon the Peril of the Penalty of Perjury.*

AN

An Act for Declaring the Rights and Priviledges of His Majesties Subjects within this Colony.

BE IT EN-ACTED *By the General Assembly of this Colony, And by the Authority of the same it is hereby Enacted,* That no Free-man shall be Taken or Imprisoned, or be deprived of his Free-hold, or Liberty, or Free Customs, or Out-Lawed, or Exiled or otherways Destroyed, nor shall be passed upon, Judged or Condemned, but by the Lawful Judgement of his Peers, or by the Law of this Colony; And that no Aid, Tax, Tailage, or Custom, Loan, Benevolence, Gift, Excise, Duty or Imposition whatsoever, shall be Laid, Assessed, Imposed, Levied or Required of or on any of His Majesties Subjects within this Colony, or upon their Estates, upon any manner of Pretence or Colour whatsoever, but by the Act and Assent of the General Assembly of this Colony.

No Free-men to be Impri-soned, or de-prived of his Liberty, &c. But by his Peers, &c. No Tax or Duty to be raised, but by the General Assembly.

AND that no Man, of what Estate and Condition soever, shall be put out of his Lands and Tenements, nor Taken, nor Imprisoned, nor Disinheretd, nor Banished, nor any ways Destroyed, nor Molested, without being for it brought to Answer by due course of Law; And that all Rights and Priviledges Granted to this Colony by His Majesties Charter, be entirely kept and preserved to all His Majesties Subjects residing, in or belonging to the same; And that all Men Professing Christianity, and of Competent Estates, and of Civil Conversa-tion, who acknowledge, and are Obedient to the Civil Magistrate, though of different Judgmnts in Religious Affairs (Roman Catholicks only excepted) shall be admited Free-men, And shall have Liberty to Chuse and be Chosen Officers in the Colony both Millitary and Civil.

No Person to be Deseised of his Lands, otherwise mo-lested, but by due Course of Law. All Persons of Estates, and Obedient to the Magi-strate, to have liberty to E-lect, and be Elected in Offices.

An Act for the Preventing of Illegal and Clandestine Purchases of the Native Indians in this Colony.

FOR ASMUCH *as divers Persons have made Purchases of Lands in this Colony of the* Indians, *without the consent or approbation of the General Assembly, which manifestly tends to the Defrauding and Manifest Injury of such* Native Indians, *as well as defeating the Just Rights of this Colony.*

All Purchases of the Natives without the consent of the Assembly, to be void.

BE It therefore Enacted by the General Assembly, *and the* Authority of the same, That no Person, or Persons for the future, shall Purchase any Lands or Islands within this Colony, of or from the Native *Indians* within the same, but such only as are so allowed to do by the General Assembly, upon Penalty of for-feiting all such Lands or Islands so purchased, to this Colony; And to Pay for every such Purchase by them so made, the Sum of Twenty Pounds as a Fine, to and for the Use of the Colony; And all such Purchases shall be Esteemed and Adjudged Null, Void, and of none Effect.

And the Per-son purchasing to be fined.

An

An Act for Punishing Criminal Offences.

BE it *Enacted by the General Assembly, and by the Authority of the same,* That no Person shall presume to take upon him, or to Exercise (or Officiate in) any Office or place of Authority : And in case any Person shall presume so to do, and be thereof lawfully convicted in any Court of Record in this Colony, That then such Offender shall be Amerced according to the Discretion of such Court, not exceeding the Sum of Ten Pounds ; And on default of Payment of the same, to be Corporally Punished, at the Discretion of the said Court.

Whosoever shall take upon him any Place in Authority, shall re fined Ten Pounds.

AND for that Respect and Obedience that is due from Inferiours to their Superiours.

Be it further *Enacted by the Authority of the same,* That if any Person shall Threaten, Assault, Strike, Abuse or refuse to Obey any General Officer, Justice of the Peace, or Warden, or any other Officer in this Colony, in the Execution of his Office, such Offender or Offenders being duly convicted thereof before any Judge, or Court of Record within this Colony, shall be Amerced as such Judge or Court of Record shall think fit, or shall be Corporally Punished at their Discretion, according to the Nature of the Offence.

Whosoever shall strike, abuse, or refuse to obey an Officer, to be fined, or punished Corporally.

AND be it further Enacted by the Authority aforesaid, That if any Child or Servant, shall contrary to their Obedience due to their Parents, or Masters, Resist, or refuse to Obey their lawful commands, they shall be sent to the House of Correction, and there to remain, until they have Humbled Themselves to their Parents or Masters Satisfaction ; AND if any Children or Servants, shall presume to Assault, or Strike their Parents, or Masters ; upon Complaint of any such Parent or Master to any Assistant, Justice of the Peace, or Warden of such Town : Such Child or Servant so Offending, shall be Whipped, at the Discretion of such Assistant, Justice or Warden, not Exceeding Ten Lashes.

Disobedient Children and Servants to be sent to the House of Correction.

And those that strike their Parents, &c. to be whipp'd.

AND be it further Enacted by the Authority aforesaid; and it is hereby Enacted, That whosoever shall be Convicted of High Treason, Petit Treason, Wilful Murder, or Man-slaughter ; shall be Punished for such Offence, according to the Statute Laws of the Realm of *England,* with Death ; the Benefit of the Clergy reserved where allowable : And shall Forfeit his Lands, Goods, and Chattels, to the Colony, according to His Majesties Charter ; to be disposed of by the Assembly, as they shall think fit ; All necessary Charges of Prosecution, Condemnation, and Execution being first duly deducted.

High Treason, Petit Treason, Murder, and Man-slaughter how punished.

And be it Enacted by the Authority aforesaid, That whosoever shall be Lawfully convicted, of Killing any Person by Chance Medly or Misadventure, shall Forfeit his Goods and Chattels, to and for the Use of the Colony ; And that the Governour as Chief Judge, shall Release to such Person his Goods and Chattels, the Charges, Prosecution, &c. being duly paid.

Chance-Medley & Misadventure, how Punished.

And

AND Be it further Enacted by the Authority aforesaid, That if any Person Portune to be Killed by a Carts going over him, or by a Horse's Kicking of him, or by any fort of Neat Cattle's Goring him or Kicking of him, or by other *What makes Deodand.* fuch like Accident, that then the Coroner of fuch Town where fuch cafual Death fhall happen to be, fhall with an Inqueft of Twelve Lawful Men, enquire into the Meanes of the Death of fuch Perfon ; and on the Coroners *A Deodand to* Return, that fuch Perfon was Killed by any of the aforefaid Accidents, &c. *go for the ufe* Then the Coroner with his faid Inqueft upon Oath, fhall Apprize the Value of *of the Poor of* fuch Cart, Horfe or Neat Beaft, &c. Which fhall be Forfeited as a Deodand, *the Town.* and given to the Overfeers of the Poor of fuch Town where fuch Cafualty fhall happen.

AND Be it further Enacted by the Authority aforefaid, That whofoever fhall Wilfully and Malicioufly cut out the Tongues, pull out the Eyes, or cut *Malicious* off the Ears, of any Perfon or Perfons within this Colony, he fhall be *Maiming of* Proceeded againft, Profecuted and [Punifhed ; *As by the Statute of the* V. *of punifhed.* Henry *the* IV. *Chap* 5th. is Ordained.

AND be it further Enacted by the Authority aforefaid, That Witchcraft *Witchcraft* is and fhall be Felony, And whofoever fhall be Lawfully convicted thereof, *punifhable* fhall fuffer the Pains of Death. *with Death.*

AND Be it further Enacted by the Authority aforefaid, That Burglary *Burglary pu-* is and fhall be Felony : And whofoever fhall be Lawfully convicted thereof *nifhed with* fhall fuffer the Pains of Death. *Death.*

AND Be it further Enacted by the Authority aforefaid, That Robbery is and fhall be Felony, and whofoever fhall lawfully be convicted thereof, fhall fuffer *Robbery pu-* the Pains of Death. And upon Complaint made to any Affiftant, Juftice of the *nifhed with* Peace, or Warden of any Town within the Colony, of a Robbery committed *Death.* therein, fhall forthwith Grant forth a Warrant to a Conftable of faid Town, *Warrants to* to make *Hue and Cry* after fuch Robber or Robbers, for the Apprehending *be granted by* and Taking of them : And fuch Proceedings fo being made in fuch Town, *and Cry to ap-* wherein any Robbery fhall be Committed, fhall not be chargeable for the *prehend Rob-* Monies, Goods and Chattles of the Perfon fo Robbed. *bers.*

AND Be it further Enacted by the Authority aforefaid, That in any Town of the Colony, where a Forceable Entry, or Detainer of Lands or Houfes, fhall happen to be committed or done by any Perfon or Perfons *Forceable En-* whatfoever, upon Complaint or Information thereof given by the Party *try and De-* Agrived to any Two or more Affiftants, Juftices of the Peace, or Wardens *tainer.* of the Town where fuch Houfe or Land lyes, The faid Affiftants, Juftices, or Wardens fhall Iffue out their Warrant to the Sheriff of the Colony, or his Deputy, requiring him in the Kings Name to Impanel a Jury of Inqueft, of *Warrant to be* Twenty Four good and lawful Men of the Neighbourhood to come before *granted to the* them, to make Enquiry upon Oath or Engagement concerning the fame ; *Sheriff or his* And in Cafe the faid Jury fhall find the Bill or Complaint againft fuch *Deputy, to* Perfon or Perfons complained of, That then fuch Affiftants, Juftices or *Impanel a* Wardens, fhall caufe fuch Force to be removed, reftore to the Perfon or *Jury.* Perfons complaining, peaceable poffeffion of the fame.

Provided Always, That fuch Complaint or Information appears to be *Forceable En-* made within three years after fuch Forceable Entry and Detainer be Commit- *try to be Com-* ed, and not after. *Provided* alfo, That if upon the faid Juries finding the *plained of* *within three* *years.*

E   Bill

A Traverse allowed to the Court of Tryals. Bill againft fuch Perfon or Perfons, That if fuch Perfon or Perfons, fhall Offer to Traverfe the faid Complaint or Infomantion, and defire to Remove the fame to the next General Court of Tryals of this Colony, there to Try the fame, and give good and fufficient fecurity to the faid Affiftants, Juftices, or Wardens, for Profecuting the fame, And to Pay all intervening Charges and Damages in cafe they fhall be Condemned at fuch general Court of Tryals. That then fuch Affiftants, Juftices, or Wardens, fhall forbear to deliver Poffeffion to the Party and Parties complaining, until they fhall receive the Order or Judgment of fuch General Court of Tryals for their fo doing.

Twenty Shillings Fine for every perfon that refufes to aid the Affiftants, Juftices, &c. AND Be it Enacted by the Authority aforefaid. That the Affiftants, Juftices of the Peace, and Wardens, in cafe of any Refiftance made in the due performing their Duties by this Act required about Forceable Entries or Detainers, may Command the Affiftance of any of His Majefties Subjects of this Colony, who are Required to Aid them therein, under the Penalty of *Twenty Shillings* to each Perfon that fhall refufe fo to do ; To be recovered by Suit, Information, before any one Affiftant, Juftice of the Peace, or Warden of this Colony.

AND the faid Fine of *Twenty Shillings* fo Recovered, to be Paid into the Town Treafury, for the Ufe of the Town, where fuch Forceable Entry, and Detainer fhall be committed.

The Complainant to pay Cofts if Caft. AND Be it further Enacted by the Authority aforefaid, That in cafe the Jury of Inqueft on inquiry as aforefaid, fhall not find the faid Bill or Complaint againft the Perfon or Perfons Complained of as aforefaid, That then the Perfon or Perfons Complaining, fhall be Condemned by the faid Affiftants, Juftices, or Wardens, To pay the Cofts of Courts as is Ufual in other Cafes.

Twenty Pound Fine to the Sheriff or his Deputy to difobey, the Affiftants Warrant. AND be it further Enacted by the Authority aforefaid, That if the Sheriff or his Deputy, to whom fuch Affiftants, Juftices, or Wardens Warrant is delivered, doth not duly Execute the fame ; That he fhall Forfeit the Sum of *Twenty Pounds,* Lawful Money, to be Recovered by Bill, Information, Suit, or Complaint, in any Court of Record within this Colony.

Rioters to fuffer 12 months Imprifonment, or a Fine of Ten Pounds. AND Be it further Enacted by the Authority aforefaid, That all Perfons that fhall be Lawfully Convicted of a Riot, fhall Suffer Twelve Monthes Imprifonment, or Pay a Fine of *Ten Pounds,* to the Ufe of the Colony.

Fine for breach of Peace, not to exceed Twenty Shillings, or to be bound over to the Court of Tryals. AND be it further Enacted by the Authority aforefaid, That any Affiftant, Juftice of the Peace, or Warden, in this Colony ; upon Convicting any Perfon or Perfons before him for Breach of the Peace, by Striking, &c. Shall and may Fine fuch Offender or Offenders at Difcretion, not Exceeding *Twenty Shillings,* or Bind them over to the General Court of Tryals, with two fufficient Sureties according as the Nature of the Offence may require.

Affault and Battery to be Tryed at Common Law. AND be it further Enacted by the Authority aforefaid, That in all Cafes of Affault or Battery, the Party Affaulted or Battered, fhall have an Action of Trefpafs at the Common Law, againft the Perfons Committing fuch Affault, or Battery, fhall Recover his Damage Received thereby.

Sodomy, Buggery or Rape, punifhed with Death. AND be it Enacted by the Authority aforefaid, That whofoever fhall Perpetrate and Commit the Deteftable and Abominable Crimes of Sodomy, or Buggery, and be thereof Lawfully Convicted, fhall fuffer the Pains of Death ; as in cafes of Felony, with the benefit of Clergy.   And

AND *Be it further Enacted by the Authority aforesaid*, That whofoever fhall Commit Fornication, and be thereof Lawfully Convicted before any two Affiftants, Juftices of the Peace, or Wardens of the Town where fuch Fact *Fornication* fhall be Committed, (the Affiftants, Juftices, or Wardens, are hereby Im- *how Tryed.* powered the Cognizance thereof,) fhall be publickly Whipped in faid Town *The punifh-* where fuch Fact fhall be Committed with Ten Stripes and no, more, or pay a *ment thereof* Fine of *Forty Shillings* into the Town Treafury, to and for the Ufe of the Poor of fuch Town.

AND Be it further Enacted by the Authority aforesaid, That whofoever *Theft.* fhall Steal or Purloyn any Moneys, Goods, Wares, or Merchandize ; And *For the firft* be thereof Lawfully Convicted, at the General Court of Tryals, (who are *Offence, to* hereby fully Impowered to have Cognizance of the fame) either by Confef- *reftore twofold* fion, or by the Evidence of two perlons upon Oath or Engagement, fhall for *to the Owner,* the firft Offence, Reftore to the Owner of fuch Moneys, Wares, Goods, *of Fined at* and Merchandizes, fo ftolen two fold ; And fhall be Whipp'd or Fined at *Difcretion.* the Difcretion of the Judges of faid Court ; And upon a fecond Conviction *For the fecond* of fuch Offence, to Reftore two fold as aforefaid to the Owners of fuch *ftore twofold* Moneys, Wares, Goods, Merchandizes, fo Stolen, and four fold to the *to the Owners,* Colony ; And be Whipp'd, or Fined at Difcretion, by the Judges *and fourfold* of faid Court. *to the Colony, to be Whipp'd, &c. as afore.*

AND Be it further Enacted by the Authority aforesaid, That if the perfon fo *faid.* Offending, and convict thereof as aforefaid, fhall not have Goods and *If there be* Chattels fufficient to fatisfy and Pay the Judgement of fuch Court as aforefaid, *not fufficient Eftate to fa-* That then and in fuch Cafes, the Offender fhall be Sold by the Sheriff, by *tisfie as aforen* the Direction of the Judges of faid Court, to fatisfy fuch Judgement as fhall *faid, the Of-* be given as aforefaid. *fender fhall be Sold to fatisfie the fame.*

AND be it further Enacted by the Authority aforesaid, That if any Officer *the fame.* within this Colony, fhall Exact or Extort any more or Greater Fees than by *No Officer to* Law is ftated him, or that under pretence of Executing his Office, fhall Levy *take more than* any more or Greater Sums of Monies, &c. Than by any Judgement, *his Fees.* Execution, Order or Decree, he is Ordered or allowed to do, and be *ty of treble* thereof Lawfully convicted, he fhall Forfeit to the party agrieved treble *Damages.* Damages, which fhall be (according to the Damage received) Recovered by the party agrieved, before any Court, of Judge of Record, by Action of Trefpafs upon the Cafe.

AND be it further Enacted by the Authority aforesaid, That if any Perfon fhall wrongfully and Malicioufly, Spoil, Burn or Deftroy any Frame *Wilful deftroy-* prepared for Building of either Houfe, Mill, or Barn, or fpoil any Cart, or *ing of Houfes* Wood heaped and prepared for Coals, or other Ufe ; or cut out the Tongue *for Coals, bar-* of any Beaft being alive ; or fhall barke Fruit Trees, or procure any of the *king of Fruit* faid Offences to be done ; The Perfon fo Offending, fhall pay the Owner *Trees, to pay* thereof Treble Damages, with coft of Court, and pay a Fine to the Ufe of *treble Dama-* the Colony, according to the Direction of the Judges of the Court, where *And Fine* fuch Offender fhall be convicted. *the Colony.*

AND if any Perfon fhall Wrongfully and Malicioufly Cut or take away Corn growing, or Rob any Orchard or Garden, or break or cut any Hedge, Pale, Rail or Fence ; or Digg up, Cut down, Spoil or carry away, any Fruit Trees, *Trefpaffes.* or fhall Cut down or Deftroy any other fort of Trees ftanding ; or fhall put any Beaft into the Field of another, without the knowledge or confent of the

The Trespasser to pay treble Damages And Fine for the same. For want of Estate, to be sent to the House of Correction.

Owner of the Field ; And shall be duly convicted thereof, shall Pay to the Party Grieved treble Damages and cost of Court: And shall pay to the Use of the Colony such Fine, as by the Judges of the Court where such Offender or Offenders shall be Convict, shall be thought reasonable for the same. And in case such Offender or Offenders have not sufficient Estate to Pay such Fines as he or they shall be Amerced, then such Offender or Offenders, shall be sent to the House of Correction, there to remain until the same be satisfied and paid.

Bargains above Ten Pounds to be void, if not in Writing.

How proved if under Ten Pounds.

Fraudulent Dealers to pay treble Damages to the person agrieved.

AND *Be it further Enacted by the Authority aforesaid,* For the preventing of Fraudulent Dealings in Bargains and Contracts ; That no Bargains nor Contracts, for above the value of *Ten Pounds,* shall be vallid and binding in Law, unless the same be reduced into Writing, and Signed by the parties contracting, in the Presence of one or more credible Witness or Witnesses ; And that all Verbal Contracts, for any matter under the value of *Ten Pounds,* shall be well and sufficiently proved, by the Evidence of one or more credible Witness or Witnesses, otherwise to be Null and Void in the Law. And that if any Person shall Use any Fraud or Deceit in Bargains or Contracts with any Person : The Person Cheated or Deceived thereby, shall have his Action of Trespass against the Person Offending therein, and Recover Treble his Damages with cost of Suit.

Fraudulent Conveyances to deceive Creditors. To be void in the Law, and the Conveyancer to pay treble Costs.

AND *be it further Enacted by the Authority aforesaid,* That all Bonds, Bills, Deeds of Sale, Gifts, Grants, or other Conveyances, or Obligations whatsoever, that shall be made by any Person with intent to defraud or deceive others, or defeat such Person or Persons Creditors, of their Just Debts and Dues. That all such Bonds, Bills, Deeds of Sale, Gifts, Grants or other Conveyances or Obligations whatsoever, shall be Null Void and of none Effect ; And the Party injured or agrieved thereby, shall Recover his double Damages, together with cost of Suit.

Conspirators & Champertors to be Imprison'd one year, and a Fine to the Colony.

AND *Be it further Enacted by the Authority aforesaid,* That in case any Person or Persons, shall be Lawfully convicted of Conspiracy, according to the Statute of the XXXIII. *Edward* the 1st. Entituled, a Definition of Conspirators, or shall be convicted of Champerty ; he or they that shall be so convicted, shall Suffer One Years Imprisonment, and make Fine to the Colony, as the Judges of the Court where such Person or Persons is Convicted shall award ; and the party agrieved, shall have his Remedy, and recover his Damages by an Action of Trespass on the Case,

PROVIDED always, That this Act shall not Extend, to any Person or Persons who Honestly and without any Unjust Design, shall assist with Monies or otherwise, such Person or Persons as are not of Estate or ability sufficient to carry on a suit in Law, for the Recovery of their Just Right and Estate.

No Juror to take a Bribe. They that are guilty of either, to forfeit five times the value of such Reward.

AND, *Be it further Enacted by the Authority aforesaid,* That in case any person or persons being Impanelled and Sworn upon a Jury, shall take any Reward to bring in a Verdict, or in case any person shall Embrace a Juror so to do, the Parties both Giving and Receiving such Reward, being thereof duly Attaint, in any Court of Record, according to the Statute of the XXXVIII. of *Edward* the 3d. CHAP. 12th. shall pay Five times the Value of such Reward ; One half to the Use of the Colony, and the other half to such Informer, as shall Sue for the same ; And on default of payment, shall be Imprisoned One Year in the House of Correction.

And

AND be it further Enacted by the Authority aforesaid, That if any Person shall Forge, Raze, Embezel or take away any Record, Writt, Return or Procefs belonging to fuch Record, or any part of the fame, By reafon where-of Judgement fhall be Reverfed ; Or fhall Forge any Deed, Obligation, Accquittance or Record, or fhall Wilfully and defignedly make falfe Entry of Pleas, or alter Verdicts, or fhall be Procuring, or Confederating or Abetting fuch Doings, Such Perfon or Perfons being thereof duly Attainted, fhall be Imprifoned, and Grievoufly Fined, according to the Difcretion of the Judges of fuch Court, where fuch Perfon or Perfons fhall be Attainted ; And fuch Perfon or Perfons, as fhall be Agrieved thereby, fhall have Remedy by Action, to Recover his or their Damages.

Forging, &c. keeping away of Records and altering Ver-dits, to be punifhed by Imprifonment and fining.

An Act for the Eftablifhing Weights and Meafures throughout this Colony.

BE it Enacted by the General Affembly, And by the Authority of the fame, That during the fitting of the General Affembly in *May* Annually, There fhall be Annually Chofe and Elected, by the General Affembly, One General Sealer, who fhall provide and procure at the Colonies charge, a Standatd of each and every of the Weights and Meafures following ; *viz.* One half Bufhel, One Peck, One half Peck, One Ale Quart, One Wine Quart, One Wine Pint, and One Wine half Pint. One Yard, One half Hundred, One half Quarter of a Hundred, One Fourteen Pound, One Four Pound, One Two Pound, One one Pound, and One half Pound Weight ; which fhall be accord-ing to the Standard of His Majefties Exchequer in the Kingdom of *England.* AND That each refpective Town fhall provide one Standard, of all the above-faid Weights and Meafures, which fhall be proved and Sealed, by the General Sealer of the Colony. AND that the Free-men of every Town, fhall at the ufual time of Election of Town Officers, Annually Chufe a Perfon, to prove and Seal all Weights and Meafures throughout fuch Town, with fuch a Seal or Mark, as fhall be by each Town appointed : who fhall be Engaged faithfully and duly to Exercife faid Office. AND if any Perfon fhall be found, to Sell or Buy by falfe Weights or Meafures, fuch Perfon being thereof duly Convicted before any One Affiftant, Juftice of the Peace or Warden, in fuch Town, fhall Forfeit and Pay to the Ufe of fuch Town, for the firft Offence, *Six Shillings* and *Eight Pence,* and for the fecond Offence, *Thirteen Shillings,* and for the third Offence, fhall Forfeit and Pay *Twenty Shillings,* and for Example to Others, fhall ftand in the Pillory, in fome Publick place in fuch Town, for the fpace of One Hour.

A general Sealer to be Annually Chofe in May.

A general Sealer to pro-cure Weights & Meafures. Each Town to provide a Standard of Weights and Meafures, to be proved by the Colony.

AND be it further Enacted by the Authority aforefaid, That if any Perfon or Perfons, of the Age of Fourteen Years or upwards, fhall either by Word or Writing, Publifh, Tell, or Declare any Lye or Lies, tending to the Defama-tion or taking away the good Name, Fame or Credit or Eftate of any Perfon, and whereby fuch Perfon may be Reafonably thought to be Hurt or Damni-fied, fuch party fo Hurt or Damnified thereby, fhall or may take his or their Suit againft fuch Offender, and Recover his juft Damages ; And the Offender therein upon Conviction, fhall be Fined by fuch Court, Affiftant, Juftice of the Peace or Warden before whom Convicted, not exceeding the Sum of *Twenty Shillings.*

A Town Seal-er to be An-nually Chofen.

F   AND

Servants not to be put away before their time be expired, without good cause, those that put them away, contrary hereunto.

AND be it further Enacted by the Authority aforesaid, That any Person whatsoever, That shall Contract and Agree with any Servant for one Years Service, or more or less time ; shall not put away his or her said Servant, before the time as Agreed on be expired, unless upon good and sufficient cause made appear, before one or more Assistant, Justice of the Peace or Warden of said Town, where said Master or Mistress Dwells ; AND if any Master or Mistress of any Servant or Servants, shall put away any such Servant, before the time Agreed be expired ; he or she so doing without a sufficient discharge from one or more Assistants, Justices of the Peace or Wardens of said Town, shall Forfeit to such Servant aggrieved, *Forty Shillings* in Money, to be Recovered before any Two Assistants, Justices of the Peace or Wardens of such Town.

No Servant to depart from his Masters Service without leave.

If a Servant depart without Licence, to be committed to Goal.

AND be it further Enacted by the Authority aforesaid, That no Servant hired as aforesaid, for any term of Time, shall depart from the Service of his said Master or Mistress, until such time of Service as agreed on between them be fully ended, without some justifiable cause, as shall be allowed of, under the Hand of one or more Assistants, Justices of the Peace or Wardens of said Town, where his Master or Mistress shall dwell ; And that if any servant, shall depart from his said Master or Mistresses Service (before his Term or Time of Service agreed on be fully ended) without Licence, first had or obtained, from one or more Assistant, Justice of the Peace or Warden of said Town as aforesaid, shall for his or her Offence, upon due proof thereof, before any one or more Assistants, Justices of the Peace or Wardens of said Town, shall be Committed to Prison, there to remain, until he or she so doing, find sufficient Surety, to perform his or her Contract, as agreed on.

Whosoever retaine Servant not lawfully discharged shall forfeit Five Pounds.

AND be it further Enacted by the Authority aforesaid, That whosoever shall Wittingly or Knowingly, Retain any such hired Servant as aforesaid, that is, not Lawfully discharged as aforesaid, shall for every such Offence, Forfeit to the Person agrieved thereby, *Five Pounds,* to be Recovered at any Court of Record, by Action of the Case.

No Artificer to leave his Work before, finished on the penalty of Five Pounds.

AND be it further Enacted by the Authority aforesaid, That no Artificer or Handicrafts-man, That shall Agree or Contract with any Person, for the Performing of any piece or parcel of Work, Relating to his or their several Occupations, or shall Agree to Work for any certain time, shall depart from his or their Work, before the same be finished.
AND That if any Artificer or Handicrafts-man, upon any Contract with any Person, for the performing any Work as aforesaid, shall Depart and Leave his said Work before finished, without the Leave or Assent of his Employer, shall Forfeit to the Person Agrieved thereby, *Five Pounds,* to be Recovered in any Court of Record within this Colony, by Action of the Case.

Each Town to provide for their own poor. And to put out to Service such as are likely to become chargeable. Overseers of the Poor to be chosen in each Town annually.

AND be it further Enacted by the Authority aforesaid, That each Town in this Colony, shall carefully provide for the Relief of the Poor, Sick, and Impotent, of such Town, who are not capable of Providing for themselves ; And also to Employ or put out to Service, all such Young and Able Persons, as are not of sufficient Estates to maintain themselves, or which through Idleness, may be likely to become a charge or damage to such Town : And for the effectual performing thereof, shall Annually at the time of Election of Town Officers, Elect and Chuse Overseers of the Poor, who are from time to time, to give in their Information to the Town Council thereof, who upon such Information, are to take such course for the Effecting thereof, as to them shall seem proper and needful, Agreeable to the Statute of the XLIII. of *ELIZABETH.* CHAP. 2d.

AND

AND B*e it Enacted by the Authority aforesaid,* That any Affistant, Juftice of the Peace or Warden, fhall and may upon Lawfully convicting of any Perfon or Perfons being Drunk, either by one fufficient Evidence, or by his own Knowledge thereof, Fine fuch Perfon fo Offending, *Five Shillings* for the firft Offence, (to be paid into the Town Treafury of fuch Town, where fuch Offence fhall be committed) or be fet in the Stocks, at the Difcretion of fuch Affiftant, Juftice or Warden, not exceeding Three Hours, and upon a fecond conviction of the like Offence, fuch Perfon fhall Pay as a Fine *Ten Shillings,* to and for the Ufe aforefaid ; And he bound to his Good Behaviour, with two fufficient Surties, in the Sum of *Ten Pounds,* to the next fucceeding General Court of Tryals.

Drunkennefs. For the firft offence to pay Five Shillings or fet in the Stocks, For the fecond offence to pay, Ten Shillings, and be bound to good behaviour.

PROVIDED always, that fuch Complaint, be made within Ten Days after fuch Offence be committed.

AND Be it further Enacted by the Authority aforefaid; That whofo-ever fhall prophanely Swear or Curfe, within the hearing of any Affiftant, Juftice of the Peace or Warden, or be thereof convicted, either by his own Confeffion, or by the Evidence of two Witneffes, upon Oath or Engagement, before any one Affiftant, Juftice of the Peace or Warden, fhall for every fuch Oath or Curfe, be Fined *Five Shillings,* to and for the Ufe of the Poor of fuch Town, where the Offence fhall be Committed, or be fet in the Stocks, at the Difcretion of fuch Affiftant, Juftice or Warden, not exceeding three Hours.

Prophane Curfing and Swearing. To be fined Five Shillings for every Oath and Curfe, or. to be fet in the Stocks.

PROVIDED always, that every Offence againft this Law, be complained of within Ten Days after fuch Offence Committed.

AND be it further Enacted by the Authority aforefaid, That no Perfon whatfoever, fhall keep any Tavern, Ale Houfe or Victualling Houfe nor Sell any ftrong Liquors of any fort whatfoever by Retail, without a Licenfe firft had and obtained of the Town Council, of fuch Town wherein fuch Perfon dwells. And if any Perfon or Perfons, fhall prefume fo to do, and be thereof Lawfully Convict, before any one Affiftant, Juftice of the Peace, or Warden of faid Town, either by his own Confeffion, or by the Evidence of two Witneffes, upon Oath or Engagement, fhall Forfeit *Forty Shillings,* for the Ufe of the Poor of fuch Town, where fuch Offence fhall be Committed.

None to Sell ftrong Liquors by Retail, without Licenfe on the penalty of Forty Shillings.

AND Be it further Enacted by the Authority aforefaid, That it fhall and may be Lawfull, for any one Affiftant, Juftice of the Peace or Warden, to fummon and convent before him any perfon or perfons, as he fhall think fit, to give Evidence againft any fuch Perfon, as fhall Sell by Retail, any Strong Liquor without Licence, and to caufe fuch perfon or perfons, to give their folemn Engagement thereto, and if fuch perfons refufe the fame ; then him or them commit to his Majefties Goal in *Newport,* until he or they purge themfelves by their Engagement.

Power to the Juftice, to Office, to Convent & Swear fuch as fhall think are knowing of the fame, and if they refufe to do, Commit them to Goal, till they purge them-felves by Oath Town Councils to grant forth Licences to

AND be it further Enacted by the Authority aforefaid, That it fhall and may be in the Power of each refpective Town Council, to Grant Licences in their Refpective Towns, for the keeping of Taverns, Ale-houfes, and Victualling-houfes ; they Granting no Licence under *Forty Shillings,* nor none above *Ten Pounds.* And to take fuch Bonds or Recognizances, as they fhall think

meet

Sell firing Liquors by Retail.

meet, of all such Persons as they shall grant Licences to, for their Regular keeping, and maintaining good orders in the same.

AND also that the respective Town Councils, shall and hereby are Impowerd, to take such Security of Strangers, coming to Inhabit in their respective Towns, as to them shall seem needful, to secure their Towns from any charge that may happen or accrue thereby.

Town Councils to take Bond of Strangers.

No Tavern-keeper to suffer an Inhabitant to sit in his House above one hour at a time, on the penalty of Ten Shillings

AND be it further Enacted by the Authority aforesaid, That no Tavern-keeper, Ale-house-keeper, &c. shall suffer any Inhabitant of the Town wherein he dwells, to sit or remain in their House, Tipling or Drinking, for above the space of one Hour at a time, on the Penalty of paying *Ten Shillings* for every such Offence, being duly Convicted thereof, before any one Assistant, Justice of the Peace or Warden of said Town, either by his own Confession, or by the Evidence of two Witnesses, upon Oath or Engagement, to be Recovered, by a Warrant of Distress, to be granted by any such Assistant, Justice or Warden.

No person to sit in a Tavern for above one hour at a time. On the penalty of 3 Shillings 4 d. for the use of the Poor.

AND That no Towns-man shall sit or remain in any Tavern, Ale-House &c. in the Town wherein he dwells, above the space of one Hour at a time; and if any Person or Persons, shall presume so to do, contrary to this Act, And be thereof duly Convicted, either by his or their own Confession, or by the Evidence of two Witnesses upon Oath or Engagement, before any one Assistant, Justice of the Peace or Warden, shall Forfeit as a Fine, for every such Offence, *Three Shillings* and *Four pence,* to and for the Use of the Poor of such Town, to be Taken by a Warrant of Distress from any such Assistant, Justice or Warden.

A N A C T for Preventing Clandestine Marriages.

None to be Married without Publication.

B E it Enacted by the *General Assembly, And by the Authority of the same,* That no Person whatsoever, shall Marry with any Female, unless he first procure Banes of Matrimony, Sign'd by an Assistant, Justice of the Peace or Warden, and duly expose them, in some Publick place in the Town, where the Persons designing to Marry dwell, for the space of Ten Days after their being first set up ; or be Published Two several times, in a Publick Assembly in said Town ; And that it shall and may be Lawfull, for any Assistant, Justice of the Peace or Warden, to Intermarry such Persons, as shall be Published as aforesaid.

And to stand up ten days, or to be twice published in a Publick Assembly. A Certificate to be given & Recorded. Fee for Marrying.

AND upon Marrying such Persons so Published, the Assistant, Justice or Warden that Marry them, shall give the Persons so Married, a Certificate of the same, (under his Hand) who shall carry the same to the Town Clerk of the Town where such Marriage shall be Solemniz'd, And place the same to Record ; And the Officer that Marries them, and give a Certificate, shall have *Three Shillings* for the same.

Five Pounds fine to him that shall Marry without being published as aforesaid.

AND be it further Enacted by the Authority aforesaid, That whosoever shall Marry with any Female as aforesaid, without duly proceeding as by this Act is Required, shall for such his Offence, Forfeit *Five Pounds,* to be paid to and for the Use of the Town, where such Offender shall dwell, to be Recovered by the Town Treasurer of said Town, in any Court of Record, upon due Conviction thereof.

AND

AND be it further Enacted by the Authority aforesaid, That the Colonies Seal, shall have Engraven thereon an Anchor. And the Motto thereof shall be the Word HOPE.

Colonies Seal to be the Anchor and Hope.

An Act for the Probate of Wills, and Granting of Administrations.

BE *it Enacted by the General Assembly, and by the Authority of the same,* That the Power of proving of Wills, and Granting of Administrations of the Personal Estate of Persons Deceased, shall be in the respective Town Councils of this Colony, where such Person Deceased last Dwelt or Inhabited ; which said Town Council, or the Major part of them, shall have the Power as Judge of Probates, to take the Probate of Wills and Testaments, and Grant Administrations, and all other matters relating thereto, to Act and do, as by the Laws of *England,* and of His Majesties Colony doth belong to the said Office.

Town Councils to Prove Wills and grant Administration.

AND Be it further Enacted by the Authority aforesaid, That all Devices and Bequests of Land or Tenaments, or of any Right or Interest in the same, shall be in Writing, and Sign'd by the Party so devising the same, And shall be Attested and Subscribed in the Presence of the said Devisor, by three or four Credible Witnesses, or else shall be Void and of none Effect.

All Wills devising Lands shall be in Writing, and shall have 3 Witnesses.

AND be it further Enacted by the Authority aforesaid, That the Town Council of each Town, may Summons and Convent before them, all and every Person named Executor or Executors, of any Testament, to the intent to prove or refuse the Testament of his or their Testator ; And to bring in Inventories of such Testators Estate ; And in case such Person or Persons, take upon him or them, the Executorship, by proving the Will, that then at the same time, such Executor or Executors, shall give Bond to the said Town Council, that within one Month after such Probate, he or they will Exhibit a true and perfect Inventory upon Oath, of the whole Personal Estate of the Deceased, as far as shall come to his or their knowledge ; And that he or they will add thereunto, what and so much as may afterwards appear.

Executors to give Bond.

And make Inventories.

AND Be it further Enacted, That such Executor or Executors, upon his or their making an Inventory of said Estate, shall call two of the next of Kin, or two other honest men, and of good Credit of the Neighbourhood, and in their Presence, and by their Direction cause to be made a True and Perfect Inventory of all the Goods and Chattels, Wares, Merchandizes, Rights and Credit of the Testator to be Exhibited to the Town Council, and there Recorded.

Inventory how made.

And to be Exhibited to the Town Council, to be Recorded.

AND be it further Enacted, That upon Probate of such Will or Testament, the Witnesses to the same, shall upon their Oaths declare, that they saw the Testator Sign, Seal, and Declare the same to be his last Will and Testament ; And that in his Presence, they set their Hands as Witnesses thereunto. And the said Testator was in his Perfect Mind and Memory,

Wills how proved.

When proved, to be Recorded.

G at

Administrati. on granted forth.

at the fame time, which faid Teftament being fo proved, And the Clerk of the faid Council, fhall Tranfcribe a Copy thereof, into the Book of Record, And deliver the Original to fuch Executor or Executors, with an Atteft of its being Recorded. And the faid Town Council, fhall without delay give to fuch Executor or Executors, under the Seal of the faid Office, a Power to Adminifter the faid Eftate.

If the Execu-tors refufe to accept, to grant Admi-niftration to the next of Kin, or to the greatest Creditor.

AND be it further Enacted by the Authority aforefaid, That in cafe the Perfon or Perfons named Executor or Executors in a Will (being duly Summoned) before fuch Town Council, to prove the Will, fhall refufe fo to do, And take upon him the charge of Executorfhip, fuch his Refufal, fhall be entred in the Regifters Book of faid Town Council, And thereupon fuch Town Council, fhall Grant Letters of Adminiftration; with the Will annexed thereto, to the Widow or next of kin to the Deceafed Perfon, that fhall defire the fame ; And upon their refufal, to one or more of the Principal Creditors, as the faid Council fhall think fit.

Adminiftrati-on of Inteftate Eftates, to be granted to the Widow, or next of kin.

AND be it further Enacted, That when and fo often, as any Perfon fhall Dye Inteftate, Adminiftration of fuch Inteftates perfonal Eftate, fhall be Granted to the Widow, or next of kin to the Inteftate, that fhall defire the fame, And in cafe of their refufal thereunto, fuch Principal Creditor or Creditors, as the faid Town Council fhall think fit.

Adminiftra-tors to give Bond, and render an Ac-compt of their Adminiftrati-on to the Town-Council, when required.

PROVIDED always, And be it Enacted, That fuch Widow or next of kin, or Principal Creditor or Creditors of fuch Inteftate, defiring the Adminiftration of fuch Inteftate Eftate, fhall at the Granting of the fame, give Bond to the faid Town Council, with two fufficient Sureties in double the Sum of what the faid Inteftates Perfonal Eftate, fhall be by the faid Town Council, Valued to be worth, for his and their true and rightful Adminiftration of the faid Eftate according to Law ; And duly Exhibiting a True and Perfect Inventory of fuch Eftate, unto the faid Town Council, and to them at all times when Required, to render a True and Faithful Account of fuch or their Adminiftration.

Appeal to the Governour & Council, as Supream Judge of Pro-bates.

AND Be it further Enacted, That if any Party fhall be Agrieved at the Judgement or Sentence of fuch Town Council, for any matters contained in this Act, that in fuch Cafe, it fhall be Lawful for fuch Perfon, to Appeal from the faid Judgement or Sentence, unto the Governour and Council of this Colony, who as the Supream Ordinary or Judge of Probates, are hereby Impowered, to hear and determine fuch Appeals, and to give fuch Judgment thereupon, as to them fhall appear right and agreeable with Law.

Appellant t give Bond.

PROVIDED always that fuch Perfon or Perfons defiring an Appeal as aforefaid, give fecurity by Bond, to faid Town Council, to Profecute fuch Appeal with Effect, and to Pay fuch Cofts, as may be Taxed againft him or them.

He that Mar-ries with an Executrix, or Adminiftra-trix to give Bond.

AND be it further Enacted by the Authority aforefaid, That if any Perfon fhall Marry with any Executrix, or Adminiftratrix, fuch perfon upon Information given thereof by any Creditor, Legatee or other perfon Interefted in fuch Eftate, to the Town Council, before whom the Will was proved, or by whom Adminiftration was Granted, fhall be Obliged by fuch Town Council, to give Bond with fufficient Sureties, in Double the Value of fuch E-ftate to fuch Town Council, and their Succeffors, for the Right, Full and Due

Ad-

Administration, of the Estate of the Testator or Intestate ; And in case *of Upon refusal* Refusal, any one or more of the Justices of the Peace or Wardens, *to be committ-* belonging to such Town Council, shall Commit such Person to his Majesties *ted to Goal.* Goal in *Newport,* there to remain until he shall have perfomed the same.

AND be it further Enacted, That upon such persons giving Bond with Sureties as aforesaid, all former Bonds given by such Executrix or Admini-stratrix, shall be delivered up to be Cancel'd.

L A W S

Made and Past by the General Assembly of His Majesties Colony of *Rhode-Island,* and *Providence-Plantations,* Begun and Held at *Newport,* the first day of *May,* in the *Eighteenth* Year of His Majesties Reign *Annoque Domini.* 1666.

A N A C T, Establishing, Settling and Regulating, the General Courts of Tryals, within this Colony, in both Civil and Criminal Causes.

WHEREAS by His *Majesties most Gracious Charter, Granted to this His Majesties Colony, full Power and Authority is Given to the General Assembly thereof, to Appoint, Order and Direct, Erect and Settle, such Court of Judicature, as shall be necessary for the Tryal and Determination of all Actions, Causes, Matters, and things, happening within the same ; And to Regulate the Proceedings thereon.*

BE *it Enacted by the General Assembly, and by the Authority of the same,* That there shall be two General Courts of Tryals, and General Goal *The Time of* delivery, Annually Held at *Newport,* for the Tryal of all Causes, Matters *the Courts* and Things both Civil and Criminal ; The one General Court of Tryals *Sitting* and Goal Delivery, to be Held the last *Tuesday* of *March* Annually, and the other on the first *Tuesday* of *September ;* which said Courts, shall be composed, and consist of the Governour, and Deputy Governour, and *And the Pow-* Assistants of this Colony, of which the Governour, or in his absence, the *er thereof.* Deputy Governour and three Assistants, to be a Quorum ; And in case of the Absence of both the Governour, and Deputy Governour, then any five of the Assistants, to be a Quorum, who shall have Cognizance of all Pleas Real and Personal and Mixt, as also Pleas of the Crown, and Causes Criminal, and Matters relating to the Conservation of the Peace, and Punishment of Offenders, and generally of all other Matters, as fully and amply, to all Intents and Purposes whatsoever ; As the Courts of Common Pleas, Kings Bench, or Exchequer, in his Majesties Kingdom of *England,* Have or ought to Have; And are hereby Impowred to give Judgment therein, and Award Execution thereupon, and make such necessary Rules of Practice, as the Judges of the said Court, shall from time to time see needful.

Provided

PROVIDED the said Rules be not Contrary and Repugnant to the known Laws of this Colony.

The Recorder to be Clerk of the said Court. AND be it further Enacted by the Authority aforefaid, That the Recorder of this Colony for the time being, fhall be Clerk of the faid General Courts of Tryals, and General Goal Delivery. And that all Writs, Procefs and Executions for Matters Cognizable by, or Iffuing out of the faid Courts, fhall be Sign'd or Sealed by him, (as need fhall require,) who during the Sitting of the faid Courts, to make due Entries of the Proceedings thereof, and fhall be Paid *Two Shillings per Diem*, out of the General Treafury, for his attendance therein.

Each Towns Quota of Jury-men. AND be it further Enacted by the Authority aforefaid, That the Town of *Newport*, fhall fend to each Refpective General Court of Tryals, and General Goal Delivery, Five Grand Jury-men, and Five Petit Jury-men; the Town of *Portfmouth*, Three Grand, and Three Petit Jury-men; the Towns of *Providence* and *Warwick*, two Grand, and two Petit Jury-men each, to be Chofen by each Refpective, at their Town Meeting, next preceeding fuch General Court of Tryals, *&c.* to the which they fhall be Chofen.

All Jury-men to be Engaged. AND be it futher Enacted by the Authority aforefaid, That every Grand Jury-man, and Petit, chofen as aforefaid, before his Acting as fuch, fhall take each his Refpective Engagement following.

Grand Juryman's Engagement. WHEREAS You A. B. are *Chofen on the Grand Inque*ft, *on the behalf of Our Sovereign Lord the King, You do here Promife and Engage, to make a true Return to this Court, of all fuch Bills, as fhall be Prefented to You, or fuch breakers of Law, as fhall come to your Knowledge. And this Engagement You make and give upon the Peril of the Penalty of Perjury.*

Engagement of Petit Jury in Civil Actions. YOU A. B. *being of this Jury of Tryals, You* fhall *well and truly try the Iffue of this Cafe, and all Cafes that fhall be Committed unto You from this Court between the Parties, Plantiff and Defendant, according to Law and Evidence; And to keep together, until You agree of a Verdict in the Cafe or Cafes Committed to You, and make true Return of the Verdict or Verdicts, unto this Court, and to keep your Own and Fellows Secrets ; And this Engagement You Make and Give, upon the Peril of the Penalty of Perjury.*

Engagement of Petit Jury in Criminal Cafes. YOU A. B. *being of this Jury of Tryals, You fhall well and truly Try, and true Delivearnce make, Between Our Sovereign Lord the King, and the Prifoner at the Bar, according to Law and Evidence, and the Light of your Confcience upon the Evidence ; And to keep together, until you are agreed of a Verdict or Verdicts, in the Cafe or Cafes, that fhall be Committed to you from this Court ; And to keep your Own and Fellows Secrets. And this Engagement you Make and Give upon the Peril of the Penalty of Perjury.*

No General Officer to be Arrefted or Attached in Actional Cafes but Summon'd. AND Be it further Enacted by the Authority aforefaid, That no General Officer of this Government, during his continuance as fuch, fhall be Arrefted or Attached, either in Body or Goods in any Actional Cafe ; And that in all Actual Cafes, that any Perfon may have againft a Genera*l* Officer, it fhall be by Summons and no otherwife ; And that all Writs of Arreft or Attachment, that fhall be Granted forth contrary hereunto, fhall be null and Void in Law: And the Defendant fhall have his Cofts and Damages Accruing thereon.

And

AND be it further Enacted by the Authority aforesaid, That all Writts of Arrest and Summons, That are taken out of the Recorders Office, and duly served Forty Days before the Court, to the which they are Directed by the Sheriff or his Deputy.   And a Declaration be Entred in the Recorders Office, Twenty Four Days before the Court by the Plantiff, then the Defendant shall put in his Anfwer thereto in the Recorders Office, Eight Days before the Court ; otherways the Plantiff may enter a *Nihil Dicit,* and Judgement shall pass against the Defendant for want of an Anfwer, *&c.*   And all Writts and Summons, that shall be taken out of the Recorders Office, within Forty Days before any General Court of Tryals, shall be Directed to the next General Court of Tryals, succeeding such Court as aforefaid.

Writts to be taken out, an Served Forty Dayes before the Court. Declaration to be filed Twenty Dayes before the Court, and anfwer Eight.

AND be it further Enacted by the Authority aforefaid, That if the Recorder for the Time being shall be abfent at any time from any Court or Courrs of Judicature, (either by Sicknefs or other Occafions) where he is Ordered and Appointed to attend ; That then and in such cafes it shall and may be Lawful for the Judges of such Court, to Appoint another Perfon, to Officiate in the Room and Stead of the Recorder, during his abfence.

In the abfence of the Recorder, the Court to Appoint a Perfon to Officiate in his room.

AND Be it further Enacted by the Authority aforefaid, That in all Civil Actions, the Plantiff or his Attorney shall Pay the Jury.

The Plaintiff to pay the Jury.

AND be it further Enacted by the Authority aforefaid, That the Sheriff and his Deputy, in the Town where such Courts shall be Held, shall Attend all General Courts of Affembly, and General Courts of Tryals, and General Goal Delivery, during the fitting of such Courts.

Sheriff to attend the General Courts.

AN ACT for the Calling of Special Courts.

WHEREAS *it many times happens, that Merchants, Seafaring-men, and other transient Perfons not being fettled Inhabitants in this Colony, and coming here to Trade and Negotiate their affairs, are much Damnified therein, upon their Suing or being Sued in Actions Perfonal, by reafon of their long attendance, until the Ufual Courts of Tryals in this Colony to Determine such controverfies, and which are many times occafioned through Malice of the other Party, to hinder them from proceeding on their Voyages, or otherways.*

For the Preventing thereof, and to the end that Juftice may be fpeedily done,

BEit Enacted by the General Affembly of this Colony, and by the Authority of the fame, That from this time and henceforth, upon the Petition of any Merchants, Seafaring Men or other Tranfient Perfons (not being fettled Inhabitants of this Colony, Praying a fpecial Court to be called, to try any Perfonal Action or Actions, that he hath or wants to Commence againft any other Perfon, or to defend such Action Commenced againft him ; It shall be in the Power of the Governour, and in his Abfence of the Deputy Governour, to Grant forth a Warrant to the Sheriff of this Colony, or in his Abfence to his lawful Deputy, for the Impannelling a Jury of Twelve Men,

The Governour and Deputy Governour, It now to Call Special Courts.

Judges appointed in Special Courts. Qualified according to Law, to meet together at such time and place, as shall be Appointed in the said Warrant, for the Tryal of such Matters as shall be brought before the said Court, which said Court, shall confist of the Governour, and in his Absence, of the Deputy Governour, and Three or more Assistants of this Colony, (whereof one to be an Inhabitant in one of the other Towns within this Colony, then that in which such Court shall be held,) which said Court shall be Appointed to be held, within Ten Days after. the Date of said Warrant.

No Appeal from Judgment save to the King in Council. *AND Be it further Enacted by the Authority aforesaid,* That upon Tryal of such Cause or Causes aforesaid at said Court, the Verdict and Judgement thereupon given, shall be final and Definitive, without any Appeal to any other Court, saving only to the Party agrieved, the Liberty of Appealing to His Majesty in Council in *England,* as in other cases is usually allowed.

Five Pound to be paid before the Granting of a Special Court. *AND be it further Enacted by the Authority aforesaid,* That such Person or Persons, Praying for a special Court, shall be at the charge thereof, and before Granting of the same, shall Pay down to the Governour, or in his Absence to the Deputy Governour *Five Pounds,* towards bearing the Expences of said Court ; which said *Five Pound,* in case Judgement is rendred for him, shall be allowed in the Bill of cofts, to be Taxed in said Court, and the General Recorder shall be the Clerk of such Court.

AN ACT for the Protection of the Members of the General Assembly, and of Persons Chosen on Juries from being Arrested or Sued, during Service.

FORASMUCH *as the Publick Service of His Majesty, and this Government, ought to be Preferred before Private Interests, and that no Person be discouraged from serving the Publick, as Members of the General Assembly of this Colony, or Jurors upon Tryals and Inquest.*

Deputies Exempted from Arrests &c.

Unless by special leave of the Assembly. BE *it therefore Enacted by the General Assembly, and by the Authority of the same,* That all and every Person and Persons, and the Estates of such Persons, as shall be Chosen to serve as Members of the General Assembly of this Colony, for any Town in the said Colony, shall be Free and Exempt from all Summons, Arrests, Attachments and Executions whatsoever, at the Suit of any private Person, to answer any Debt or Damages, Due or pretended to be Due to such private Person, from the Time he is so Chosen, until he be Dismift from such his Station and Employ, without the special Leave and Permission of the said Assembly, first had and Obtained.

Jurors Exempted from Arrests, &c. *AND be it further Enacted,* That all Persons whosoever, that shall hereafter be Lawfully Chosen, to serve on any Grand Jury, Petit Jury, or Jury of Inquest in this Colony, they and their Estates shall likewise be Free, and Exempt from all Summons, Arrests, Attachments and Executions, in the same manner as the Members of the General Assembly are, from the time of their being Chosen, to serve in such Place or Station, until they be Legally Discharged or Dismift from the same, and a reasonable Time for their return to their Habitations again. *And*

AND be it further Enacted by the Authority aforesaid, That all and every Summons, Writ, Executions, or other Procefs, which fhall or may be ferved upon any of the Perfons aforefaid contrary to this Act, fhall be Null and Void and of none Effect in the Law whatfoever ; and that any Officer that fhall knowingly Grant, Execute or Serve, any fuch Writ, Summons, Execution or other Procefs, whereby the Perfon or Eftate, of any Perfon fhall be contrary to this Act Arrefted, Imprifoned, Attached or Seized; fuch Officer upon Complaint of Perfons damnified, or molefted or damnified thereby, to the General Affembly or General Court of Trials, of this Colony, fhall be liable to be Fined according to the Difcretion of either of the faid Courts, not Exceeding the Sum of *Five Pounds,* to be Levied on fuch Offenders Goods and Chattles, by a Warrant or Order from faid Court to whom fuch Complaint fhall be made.

All Writs, Summons &c. granted contrary hereto the Officer be fined not exceeding Five Pounds.

AN ACT for the Eftablifhing and Regulating of Fees.

AND *be it Enacted by the General Affembly of this Colony, and by the Authority of the fame ,* That the Eftablifhment, of the Fees of the feveral Offices, in the Colony hereafter mentioned, fhall be as followeth.

Fees for Probate of Wills, &c.

	£	s.	d.
FOR the Probate of Wills where the Inventory exceeds not One Hundred Pounds, *Six Shillings.*	00	06	00
For every Hundred Pounds above one Hundred Pounds, *Two Shillings* to the Town Council.			
For Probate of Inventory, where no Will appears and when the Inventory exceeds not one Hundred Pounds. *Six Shillings.*	00	06	00
If Above, for every Hundred Pounds more, *Two Shillings* to the Town Council.			

Clerks Fees.

	£	s.	d.
FOR Entering A Caveat againft the Probate of a Will, or Granting of Adminiftration.	00	01	06
For taking Bond and Granting Adminiftration under the Seal of the Town Council.	00	04	00
For Regiftring a Will or Inventory, not exceeding one Page.	00	01	06
If above one Page, for every Page Twenty five lines In a Page.	00	01	00
For a Copy of Ditto from the Record, if not above one Page.	00	01	06
If above one Page, for every Page Twenty-five lines in a Page.	00	01	00
For every Citation and Summons.	00	00	06
For Bond and Granting Licence under the Town-Council Seal.	00	05	00
For Bond of every Perfon that comes to dwell in the Town.	00	01	00
To the Town Sergeant or Conftable, for Serving every Summons or Citation if not above a mile from home.	00	01	00

If above one Mile from home, for every Mile *Three-pence.*
And the Town Clerk fhall have and take the fame Fees, as the Clerk of the Council for Recording of Inftruments, and Granting copies of the fame.

Re-

Recorders Fees.

FOR Attending the General Affembly, the General Courts of Tryals, General Goal Delivery, and fpecial Courts, *Two Shillings* per *Diem* out of the General Treafury.

	l.	s.	d.
For fixing the Colony Seal.	00	02	06
For every Commiffion.	00	03	00
For a Writ or Summons.	00	01	04
For filing a Declaration.	00	01	00
For a copy of Ditto not exceeding one Page.	00	01	06
If above one Page, for every Page Twenty-five lines in a Page.	00	01	00
For filing of an Anfwer.	00	01	00
For copy of Ditto not exceeding one Page.	00	01	06
If above one Page, for every Page Twenty-five lines in a Page.	00	01	00
To try Action called in Court.	00	01	00
For copy of Record not exceeding one Page	00	01	06
If above one Page, for every Page Twenty-five lines in a Page.	00	01	00
For a copy of every Depofition.	00	01	00
For entering a *Nihil Dicit.*	00	01	00
For a *Scire Facias.*	00	01	04
For Entring Verdict.	00	01	00
For Recording Judgement and Iffue	00	01	08
For a Writ of Execution.	00	02	06
For a Diftringus.	00	01	00
For Acquital of Felony or Sufpicion thereof.	00	01	00
For Entering a Rule of Court.	00	01	00
For Bond in the Recorders Office.	00	02	00
For Entering Traverfe upon Indictment.	00	01	00
For filing an Inventory of Goods taken by Execution.	00	01	00
For a Writ of Accompt.	00	01	08
For Entering an order of Court for Reference to Auditors.	00	01	08
For every Perfon Summoned.	00	00	04
For a Writ of Error.	00	03	00
For a Writ of Attaint.	00	03	00
For filing every Return in Court.	00	00	08
For Entering a Proteft in Court.	00	01	00
For every Evidence Read in Court.	00	00	04
For Withdrawing an Action.	00	01	00
For the Difcharge of any Pefon upon Bail to the Peace, &c.	00	01	00

Sheriff's Fees.

	l	s	d
FOR Serving a Writ if not above a Mile from home.	00	01	04
If above one Mile *Two-pence* per Mile forward & backward.			
For Attending a Prifoner before Imprifon'd per *Diem.*	00	02	06
For copy of Writ.	00	01	00
For Attending of the Court per *Diem* out of the General Treafury.	00	02	00
For Attendance on every Action,	00	01	00
For difcharge of every Perfon upon Bail to the Peace, &c.	00	01	00
For every Evidence Read in Court.	00	00	04
For Bail Bond in Actional cafes.	00	02	00
For Bond to the Peace or Good Behaveiour.	00	04	00

For ferving Execution if not exceeding *Ten Pounds, one Shilling* and *Six-pence* per Pound.

If above *Ten Pounds* and not exceeding *Fifty Pounds, Twelve-Pence* per Pound.

If above *Fifty Pounds,* and not exceeding one *Hundred Pounds, Nine-pence* per Pound.

If above one *Hundred Pounds*, and not exceeding two } *Hundred Pounds*, Six-*pence per* Pound.
If above two *Hundred Pounds*, and not exceeding three } *Hundred Pounds*, Four-*pence per* Pound.
For all Executions above three *Hundred* } *Pounds*, Two-*pence per* Pound.
For all Executions Served out of the Town where the Sheriff }
Lives *Two-pence per* Mile forward and backward. }
For turning the Key on every Prisoner Commited.   00 03 04
For Discharge of every Person upon Bail to the King.   00 01 00

Attorney General's Fees.

	l	s	d
FOR every Bill of Indictment Drawn and Plea upon Traverse.	00	13	04
For every Ditto Drawn and Pass'd the Court if not found by the Grand Jury.	00	03	00
For every Criminal Executed to Death.	01	00	00
For Discharge of every Person upon Bor to the Peace.	00	02	00
For every Days Attendance on the Court.	00	03	00

Other Fees Allowed in Court.

	l	s	d
FOR Entering every Action, to the Judges.	00	05	00
For Attorney's and Council's Fees.	00	12	00
For Drawing Bill of Costs.	00	01	00
For Taxing Ditto.	00	01	00
For every Case Tryed ; to the Jury.	00	12	00
For every Persons Discharged, upon Bail to the King, to the Sergeant.	00	01	00
For every Evidence attending the Court per *Diem*.	00	01	06
For every Action called, to the Sergeant.	00	01	00
For every Days Attendance by the Sergeant.	00	03	00

An Act for Regulating the Proceedings on Executions, and Distraints on Goods and Chattels.

BE it *Enacted by the General Assembly, and by the Authority of the same,* That in all civil Cases, where Execution shall be Levied on any Persons Goods or Chattels, the Goods and Chattles so Executed upon, shall be kept *Goods taken* in the Officers Hands Ten Days, before they shall be Offered or Exposed to *by Distres, to* Sale, so that the Person that Owned such Goods or Chattles, so taken *be kept ten* by Execution, may within the said time (if he think fit) Pay the Money *days before* due, together with the charges accruing on such Execution, and thereupon *Exposed to* *Sale.* shall have his said Goods delivered to him again.

AND Be it further Enacted by the Authority aforesaid, That in Case any Officer for Rates, or other justifiable Cause, shall Distrain the Goods or *And also all* Chattels of any Person ; that then and in such Case, the said Officer shall *Goods taken* keep the said Goods and Chattles, for the space of Ten Days, at the Charge *by Distress.* of the Owner of said Goods and Chattles, who within the said Ten Days, Paying the Money due, and the Charges accruing thereon, shall have the same Delivered him again ; But in Case the Owner shall not Redeem them as aforesaid, that then the Officer may Sell the same by Publick Vendue or

1   Outcry

Outcry, and what overplus shall remain, after the Debt and Charges are satisfied and Paid, shall be retruned to the Owner thereof.

Fines to be paid into the General Trea-fury, by the Sheriff. Five Pounds for every Months neg-lected.

AND be it further Enacted by the Authority aforesaid That all Fines and Forfeitures, shall be Levied by the Sheriff or his Deputy, by Order of the General Assembly, General Court of Tryals, and General Goal Delivery; shall be by him (as by Law is required) Paid into the General Treasury, to and for the Use of the Colony. And if the Sheiff shall refuse or neglect to Pay the same as aforesaid, by the space of one Month, he shall Forfeit for such Offence, Five Pounds, to and for the use of the Colony, to be rcover-ed by the General Treasurer for the time being, in any Court of Record.

Fines to be paid into the Town-Treasu-ry, by the Constable, &c. within one Months tim after Levied, on the penal-ty of Five Shillings per Month

AND that all Constables, and other Officers of the Respective Towns within this Colony, who are legally Authorized and Appointed to Collect and Gather any Fines or Forfeitures, which of Right ought to be Paid into the Town Treasury. And shall after the Levying and Collecting of the same, Neglect or Refuse so to do, by the space of one Month, he shall for every Month after the Expiration of the aforesaid time, Forfeit Five Shillings, to and for the Use of such Town, to be Recovered by Complaint or Infor-mation, before any one or more Assistants, Justices of the Peace or Wardens, of such Town.

An Act for the due Recording, Preserving and Keep-ing the Acts of the General Affembly of this Colony.

The Recorder to Register the Acts of Assembly,..and send Copies to the Towns, on the penalty of Five Pounds for every Of-fence.

B E it Enacted by the General Affembly, and by the Authority of the. same, That the General Recorder of the Colony for the time being, shall Re-cord all the Acts of the General Assemblies of this Colony in a Book, and send forth true Copies of the same, to the several Towns in the Colony, with the Colonies Seal affixed thereunto, by the several times, as by the General Assemblies shall from time to time be Ordered ; on the Penalty of Five Pounds, for every such Offence that he shall be wilfully guilty of, to be paid into the General Treasury, to and for the Use of the Colony.

AN ACT Establishing the Election of Town Officers, in each Respective Town in the Colony.

Each Town to Elect Town Council-men, and other Town Officers, who shall make a Town-Coun-cil.

B E it Enacted by the General Affembly, and by the Authority of the same, That every Town within this Colony, shall once in every Year, (on a Day to be by the Free-men of each Respective Town appointed,) chuse and elect such and so many Town Officers, as by the Laws of this Colony are or shall be required. And that on such a Day, by them appointed, they shall Annually chuse and elect, six good and sufficient Free-holders of each Town, for the constituting of a Town Council for each Town, who together with such Assistants, Justices of the Peace and Wardens, as shall Dwell and In-habit in said Town, with the Governour and Deputy Governour, and each of them in such Town or Towns where they shall Inhabit or Reside. shall be and they hereby are constituted and appointed, a Town Council for such Town ; And they or the Major part of such Town Council, shall be a

Their power.

Quorum, and have full Power to Manage the Affairs and Interest of said Town.

Town. And in all matters to Act, Do, Transact and Determine, all and every thing or things, which shall fall within the Jurisdiction of the same.

AND be it further Enacted, by the Authority aforesaid, That the Free-men of each respective Town, shall Annually on the Day of Election of Town Officers, Elect a Town Clerk, (who shall be Clerk of the Town Concil,) a Town Treasurer, a Town Sergeant, a Town Packer, a Town Sealer of Weights and Measures, and so many Constables, Rate-makers, Overseers of the Poor, Surveyors of Highways, Viewers of Fences, and all other Officers, as each or any Town in this Colony, shall have Occasion for. *What Officers shall be Annually Elected.*

AND be it further Enacted by the Authority aforesaid, That the Free-men of each Respective Town, on their Respective Town meeting Days, as shall be by them appointed, shall and they hereby have full Power Granted them to Admit so many Persons Inhabitants of their Respective Towns, Free-men of their Towns, as shall be by them Adjudged deserving thereof; And that the Town Clerk of each Town, shall once every Year send a Role or List of all Free-men so Admitted in their Respective Towns, to the General Assembly to be held for this Colony at *Newport,* the Day before the General Election, and also such Persons that shall be so return'd and Admitted Free-men of the Colony, shall be inrolled in the Colonies Book, by the General Recorder. *Towns power to make Free-men.*

AND be it further Enacted, by the Authority of the same, That whoso-ever shall be Legally chosen and Elected to the Office of a Constable, within any Town within this Colony, and shall refuse to serve in said place, shall Pay as a Fine, the Sum of *Three Pounds, Six Shillings and Eight Pence,* to be paid into the Town Treasury, to and for the Use of such Town; And if the Person so chosen shall refuse to Pay the same, that then it shall & may be Lawful for any Assistant, Justice of the Peace or Warden of such Town, to Grant forth a Warrant of Distress, to Distrain and Levy so much of said Persons Goods and Chattels, as shall Pay the same, and the said Fine so Levied, to be paid into the Town Treasury as aforesaid. *Constable's Fine, if refuses to Serve, 3 Pounds, Six Shillings and Eight Pence.*

AND be it further Enacted by the Authority aforesaid, That whosoever, shall be duly Elected to the Office of Town Sergeant, or Ratemaker in any Town within this Colony, and shall refuse therein as by Law required, shall Pay as a Fine *Forty Shillings,* into the Town Treasury, to and for the Use of such Town, and if such Persons shall refuse to Pay the same, then it shall be taken by Distraint in manner as aforesaid. *And Town Sergeants and Rate-makers, Forty Shillings.*

AND Be it further Enacted by the Authority aforesaid, That every Person that shall be chosen and elected to any Town Office, in any Town with n this Colony, shall take the following Engagement, before he act in his said Office. *Town Officers to be Engaged.*

YOU A. B. *Do hereby solemnly Engage, true Allegiance unto His Majesty His Heirs and Successors to bear; And that You shall well and truely Execute the Office of for this ensueing Year, or until another be Engaged in your room, or You be Legally Discharged thereof, and this Engage-ment, You make and Give upon the Peril of the Penalty of Perjury.* *The Form of their Engage-ment.*

I 2 An

AN ACT for the Regulating of Fences, throughout this Colony.

FOR*ASMUCH as Difputes and Differences, has arifen, and daily doth arife between the Owners and Proprietors of Lands within this Colony, about the making their proportionable parts of Fence, where their Lands joyn and are under Improvement.*

For the Regulating whereof,

Partition Fences to be equally maintained.

BE it therefore Enacted by the General Affembly, and by the Authority of the fame, Tha* all Partition Fences, between Lands under Improvement, fhall be made and maintained from time to time in equal halfs, by the Proprietors or Poffeffors of fuch Land refpectively, and in Cafe any Proprietor of any Land, fhall Improve his Land, (the Land adjoining, being unimproved,) and make the whole Partition Fence; in fuch Cafe, the Proprietor or Poffeffor of the Land adjoining and unimproved fhall upon his Improvement of the fame, Pay for the one half of fuch Partition Fence, according to the value thereof at that time, and fhall keep up and maintain his half part thereof for the future. And in Cafe either of the Proprietors or Poffeffors of adjoining Lands, fhall refufe fo to do ; That then upon Complaint of the party agrieved thereby, to the Viewers of Fences in faid Town, any Two of the faid Fence Viewers, are to take a View of fuch Fence fo wanting, or not kept in Lawful repair, and upon their certifying the fame under their hands ; The faid party agrieved may make or repair the Fence fo certified to be wanting, and recover the charge and damage thereof, if not exceeding *Forty Shillings*, by Action to be brought before any Two Affiftants, Juftices of the Peace or Wardens in faid Town, and if the charges or damages are above *Forty Shillings*, then at the General Court of Tryals,

Upon neglect, how to be profecuted.

Any one that withdraws his Fence, fhall yet maintain one half of his Line.

AND be it further Enacted by the Authority aforefaid, That if any Perfon fhall withdraw his Fence from the Line, between himfelf and neighbour, the party fo doing, fhall make and maintain the one half of his faid neighbours Fence notwithftanding, faving to every Perfon fuch Agreement, for the maintainance of their divifional Fence, as fhall be by them made.

What Fence fhall be deemed lawful Fence.

AND Be it further Enacted by the Authority aforefaid, That all the feveral forts of Fences hereafter mentioned and made, as is hereafter expreffed, is and fhall be deemed and adjudged Lawfull and fufficient Fence, for the Fencing in of any Lands, and that all other forts not here exprefly mentioned, that fhall upon the View of the Fence Viewers, be adjudged as good and fufficient as thefe that are hereafter mentioned, fhall be demeed Lawfull Fence, againft Horfes, Neat Cattle, Sheep &c. A Hedge with Ditch, fhall be Three-foot high above the top of the Ditch, and well ftaked at the diftance of every foot and half, bound together at the top and well fill'd. A Hedge without a Ditch fhall be ' four foot high, ftaked bound and filled as a Hedge with a Ditch ; and Poft and Rail Fence on a Ditch or Bank, fhall be four Rails high, well fet in Pofts, and all Poft and Rail Fence without a Ditch or Bank, fhall be made five Rails high, and well fet in Pofts. And that if the above fpecified forts of Fence, and other forts not herein Exprefly mentioned, be not ajudged or deemed equialent thereunto, by the Fence Viewers as aforefaid, fhall be
deemed

deemed unlawful Fence, and the party that shall be agrieved thereby, shall have and recover his Damages accruing thereon, against the Possessor of such Land.

AN ACT, for Preventing any Inhabitants of this Colony, from subjecting their Lands under any other Government.

BE it *Enacted by the General Assembly, and by the Authority of the same,* That if any Person or Persons, Inhabiting within, or having any right to any Lands lying within the Limits of this Colony ; shall Subject, Put, or Endeavour by any ways or means to Put, or Subject such Lands, under the Jurisdiction or Authority of any other Government or Colony ; That such Person or Persons, being duly convicted thereof, shall Forfeit to and for the Use of this Colony, and towards the Support thereof, all such Lands by him or them so Subjected, or Put, or Endeavoured to be Subjected or Put under any other Government or Colony ; and be further Fined, at the Discretion of the Judges of such Court, before whom Convicted ; and whoever shall be Procuring, Aiding, Abetting or Assisting, any other Person or Persons in any of the aforesaid Offences, and being thereof duly Convict, shall be Fined at the Discretion of the Judges of the Court before whom Convicted.

(margin: No person shall subject any Land with this Colony under any other Government, On the Penalty of forfeiting all such Lands, and being fined at discretion.)

AN ACT, to prevent excessive Riding in any of the Streets or Highways of the Towns of *Newport* and *Providence.*

WHEREAS *several Persons have had their Bones Broke, and received other Damages, by excessive Riding in the Streets or Highways of the Towns of* Newport *and* Providence.

For the preventing whereof for the future,

BE it *Enacted by the General Assembly, and by the Authority of the same,* That whosoever shall Ride after then a common Travelling pace, in any of the Streets or Highways, of the Town of *Newport,* or shall Ride a Gallop, in the Streets or Highways of the Town of *Providence,* shall for every such Offence, Forfeit *Five Shillings,* the one half to the Informer, and the other half to and for the Use of the Poor of the Town, where such Offence shall be committed, to be Recovered upon Complaint thereof made before any one Assistant, or Justice of the Peace, of the Town where such Offence shall be Committed, together with the reasonable charge accruing thereon, unless Justifiable excuse shall be made to appear before the said Assistant, or Justice, that shall Try the same.

(margin: Excessive Riding to be punished by paying not exceeding five Shillings.)

K   AN

AN ACT, Directing what Bonds the Sheriff shall take of Persons Arrested in Civil Actions.

One Hundred Pounds Real Estate to be Security for the Person Arrested.

BE it Enacted by the General Assembly, and by the Authority of the same, That all Persons whatsoever, that are Inhabitants of this Colony, and have a Visible Real Estate of Free-hold in the same, of the Value of one *Hundred Pounds*, his or their own Bond shall be taken by the Sheriff, to answer such Action.

AN ACT, Establishing Pounds and Stocks, &c.

Every Town to have a Pound, and Cage or Stocks. On the penalty of Ten Pounds.

BE it Enacted by the General Assembly, and by the Authority of the same, That Each Respective Town in the Colony, shall Erect, Build, Make and Maintain at their own charge, one Publick Pound, for the Impounding of Horses, Neat Cattle, Sheep, &c. and one good sufficient Pair of Stocks or Cage, for the Punishing and Securing of Offenders, in such place or places of each Respective Town, as shall be to them most convenient, on the Penalty of Forfeiting *Ten Pounds*, to and for the Use of the Colony, by every Town as shall neglect the same.

L A W S

Made and Past by the General Assembly of His Majesties Colony, of *Rhode-Island*, and *Providence-Plantations*, Held at *Newport*, the first day of *May*, 1669.

AN ACT, for Erecting a Township in the *Narraganfett* Country, to be called *Westerly*.

WHEREAS the Inhabitants of a certain Tract of Land, in the Narraganfett Country, called and known by the Name of Misquamacuk, alias Pawcatuck, Bounded Westerly on the Colony, and Southerly on the Sea; Have Petition'd this Assembly to be Incorporated into a Township; and there being a sufficient number of Inhabitants already settled thereon, and Land convenient for the same,

Westerly Erected a Township.

BE it therefore Enacted by the General Assembly, and by the Authority of the same, That the aforesaid Tract of Land be, and it is hereby Incorporated a Township, and called by the Name of *Westerly*: And the Inhabitants thereof, shall have and Enjoy all the Rights, Immunities, Priviledges and Powers, as other Towns in this Colony have or do Enjoy.

L A W S

Made and Paſt by the General Aſſembly of His Majeſties Colony of *Rhode Iſland,* and *Providence-Plantations* in *New-England,* Held at *Newport* the Second Day of *May* 1671.

AN ACT, for Subſiſting of Poor Priſoners Committed, at the Kings Suit.

BE it Enacted by the *General Aſſembly,* and by the *Authority of the ſame,* That all Perſons that ſhall be Committed to Goal in this Colony, or Criminal Offences, and are Poor, and have not wherewithal to ſubſiſt themſelves, ſhall be allowed *Five-pence per Diem,* out of the General Treaſury of this Colony, for their Subſiſtance, during their Impriſonment. *Provided* they demand the ſame.

Poor Priſoners at the King's Suit allowed Five pence per Diem.

L A W S

Made and Paſt by the General Aſſembly of His Majeſties Colony of *Rhode-Iſland,* and *Providence-Plantations* in *New-England,* Held at *Newport,* the Second Day of *May,* 1672.

AN ACT for Incorporating the Lands on *Block Iſland,* A Townſhip to be called *New Shoreham.*

WHEREAS the *Inhabitants* of Block Iſland, *have Petitioned this Aſſembly,* to be *Incorporated a Townſhip, and there being a ſufficient Number of Inhabitants already Settled thereon, and Land Convenient for the ſame,*

BE it therefore Enacted by the General *Aſſembly, and by the Authority of the ſame,* That all the Lands of *Block-Iſland,* be, and they hereby are Incorporated a Townſhip, and called *New-Shoreham* ; and the Inhabitants thereof, ſhall have and Enjoy all Franchiſes, Immunities, Priviledges and Powers. as in their Charter Granted them by this Aſſembly is more largely ſet forth.

Block-Iſland Erected a Townſhip. and called New-Shore-ham.

Made and Paſt by the General Aſſembly of His Majeſties Colony of *Rhode-Iſland,* and *Providence-Plantations* in *New-England,* Held at *Newport,* the Twenty Eighth Day of *October,* 1674.

A N A C T, Incorporating a certain Tract of Land in the *Narraganſett* Country into a Townſhip, to be. called *Kingſtown.*

WHEREAS the Inhabitants *of a certain Tract of Land in* the Narraganſett Country, *Bounded Eaſt by the* Narrraganſett-*Bay, Southerly the Sea or* Ocean, *and Weſt by the Townſhip of* Weſterly, *have Petitioned this Aſſembly, to be Incorporated a Townſhip ; and there being a Sufficient Number of Inhabitants already ſettled thereon, and Land convenient for the ſame,*

Kingſtown Erected.

BE .it therefore Enacted *by the General Aſſembly, and by the Authority of the ſame,* That the aforeſaid Tract of Land in the Narraganſett-Country, be, and hereby is Incorporated a Townſhip, and called *Kingſtown,* and the Inhabitants thereof, ſhall have and Enjoy all ſuch Immunities, Priviledges and Powers, as in their Charter Granted them by this Aſſembly, is more largely and amply ſet forth.

L A W S

Made and Paſt by the General Aſſembly of His Majeſties Colony of *Rhode-Iſland,* and *Providence-Plantations,* Held at *Newport,* the Thirty Firſt Day of *October,* 1677.

WHEREAS *there is a certain Tract of Land in the* Narraganſett Country, *Bounded Northerly upon the Town of* Warwick, *and Eaſterly upon the* Narraganſett-*Bay, Southerly and Weſterly as by Plat, Returned to this Aſſembly, by* Meſſieurs Peleg Sanford, *and* John Smith, *Serveyors, eſpecially Impowered thereto.*

Eaſt Greenwich Incorporated a Townſhip.

BE it therefore Enacted *by the General Aſſembly, and by the Authority of the ſame,* That the aforeſaid Tract of Land be, and it hereby is Incorporated a Townſhip, and called *Eaſt Greenwich,* and the Inhabitants thereof, ſhall have all ſuch Immunities, Priviledges and Powers as other Towns in this Colony, generally have or do Enjoy.

An

An Act for Granting of Rehearings.

BE it *Enacted by the General Assembly, and by the Authority of the same,*
That either *Plaintiff* or Defendant, that shall be agrieved, at the General
Court of Tryals by Judgement given against either of them, shall and
may have Liberty of one Rehearing, to the next succeeding General Court
of Tryals. *Provided* he or they so Rehearing, shall Pay into the
Recorders Office, (within ten days after such Judgement rendred) such
Costs as shall be Taxed against him or them at such Court, and give sufficient
Bond to the Recorder, to prosecute such Rehearing with Effect, and Pay
all such Costs as shall be Awarded against him or them, at such succeeding
General Court of Tryals.

*Plaintiff or
Defendant
may have a
Rehearing, they
giving Bond
in the Recor-
ders Office, to
prosecute the
same, &c.*

AN ACT to Enable private Persons to Recover their Debts due from any Town by Action, against the Town Treasurer.

BE it *Enacted by the General Assembly, and by the Authority of the same,*
That all Persons whatsoever, That shall have any Money due to him
or them, from any Town in this Colony, for any matter, cause or thing
whatsoever, shall take the following Method for the obtaining of the same,
(to wit) such person or persons, shall Present to the Town Meeting, a
particular Account, of such Debt or Money due, and how Contracted ; which
being done in Case Just, and due satisfaction is not made him or them by
the Town Treasurer of such Town, within one Months time after such account be given in as aforesaid, that then it shall be Lawful for such person
or persons, to Commence his or their Action against such Town Treasurer,
for the recovery of the same, and upon Judgement Obtained for such Debt
or Mony due, in Case the Town Treasurer shall not have sufficient of the
Towns Money in his hands, to satisfy and pay the Judgment Obtained against
him, and the charges expended in defending such Suit ; That then upon
Application made by such Town Treasurer, to any one Affistant, Justice of
the Peace or Warden of such Town, such Affistant, Justice or Warden, shall
grant forth a Warrant, to the Town Sergeant of such Town, Requiring him
to Warn the Inhabitants of such Town, to hold a Town Meeting, at such
time and place as shall be Appointed, for the speedy ordering and making
a Rate, to be Collected for the Reimbursement of such Town Treasurer ; And
in Case such Town upon due Warning given them, shall not take due,
speedy and effectual care to Reimburse, Pay, or Satisfy such Town Treasurer
such Moneys, Costs and Charges by him Expended or Recovered against
him ; That then upon Information or Complaint thereof by him made, to
the next General Affembly of this Colony, such order shall be given therein, for
the said Treasurers Reimbursement, with allowance for all incident costs, charges and trouble occasioned thereby ; and such Town shall be Fined, at the
Difcretion of the said General Affembly.

*How Debts
due from a
Town may be
recover'd.
To be
Exhibited to
the Town.
Meeting, and
then the Town
Treasurer to
be Sued for
the same.
If the Town
Treasurer have
not sufficient,
to pay the
same, to give
Information
thereof to an
Affistant, &c.
who is to call
a Town Meet-
ing, to make
a Rate for
the same.
Town shall
neglect so to
do, such Town
shall be fined
by the Gene-
ral Affembly.*

L　　　　　　　　　　　　　　　An

AN ACT, Enabling the Sheriff to Appoint and Conſtitute a Deputy or Deputies.

B E *it Enacted by the General Aſſembly, and by the Authority of the ſame,* That the Shiriff of this Colony for the time being, ſhall at all times hereafter have Power and Authority, to Conſtitute and Appoint one or more Deputies under him, for the due Serving or Executing any Writ, Warrant, or Execution, belonging to his Office, as alſo to Collect Fines and Amercements.

The Sheriff to appoint a De- puty.

PROVIDED always, and it is Enacted, That ſuch Sheriff ſhall be Reſponſible for any neglect or miſdoing, of ſuch his Deputy or Deputies, in the Matters and Truſts committed to him or them.

And to be re- ſponſible for him.

An Act, for Amercing Perſons Choſen to Serve as Jurors at any Court in this Colony, for Non-Appearance.

B E *it Enacted by the General Aſſembly, and by the Authority of the ſame,* That in Caſe any Perſon ſhall be duly Choſen by any Town in this Colony, ſerve on a Jury at any Court in this Colony, and ſhall not make his due Appearance at ſuch Court as by Law he ought; that then ſuch Perſon ſhall (for ſuch his default) be Amerced the Sum of *Thirteen Shillings* and *Four-pence,* by the Judges of ſaid Court, unleſs they ſhall ſee reaſonable cauſe to mitigate or remit the ſame.

Jurors upon non-appea- rance, to be fined Thir- teen Shil- lings and Four-pence. Towns fined, if they don't chuſe and ſend their Quota of Qualified Jury-men. To be taken by Diſtreſs.

AND be it further Enacted by the Authority aforeſaid, That in Caſe any Town ſhall neglect to chuſe, and ſend their number of Jury-men, or neglect and ſend Perſons not qualified according to Law ; that then ſuch Town ſhall be Amerced, for every ſuch Perſon ſo Omitted to be ſent, or un- qualified as aforeſaid, the Sum of *Twenty Shillings,* to be Levied by Diſtraint up- on the Eſtate of the Treaſurer of ſuch Town, by Warrant from the General Recorder, directed to the Sheriff of this Colony, or his Deputy, the ſaid Treaſurer to be Reimburſed by ſuch Town.

AN ACT, Directing the Duty of His Majeſties Attorney General in this Colony.

B E *it therefore Enacted by the General Aſſembly, and by the Authority of the ſame,* That His Majeſties Attorney General for this Colony, ſhall conſtantly give his Attendance at all General Courts of Tryals, and Goal Delivery, where his Attendance is by Law required, for the ſervice of His Majeſty : And is to give unto ſuch Court or Courts, due Advice and Information, concerning any Crimes, Breaches of the Peace, or Wrongs done to His Majeſty, or any of His Subjects, that ſhall come to his knowledge ; and to draw up and preſent to ſuch Courts, all Informations and Indictments, or other Legal Proceſs, againſt any ſuch Offenders as by Law is Required, and diligently by a due courſe of Law, to Proſecute the ſame, to final Judgement and Execution.

Attorney Ge- neral to at- tend theCourts de Die in Diem, and to draw all In- dictments, and proſecute the ſame.

An

AN ACT, for the Protection of Witnesses from Arrest, that shall come from another Government to give Evidence.

WHEREAS *many times it falls out, that Persons Living in other Governments, can give Evidence against Criminals, but for fear of being Arrested, are discouraged from giving their Personal Attendance in the Courts of this Colony, as is needful and requisite in such Cases.*

BE it therefore Enacted by the General Assembly, and by the Authority of the same, That where any Person shall by Notification in Writing from any Assistant, Justice of the Peace, Warden, or from the General Recorder of this Colony, be desired to Appear before such Assistant, Justice of the Peace or Warden, or before any Court in this Colony, to give in Evidence in any matter relating to any Criminal Offence ; That such Person shall be Protected, and free from all Arrest in Civil Actions, during the necessary time of his coming and giving Evidence, and returning out of this Government again.

Persons coming from another Government to give Evidence, not to be Arrested.

L A W S

Made and Past by the General Assembly of His Majesties Colony of *Rhode-Island,* and *Providence-Plantations.* Held at *Newport,* the Thirtieth Day of *May* 1678.

AN ACT, for Incorporating the Island of *Conanicut* a Township, to be called *James-Town.*

WHEREAS *Mr.* CalebCarr, *Mr.* Francis Brinly, *and other Inhabitants of the Island of* Conanicut, *Have Petition'd this Assembly, to be Incorporated a Township ; and there being a sufficient number of Inhabitants thereon, and Land convenient for the same,*

BE it therefore Enacted by the General Assembly, and by the Authority of the same, That the abovesaid Island of *Conanicut,* be, and it is hereby Incorporated a Township, and called *James Town,* and the Inhabitants thereof, shall have and Enjoy all such Franchises, Liberties, Priviledges and Powers, as the Town of *New Shoreham,* in this Colony Have, Do, or ought to Enjoy,

Conanicut Island Incorporated a Township and called James Town.

Made and Paſt by the General Aſſembly of His Majeſties Colony of *Rhode-Iſland,* and *Providence-Plantations.* Held at *Newport,* the Sixth Day of *May,* 1679.

AN ACT, Prohibitng Sports, and Labours on the Firſt day of the Week.

BE it Enacted by the *General Aſſembly of this Colony, and by the Authority of the ſame,* That noPerſon nor Perſons within thisColony,ſhall do or exerciſe any Labour or Buſineſs,or Work of their ordinary Calling,nor Uſe any Game, Sport, Play or Recreation, on the Firſt Day of the Week, nor ſuffer the ſame to be done, by their Children, Servants or Apprentices (works of Neceſſity and Charity only excepted) on the Penalty of *Five Shillings,* for every ſuch Offence, to be Levyed on due Conviction thereof, by Warrant of Diſtreſs, from any one Aſſiſtant, Juſtice of the Peace, or Warden, to the Conſtable of ſuch Town, where ſuch Offence ſhall be committed, to and for the Uſe of the Poor of ſuch Town, together with the reaſonable charges accrueing thereon. And in Caſe ſuch Offender ſhall not have ſufficient to ſatisfy the ſame, then to be ſet in the Stocks, by the ſpace of Three Hours. And that whoſoever ſhall Improve, ſet to work or encourage any other Perſon's Servant, to Commit any of the aforeſaid Offences, ſhall ſuffer the like Puniſhment as aforeſaid.

AN ACT, for Preventing Sailors, from being Truſted or Credited for Strong Liquors.

WHEREAS *it is the frequent Complaint of Maſters and Commanders of Ships and other Veſſels, of Great Damage ſuſtained by them, by reaſon of the Entertaining and Truſting of Sailors, (Ship'd in their Employ,) by Tavern-keepers and others, whereby their Voyages are many ways hindred.*

BE it Enacted. by the *General Aſſembly, and by the Authority of the ſame,* That if any Perſon or Perſons, keeping any Tavern, Ale-houſe, Victualling-houſe or Ordinary, ſhall Truſt or give Credit to any Sailor, Ship'd on Board any Ship or other Veſſel, without the knowledge and Conſent or Order of the Maſter or Commander of ſuch Ship or Veſſel, whereunto ſuch Sailor ſl all then belong, for any more or greater Sum than *Five Snillings.* And ſuch Perſon or Perſons giving Credit, or Truſting ſuch Sailor for more, ſhall be wholly barr'd, during the time ſuch Sailor ſhall remain in ſuch Commander or Maſters Service, from bringing any Action for the ſame; & in caſe ſuch Perſon ſhall cauſe ſuch Sailor to be Arreſted,detained or hindred, from following his Commanders or Maſters Employ on ſaid Voyage.

Voyage, contrary to this Act ; fuch Commander or Mafter fhall have his Action againft fuch Perfon thereupon, and recover his full Damages with Cofts.

LAWS

Made and Paft by the General Affembly of His Majefties Colony of *Rhode-Ifland,* and *Providence-Plantations,* Held at *Newport,* the Fifth Day of *May,* 1680.

AN ACT, Granting Appeals to the General Affembly, from the General Courts of Tryals.

BE it *Enacted by the General Affembly, and by the Authority of the fame,* That in all Perfonal Actions, where either Plantiff or Defendant, fhall Obtain two Judgments for him at the General Court of Tryals in one Action and Caufe brought to the faid Court : The other Party againft *Plaintiff or* whom faid Judgments were given, fhall have Liberty to Appeal to the *Defendant* next General Affembly, from the laft Judgment for Relief, who may if they *may have an* fee Juft and Reafonable Caufe, Confirm, Alter, Amend, or Reverfe fuch *Appeal from* Judgments, and give a new Judgment thereupon, as to the faid Affembly *the General* fhall appear to be agreeable to Law and Equity : And that each or either *Court of Try-* Appellant or. Appellee, fhall and may have Liberty of giving in new *als.* Evidence upon fuch Appeal.

PROVIDED Always, the Party defiring an Appeal, fhall within the *They giving* fpace of Ten Days, after Judgment given in faid General Court of Tryals, *Bond, &c.* Enter his Appeal with the Recorder of this Colony, and Pay into the *days after* faid Recorders Hands, *Three Pounds,* to and for the Ufe of the faid *Judgment.* Affembly, for the Entering thereof, and fuch Cofts as was Awarded on faid Judgment, and give Sufficient Bond to faid Recorder, for the due Profecution of fuch Appeal with Effect. And in mean time Execution fhall be ftayed, until the Determination and Decree of faid Affembly be given thereon.

AND be it further Enacted by the Authority aforefaid, That the Party *The Appel-* Appealing, fhall take out copy of the whole Record of faid Judgment, from *lant to take* out of the Recorders Office, Signed to by faid Recorder, to be Prefented *out a Copy* unto fuch General Affembly, and alfo fhall Ten Days before meeting of fuch *of the Cafe.* General Affembly, File his Reafons of Appeal with the Recorder, that the Appellee may have a copy thereof, and have due time to put in his An-fwer thereto, at the firft Opening of faid Affembly,

M AN

AN ACT, to Inforce the Election of Town Officers, at their Uſual Days of Election.

If any Town neglect to chuſe Town Officers. The General Court of Tryals to order the chuſing of the ſame.

BE it Enacted by the General Aſſembly, and by the Authority of the ſame, That if the Freemen, of any Town in the Colony, ſhall Neglect on their Uſual Days of Election, to chuſe and elect, ſo many Town Officers, as by them have been Uſually Elected, for the Management of their Prudential Affairs ; That then and in ſuch Caſes, upon any. ſuch Town being Preſented to the General Court of Tryals, by the Grand Jury, and duly Convicted thereof ; ſuch Town or Towns, ſhall be Fin'd at the Diſcretion of the Judges of ſuch Court, not. Exceeding *Fifty Pounds*, and the Judges of ſaid General Court of Tryals, ſhall give forth and order, appointing and ordering them to chuſe and elect their Town Officers as Uſual, for the remaining parts of ſaid Year, at ſuch time as ſhall be by them Enjoyned.

L A VV S

At the General Aſſembly of His Majeſties Colony of *Rhode-Iſland,* and *Providence-Plantations,* Held at *Newport,* the Third Day of *May,* 1682.

AN ACT for Eſtabliſhing A Naval Office.

WHEREAS by Letters from His Moſt Gracious Majeſty, to this Colony, Dated the Twelfth Day of November, in the Thirty Firſt Year of His Reign, It is Ordered and Commanded, That a Naval Office be Erected in this Colony.

The Governour to Conſtitute a Naval Office. The Naval Officers Duty.

BE it therefore Enacted by the General Aſſembly, and by the Authority of the ſame, That the Governour of this Colony for the time being, ſhall, and hereby is Impowered to appoint one or more Naval Offices, in ſuch Place or Places in this Colony, as he ſhall think fit and needful, and ſhall Annually appoint a proper Perſon or Perſons as Naval. Officer or Officers therein, to take Entries of Veſſels, and in all things belonging to ſaid Office, to take care that the Laws Relating to Navigation or Cuſtoms and Duties on Goods and Merchandize, be duly obſerved.

A N

A N A C T, Confirming the Grants heretofore made
by the Inhabitants of the Towns of *Newport,* *Provi-*
dence, Portſmouth, Warwick, and *Weſterly,* and to Ena-
ble ſaid Towns to make Prudential Laws and Orders,
for their better Regulating their Town Affairs.

WHEREAS *in the Fifteenth Year of the Reign of our Royal Sovereign*
Lord Charles *the Second, of Bleſſed Memory, there was a Charter*
Granted to this his Majeſties Colony of Rhode-Iſland, *and* Providence-Plantations
in New-England, *In which was contain'd many Gracious Priviledges, Granted to*
the Free Inhabitants thereof ; and amongſt others of the ſaid Priviledges, there
was Granted to the General Aſſembly of ſaid Colony, full Power and Authority
to Make and Ordain Laws, ſuiting the Nature and Conſtitution of the Place ;
and in Particular to Direct, Rule and Order all matters Relating to the Purchaſes
of Lands of the Native Indians. And this Preſent Aſſembly, Taking into The Purchaſes
their ſerious Conſideration, That the Lands of the ſeveral Towns of Newport, *made by the*
Providence, Portſmouth, Warwick *and* Weſterly, *were Purchaſed (by the* Towns of
ſeveral Inhabitants thereof,) of the Native Indians, Chief Sachams of the Country, Newport,
before the Granting of the ſaid Charter ; ſo that an Order or Direction from the ſaid &c. confirmed.
Aſſembly could not be obtain'd therein, and it being thought Neceſſary and
Convenient for the reaſons aforeſaid, That the Lands of the aforeſaid Towns ſhould
be by an Act of the General Aſſembly, of this His Majeſties Colony, Confirmed
to the Inhabitants thereof according to their Several and Reſpective Rights
and Intereſt therein.

BE *it therefore Enacted by this Preſent Aſſembly, and by the Authority*
thereof it is Enacted, That all the Lands Lying and being, within the
Limits of each and every of the aforeſaid Towns, of *Newport, Providence,*
Portſmouth, Warwick, and *Weſterly,* according to their Several Reſpective
Purchaſes thereof made and obtain'd of the Indian Sachems ; Be and hereby
is Allowed of, Ratified and Confirmed, to the Proprietors of each of the
aforeſaid Towns, and to Each and Every of the ſaid Proprietors, their ſeveral
and Reſpective Rights and Intereſts therein, by Virtue of any ſuch Purchaſe
or Purchaſes as aforeſaid, TO HAVE AND TO HOLD, all the aforeſaid
Lands, by Virtue of the ſeveral Purchaſes thereof, with all the Appurtenances,
Priviledges, and Commodities thereunto belonging, or any wiſe Appertaining,
to them the aforeſaid Proprietors, their Heirs and Aſſigns for ever, in as
Full, Lawful, Large and Ample manner to all Intents, Conſtructions and
Purpoſes whatſoever, as if the ſaid Lands, and every part thereof, had been
Purchaſed of the Indian Sachams, by Virtue of any Grants or Allowance
Obtained from the General Aſſembly of this Colony, after the Granting
of the aforeſaid Charter ; and whereas there is within ſeveral of the Towns
within this Colony, confiderable of Lands, Lying yet Uncommon or
Undivided ; And for the more orderly way and manner of the ſeveral
Proprietors, their managing the Prudential Affairs thereof : And for the
more effectual making of Juſt and Equal Diviſion or Diviſions of the ſame, ſo
that each and every of the Proprietors may have their True and Equal part
or proportion of Land, according to his or their proportion of Right, and
that

that the Exact Boundaries of each and every Mans Allotments, when Laid to him may be kept in *Perpetuam.*

How they shall divide their Commons.

It is further Ordered and Enacted by the Authority aforesaid, That it shall and may be Lawful for the Proprietors, of each and every such Town within this Colony, being convened by a Warrant from under the Hand and Seal of an Assistant or Justice of the Peace, in such Town, the Occasion thereof being specified in the Warrant, for them or the Major part of them so met, to chuse and appoint a Clerk, and a Surveyor or Surveyors, and such or so many other Officers, as they shall Judge needful and convenient, for the orderly carrying on and management of the whole Affairs of such Community, and in like manner to proceed from time to time, as often as need shall require.

The aforesaid Towns to make Acts and Orders for their prudential Affairs.

And it is further Ordered, That each and every Town within this Colony, shall, and are hereby fully Impower'd to Make and Ordain, all such Acts and Orders, for the well Management, Rule and Ordering all Prudential Affairs, within their, and each of their Respective Bounds and Limits, as to them shall seem meet and convenient. Always Provided, and in such Cases, such Acts and Orders, are not Repugnant or Disagreeable, to the Laws of this Colony.

L A W S

Made and Past by the General Assembly of His Majesties Colony of *Rhode-Island,* and *Providence-Plantations,* Held at *Newport,* the Sixth Day of *May,* 1690.

AN ACT, for Establishing Justices of the Peace, in the Respective Towns of this Colony.

Justices of the Peace to be Elected for the several Towns.

BE it Enacted by the General Assembly; and by the Authority of the same, That the General Assembly that is Yearly Held at *Newport,* the First Wednesday of *May,* shall during their Session, Annually chuse and Elect so many Justices of the Peace, for each Respective Town in the Colony, as to them shall seem needful and requisite, for the better Administration of Justice, in each Respective Town.

Their Engagement.

AND be it further Enacted by the Authority aforesaid, That whosoever shall be Elected to the Office of Justice of the Peace in this Colony, shall take the same Engagement, as the General Officers take, before he shall Act or Officiate in said Office, and that every Justice of the Peace shall be Commissionated before his Acting in his Office; by the Governour of this Colony for the time being, under the Seal of the Colony, which Commission shall be in the following Form, (*to Wit.*)

Their Commission.

YOU A. B. *being Chosen by the General Assembly, of this their Majesties Colony of* Rhode-Island *and* Providence-Plantations, *to the Place and Office of a Justice*

Justice of the Peace, for the Town of   *You are hereby in their*
Majesties Name   *by the Grace of God over* England,
Scotland, France, *and* Ireland, *King and Queen, Defenders of the Faith &c.*
Commissionated to take care for Keeping and Preserving the Peace, and Administring
the Laws throughout the Township, for the which You are Chosen, according to the Laws
of the Colony, and Statutes in such Cases Provided and made, and to appear at
all Courts of Tryals, or make Return thereunto, concerning all Delinquents, or such
whom by Virtue of your Power, by the Laws you shall Bind over unto such Courts,
and upon Especial Occasion to send forth Your Warrants, to make Hue and Cry, to
Apprehend any Malafactor, upon Complaint unto You made, in behalf of their
Majesties ; which Warrants are strictly to be Observed and Pass throughout this
Colony, for the Apprehending any Person, to Answer at the Kings Suit. And for your
so Doing, This Commission shall be your Sufficient Warrant and Discharge.

Given under my Hand, *&c.*

AN ACT, Establishing the Proceedings and Tryals of all Actions, not Exceeding *Forty Shillings.*

BE it *Enacted by the General Assembly, and by the Authority of the same,*
That all manner of Debts, Trespasses and other Actions, not Exceed- *Actions not*
ing *Forty Shillings,* (wherein Title of Lands is not concern'd) shall and may *exceeding*
be Heard, Tryed, Adjudged and Determined, by and before the Assistants, *Forty Shil-*
Justices of the Peace, or Wardens of the Town, where the Defendant shall *lings, how*
live or be Arrested, or by any two of them, who are hereby Impowered upon *Tryed.*
Complaint made of any such matter or cause as aforesaid, to Grant forth a
Warrant or Summons, against the Party complained of, to be Directed to
the Constable or Town Sergeant of such Town, where such Defendant shall
be at the time of Granting forth such Warrant or Summons, and then to *A Warrant of*
Adjudge of such Case in Dispute, between the Parties, Plantiff and Defendant, *Summons to*
Hearing, Examining and taking according to Law, all such Evidences as shall be *be granted*
by either Party produced ; and after Judgment given, to Grant forth an *out.*
Execution, to the Constable or Town Sergeant as aforesaid, to Levy the said
Fine, Debt or Damage, with the charges accruing thereon, upon the Defen-
dants Goods and Chattels, (unless the Defendant satisfie and Pay down the *Upon Con-*
Judgment and Costs Awarded against him,) and such Goods and Chattels *viction Exe-*
so taken by Distraint, shall be Exposed to Sale, returning the overplus if any *cution to go*
there be, to the Defendant, and for want of such Goods and Chattels, to *forth.*
make such Distress upon, and to take the Body of such Defendant into
Custody, and him to Commit to any of their Majesties Goals within this
Colony, there to remain until the said Fine, Debt or Damages, with Costs *For want of*
be fully satisfied and Paid ; and in Case the Plaintiff be Non-Suited, or *Estate to sa-*
Judgment pass against him, then the said Assistants or Justices, *&c.* are *tisfie, to be*
thereby Impowered to Assess the Defendant, reasonable Costs against such *Committed to*
Plaintiff, to be Levyed and Recovered, in the same Manner and Form as is *Goal.*
above expressed, and the said Assistants and Justices, are hereby Required to *The Plaintiff*
keep fair Records of all their Proceedings therein from time to time. *to pay Costs*
                                                       of Non-Suit.

N   And

*And be it further Enacted by the Authority aforesaid,*That either Party,whether Plaintiff or Defendant, shall and may ·have Liberty, to Appeal from any such Judgment, to the next succeeding General Court of Tryals, to be Held for the Colony, he entering into Bond with one sufficient Surety, in double the Debt and Damages Sued for, and sufficient to answer all Costs that shall arise on the Prosecution of his said Appeal with Effect, and abide the Judgment of said Courts, where said Appeal shall be Tryed, and Receive a final Issue, without any further Rehearing or Appeals, and such Recognizance taken as aforesaid, shall be by such Assistants, or Justices of the Peace, returned into the Recorders Office, at the Sitting of such Court as aforesaid.

Plaintiff and Defendant have either Liberty of Appeal to the General Court of Tryals. Whose Judgment shall be final.

AND the Party Appealing, shall bring the Copies of the whole Case, to such Court of Tryals Appealed unto, where such Party shall be allowed the benefit of any further Plea or Evidence, and if upon such new Plea or Evidence, the Judgment shall be Reversed, the Appellant shall have no Costs Granted him for the first Tryal : And the Assistants and Justices, and other Officers concerned in the Proceedings or Tryal of such Actions as aforesaid, shall take these following Fees, hereafter Stated, and no more.

Fees in Actions not Exceeding *Forty Shillings.*

Assistants and Justices Fees.

	l.	*s.*	*d.*
FOR a Warrant of Arrest.	00	01	00
For every Summons.	00	01	00
For Judgment.	00	04	00
For Recording of Judgment.	00	04	00
For Bond to the Peace or good Behavior.	00	02	06
For Recognizance on Appeals.	00	01	06
For Execution.	00	01	06
For Copy of the Case, the same as the Recorder.			

Constable and Town Sergeants Fees.

FOR Serving of every Warrant, if not above one Mile from Home.	00	01	00

If above one Mile *Two-pence per* Mile, Forward and Backward,

For every Person Sumoned, if not above one Mile from Home.	00	00	06

If above one Mile *Two-pence per* Mile Forward and Backward,

For every Execution Served upon Personal Estate, not above one Mile from Home.	00	01	00

If above one Mile *Two-pence per* Mile, Foreward and Backward.

For every Execution upon the · Body.	00	01	00

If above a Mile distance from Goal, *Two-pence per* Mile Forward and Backward.

The Constable and Town Sergeant to be allowed for attendance, at the Discretion of the Court.

To every Evidence for taking Engagement.   00   01   00
To every Witnefs for Attendance *per Diem.*   00   01   00.
If above one Mile from home *Two-pence per* Mile Forwards & Backwards.

AN ACT, for Regulating the Ferrys.

BE it Enacted by the General Affembly, and by the Authority of the fame, That all and every perfon or perfons, keeping a Ferry within this Colony, fhall at all feafonab e times carry and Tranfport over fuch Ferry or Ferries, the perfon Riding Paft, and all Officers, and all others Travelling Backwards and Forwards, up n the Publick Service of the Colony, without demanding any thing for Tranfportation.

All Perfon on Publick Service, to be carried over the Ferries, Ferriage free.

LAWS

Made and Paft by the General Affembly of His Majefties Colony of *Rhode Ifland,* and *Providence-Plantations.* Held at *Newport,* the Fifth Day of *May 1696.*

AN ACT, Regulating the Granting of Commiffions to Private Men of War.

FOR the Preventing of any Illegal Actions, or Depredations by Privateers, "Commiffionated by the Governour or Deputy Governour o this Colony "on any of His Majefties Subjects, or others in Alliance with his Majefty.

BE it Enacted by the General Affembly, and by the Authority of the fame, That no perfon or perfons, fhall have any Commiffion given him or them, by the Governour or Deputy Governour of this Colony, for the Equipping or Fitting out any Veffel or Veffels, for the Annoying, Taking, Seizing or Deftroying His Majefties enemies, before fuch Perfon or Perfons defiring fuch Commiffion, give Bond of One *Thoufand Pounds,* Sterling Money of *England,* with good Sureties for the due Obferving and Acting according to fuch Commiffion ; and that neither fuch perfon or perons or any under his or their Command, fhall at any time or place Commit any Acts of Hoftility, Depredation or Injury, to or againft any of His Majefties Sbjects or his Allies, or that are or fhall be at fuch time in Alliance with his faid Majefty, but in all things fhall Act againft His Majefties enemies, according to the Commiffion given him or them, and that all Prizes by him or them Taken from His Majefties Enemies, fhall be brought into fome Port within His Majefties Dominions, there to receive fuch Examination, Tryal and Condemnation, as by the Judge or Judges Appointed by His Majefty, fhall be Adjudg'd Lawful.

Captains of Private Men of War to give a Thoufand Pound Bond.

AN ACT, for Collecting of Rates, where the Person Rated hath no visible Estate.

If no visible Estate to pay Rates, to be Committed to Goal, until the same be paid.

BE it *Enacted by the General Assembly and by the Authority of the same,* That if any Person in this Colony, being Legally Rated in any Town, and shall Refuse or Neglect to Pay such Rate, being by the Officer to whom such Rate shall be committed to Collect, Legally Demanded of such person (in Case no visible Estate can be found by such Officer sufficient for the Payment thereof whereon to Distrain) shall be by such Officer, (who is hereby Impowered) Committed to His Majesties Goal in *Newport,* there to Remain until the same be satisfied.

AN ACT, for Regulating the Sitting of the General Assembly.

WHEREAS *it hath been found by long Experience, That the Governour, Deputy Governour and Assistants, sitting with the Deputies for the several Towns, hath been a great hindrance in the Managing of the Publick Affairs of the Government.*

For the Preventing whereof for the Future,

Governour, Deputy Governour and Assistants to Compose the Upper House, and Vote apart.

BE it *Enacted by the General Assembly, and by the Authority of the same,* That at all times hereafter, During the Sessions of the General Assembly of this Colony ; The Governour, Deputy Governour & Assistants, shall Sit apart from the Deputies of the several Towns, and Debate and Vote in all Publick Affairs of the Colony by themselves, and shall be Term'd and Called the Upper House.

The Deputies to Sit & Vote by themselves.

AND that the Deputies of the several Towns in this Colony, shall also Sit, Debate and Vote, in all Publick Affairs of this Colony, During each Session by themselves, and shall be Term'd and Be the Lower House, and shall Elect their Speaker and Clerk, for and During the continuance of such Assembly ; and in Case the said Upper and Lower House (for the Tryal of any Appeal, or other Occasion) shall see cause, it shall and may be Lawful, for them to Resolve themselves into a Grand Committee, and Sit and Vote together, for the better Determining of the same.

An

AN ACT, for Preventing of any Intrusion into the Lands in the *Narragansett* Country.

WHEREAS *sundry Persons, have settled themselves and Families, in the Narragansett Country, without any Legal Title to any Land therein, and without the Consent and Approbation of the General Assembly of this Colony.*

For the Preventing the Ill Consequences thereof, and the like Intrusions for the Future,

BE it Enacted by the General Assembly, and by the Authority of the same, That all Possessions of any Lands in the *Narraganset* Country, obtained by Intrusion, without the consent and approbation of the General Assembly, be , Deem'd and Adjudged Illegal and Void in Law, and shall not give unto such Possessors, any Right, Title, Interest, Property or Claim therein or thereunto; and the Assistants, and Justices of the Peace, of the Towns of *Kingstown*, *Westerly*, and *East-Greenwich*, shall return the Names of all such Persons, that have Intruded as aforesaid, (or that shall Intrude thereon hereafter) to the General Assembly from time to time, that they may in such Legal manner, as they shall think fit, order the Removal of such Intruders, and Preserve the Just Rights, of this Colony thereunto. *All Possession of Lands in Narragansett, without the Consent of the Assembly, to be void.*

L A W S

Made and Past by the General Assembly of His Majesties Colony of *Rhode Island*, and *Providence-Plantations*, &c. Held at *Newport*, the Fourth Day of *May*, 1698.

AN Additional Act to an Act, for Establishing Weights and Measures throughout this Colony.

WHEREAS *several Towns in the Colony have been deficient, and have Neglected to Provide Weights and Measures, pursuant to an Act of Assembly, Past in this Colony*, March the First, 1663. *Entituled*, An Act, for Establishing Weights and Measures.

For the better Inforcing whereof,

BE it Enacted by the General Assembly, and by the Authority of the same, That the Town Treasurer of each respective Town, shall at the proper costs and charges of each Town, provide & procure the several Weights and Measures, as is Specified in the afore-cited Act, *The Town Treasurer of each Town to provide Weights and Measures. Past*

O

(Paft the Firft Day of *March*, 1663.) within the fpace of one Year after the Date hereof, (if not already fupplied) which fhall be Proved and Sealed, by the General Sealer of the Colony, with the Stamp of an Anchor, and every Town that fhall Neglect the fame, fhall Pay as a Fine, *Five Pounds* into the General Treafury ; To and for the Ufe of the Colony, and the General Sealer, fhall be paid for every half Bufhel, by him Proved and Seal'd, *Six-pence* ; and for every other Weight and Meafure *Three-pence* each, and the Town Sealer for every Weight and Meafure by him Seal'd, *Three-pence*, to be- Paid by the Owner thereof.

Fees for the Sealer.

And be it further Enacted by the Authority aforefaid, That whofoever fhall Sell by any other Weights, then are agreeable to the afore-cited Act, fhall Suffer the Penalty, as is therein mentioned.

AN ACT, for Punifhing of ' fuch as fhall Refufe to Aid or Obey, the Affiftants, Juftices of the Peace, Wardens or Conftables, in the due Execution of their Office

Whofoever fhall refufe to Aid an Officer in the Execution of his Office. fhall be fined Ten Shillings

BE it therefore Enacted by the General Affembly, and by the Authority of the fame, That whofoever fhall Refufe to give Aid, or duly Affift, any Affiftant, Juftice of the Peace or Conftable in this Colony, in the due Execution of their Refpective Offices, when thereunto lawfully Required ; and be duly Convicted thereof, before any Affiftant, or Juftice of the Peace, &c. fhall for every fuch Offence, Pay as a Fine *Ten Shillings*, into the Town Treafury of fuch Town, where fuch Offence fhall be Committed ; and if the Party fo Offending Refufe to Pay the fame, then it' fhall be taken by a Warrant of Diftrefs, and be difpofed of as aforefaid.

AN ACT for Preventing of Sheep and other Cattel, from being Worried and Torn by Dogs.

WHEREAS great *Damage has been done to many Perfons, by Dogs. Ligging, Worring, and oftentimes Killing their Sheep and other fmall Cattel.*

For the Preventing whereof,

No Dog to worry Sheep. &c. On the Pe- nalty of the Owners pay- ing the Da- mages for the fifft Offence And for the fecond Offence, double Da- mages.

BE it Enacted by the General Affembly, and by the Authority of the fame, That in Cafe any Perfon, fhall have any Sheep or other Cattle, Worried, Torn or Killed by any Dog or Dogs, that the Owners of fuch Sheep or Cattle, fhall Recover againft the Owner of fuch Dog or Dogs, by Action of the Cafe with cofts of Court ; and that if afterwards, any further Damage be done by fuch Dog or Dogs to any Sheep or Cattle, in like manner that the Owner of fuch Dog or Dogs, fhall Pay to the Party agrieved thereby, double Damages, to be Recovered in like manner as aforefaid with Cofts, and that fuch Dog or Dogs be Killed.

AN

AN ACT, for the Impounding of Cattle, Sheep, &c. and for Recovering the Damages that shall be done by them.

BE it *Enacted by the General Assembly, and by the Authority of the same,* That if any Neat Cattle, Horse, Sheep or Hogs, shall break into the Grounds of any Person through Lawful Fence, the Party agrieved, shall have his Liberty, either to Recover his Damages by Action against the Owner or Owners of the same, or otherwise to Impound the same, in the Publick Town Pound, and forthwith upon such Impounding, to get Two Free-holders of such Town, to Apprize the Damages done, and such Cattle Horses, Sheep or Hogs, to be kept in such Pound, until the Damage and Charge of Impounding be Paid by the Owner thereof.

The Person agrieved by, ing into his Grounds, to recover his Damage by Action, or otherwise to Impound.

PROVIDED always, and it is Enacted, That in Case the Owner or Owners of such Cattle, &c. shall see cause to Replevin the same, that it shall be Lawful for him so to do, he giving Bond to the Assistants, or Justices of the Peace granting such Replevin, to prosecute the same with Effect, if the Damage Apprized Exceed not *Forty Shillings,* before Two Assistants, or Justices of the Peace, in said Town, and if the Damage be above *Forty Shillings,* then to be prosecuted at the next succeeding General Court of Tryals.

Upon Replevin, Bond to be given

AND the said Assistant, or Justice of the Peace, granting such Replevin, shall return the same, with the Bond by him taken, (if Tryable at the General Court of Tryals) to the Clerk of said Court, Twenty Days before the Sitting of such Court : And if Tryable, before the Assistants or Justices, then Ten Days before the Day appointed for Tryal ; and thereupon the Party Distraining, shall put in his Avowry or Justification of Impounding, into the General Court of Tryals, Eight Days before the Sitting of said Court, with the Clerk of said Court ; and if before the Assistants or Justices, Four Days before the time appointed for the Tryal of the same, with one of the said Assistants or Justices.

AND be it further Enacted, That in case the Owner or Owners of such Cattle, &c. Impounded, shall not within Ten Days after the Impounding the same, pay or satisfie the Damages appraised, and Charge of Impounding and Feeding such Cattle, &c. or otherwise Replevin the same as aforesaid ; that then so many of said Cattle, &c. shall be Sold by Publick Outcry, as will pay and satisfie the Charge and Damages.

If not replevin'd within ten Days, to be Sold to pay Damages, &c.

AND be it further Enacted, That the Pound-Keeper shall feed such Cattle, &c. Impounded, at the Charge of the Owner thereof, and shall be allowed and paid for every Neat Beast, or Horse-kind Impounded, *Four-pence,* and for every Sheep or Hog, *One Penny,* before Discharged from the Pound.

AND be it further Enacted by the Authority aforesaid, That no Hog or Hogs, shall run at large in any Town in the Government, from the first of *February,* to the middle of *October* Annually, Unyoked or Unringed, (unless by Act of any Town, for such Town it be ordered otherwise,) and it shall & may be lawful for any Person or Persons, to Impound any Hog or Hogs, running loose contrary to this Act, and the Owner of such Hog or Hogs, shall Pay the Poundage thereof, before they be from Pound discharged.

No Hog to run at-large. The Penalty thereon.

An

AN ACT, for the Preventing Fires doing damage in the Town of *Newport.*

FORASMUCH as the Buildings in the Town of Newport, are contiguous and adjoining to one another, in most parts of said Town, whereby Fire in breaking out may do unspeakeable damage, unless timely Provided for.

Every House to provide one good Ladder, within six Months. On the Penalty of One Shilling per Mon. h.
BE it Enacted by the General Assembly, and by the Authority of the same, That the Owner or Owners, of each and every Dwelling-House, in the Town of *Newport*, from the Pound at the North-east end of the Town, down to the Sea side, and so Southward and Northwad, as far as the Buildings are contiguous or adjoining one to another; shall provide and procure (within Six Months from the Date hereof) for each Dwelling-House, one good Ladder of sufficient Length, to reach to the Ridge of his or their Dwelling-House ; and the same corinually keep in repair ; that every Owner or Owners of any Dwelling-House shall neglect to do the same, he, she or they so neglecting, shall for every Month after said Six Months are Expired, Forfeit as a Fine to and for the Use of said Town, *One Shilling per* Month, to be recovered up in Complaint made, and Convicted thereof before any Assistant, or Justice of the Peace of said Town, by Warrant of Distress ; excepting out of this Act, all such Houses which have Walks or Turrets thereon, or other Conveniency, as shall be adjudged and deemed equivalent thereunto.

AN ACT, for Prevening Fraud in Fire-Wood, Exposed to Sale.

Fire-Wood to be four Foot long, & the Cord eight foot long.
BE it Enacted by the General Assembly, and by the Authority of the same, That all Fire-wood Exposed to Sale in this Colony, shall be Four Foot Long, Measuring to one Half of the Cart, and shall be Sold by the Cord ; and that the Cord shall be Eight Foot Long, Four Foot High, well stowed and closely laid together.

Every Town to Chuse a Corder of Wood.
AND that in every Town in this Colony, where Wood is Exposed to Sale by the Cord, the Free-men of said Town shall (if they think fit) Annually chuse and Elect, one Wood-Corder, who shall take the same Engagement to his Office, as other Town Officers do ; and shall have *Four pence per* Cord, for every Cord by him Corded, from the Seller of said Wood.

All Wood Exposed to Sale, that is not four foot long, shall be forfeited.
And be it further Enacted by the Authority aforesaid, That whosoever shall Sell or Expose to Sale, any Wood that is not of the Length as aforesaid, shall upon due Conviction thereof, before any Assistant, or Justice of the Peace of such Town, where such Offence shall be committed ; Forfeit all such Wood so Exposed to Sale ; the one half to the Informer, and the other half to and for the Use of such Town ; to be taken by a Warrant of Distress, to be Granted by such Assistant or Justice, to whom Complaint shall be made.

An

AN ACT, for Preventing the misapplying of the Rates and Taxes, that shall be hereafter Assessed and Levied in this Colony.

BE it Enacted by the General Assembly, and by the Authority of the same, That all Rates and Taxes, that shall be Assessed and Levied in this Colony for the future, shall be applied to no other Use or Uses whatsoever, then those for which the same shall be Assessed and Levied: Any Custom or Usage to the contrary hereof notwithstanding.

No Rates to be misapplied.

AN ACT, for Building A Goal in the Town of *Providence*.

BE it Enacted by the General Assembly, and by the Authority of the same, That there shall be a Goal Erected and Built in the Town of *Providence*, for the securing such Criminals and Prisoners for Debt, as as shall be by lawful Authority Committed thereto, and that the Sheriff of this Colony for the time being, and in his absence, the Town-Sergeant of said Town for the time being, shall have the Care and Custody of the same.

A Goal to be Built in the Town of Providence.

L A W S

Made and Past by the General Assembly of His Majesties Colony of *Rhode-Island*, and *Providence-Plantations*, &c. Held at *Newport*, the Thirtieth Day of *April*, 1700.

AN ACT, for putting in Force the Laws of *England* in all Cases, where no Particular Law of this Colony hath Provided a Remedy.

BE it Enacted by the General Assembly, and by the Authority of the same, That in all Actions, Matters, Causes and things whatsoever, where no Particular Law of this Colony is made to Decide and Determine the same; that then and in all such Cases the Laws of *England* shall be put in Force to Issue, Determine and Decide the same. Any Usage, Custom or Law to the contrary hereof notwithstanding.

A r

A N A C T, for the Enabling the Governour of this Colony, to put in Execution the Statute of Trade and Navigation.

All Vessels that Arrive in this Government, to make their Report to the Governour, &c.

BE it Enacted by the General Assembly, and by the Authority of the same, That from and after the Publication of this Act, no Master of any Ship or Vessel that shall come into any Bay, River or Port within the Precincts of this Colony, shall, or do presume to Land, Unlade and put on Shore, any Wares, Goods or Merchandizes, before he hath made Report thereof to the Governour, or in his absence, to the Deputy Governour ; and have lawfully Entered the same in the Collectors Office ; under the Penalty made and Enacted by the Parliament of *England*, in the Fifteenth year of King *Charles* the Second, for preventing of frauds, and Regulating abuses in the Plantations.

None to Land any Passenger without leave.

And be it further Enacted by the Authority aforesaid, That if any Master or Commander of any Ship or Vessel, shall Land, or put on Shore, in this Colony, any Person, or Passengers, that shall not be admitted or Received to Inhabit in this Colony; that then and in such Cases, it shall and may be in the power of any Assistant or Justice of Peace, &c. of such Town, where such Passenger, &c shall be Landed, To Require, and Command such Master or Commander, to take on board his Ship or Vessel, such Passenger or Passengers, as have been by him Landed, and him, he, she or them so taken on Board, to Transport and Carry out of this Colony ; and if any Master or Commander of any Ship or other Vessel, shall refuse or neglect so to do, that then it shall and may be lawful for any Assistant or Justice of the Peace, &c. to Grant forth a Warrant, for the Apprehending of such Master or Commander, and him Commit to his Majesties Goal in this Colony, until that he give in one *Hundred Pound* Bond, with Security to perform the same.

AN ACT, for Preventing of Clandestine Transportations of any Person or Persons out of this Colony.

WHEREAS divers Masters of Ships, and other Vessels, do from time to time Transport and Carry away out of this Colony, many Persons who are Indebted to several Inhabitants of this Colony, without giving any Account of the Names of such Persons by them so Carried ; which is a manifest Injury to the Creditors of such Persons, and some of them are hereby undone ; for the preventing whereof for the future,

None to be Transported out of the Colony, without a Certificate, under the Penalty of Fifty Pounds.

BE it Enacted by the General Assembly, and by the Authority of the same, That no Master or Commander of any Ship or Vessel whatsoever, shall Transport or Carry out of this Colony, any Family, or Person or Persons that have not for the space of ten Days before their Departure, fix'd up his, her or their Name or Names in Writing, in some Publick Place of the Town wherein they Reside, and of their intent to Depart the Colony ; and that the same be Certified under the Hand of an Assistant, or Justice of said
Town

Town, under the Penalty of Forfeiting, to and for the Use of the Colony, *Fifty Pounds*, in Money, to be Recovered by the General Treasurer, upon due Conviction thereof, in the General Court of Trials.

And be it Enacted by the Authority aforesaid, That the Assistant, or Justice, &c. that shall give such Certificate as aforesaid, shall Transmit a Copy thereof, to the Naval Officer in *Newport*, who shall keep a fair Register thereof, and of the Time of Departure, and of the Masters and Vessels name wherein Transported ; and shall be paid *Twelve-pence* for the same by the Person or Persons desiring to be Transported.

L A W S

Made and Past by the General Assembly of His Majesties Colony of *Rhode-Island,* and *Providence-Plantations,* &c. Held at *Warwick,* the Twenty Ninth Day of *October,* 1701.

AN ACT, in Addition to an Act, for Preventing of Clandestine Marriages · And also for the Registring of Marriages, Births and Burials.

BE it Enacted by the General Assembly, and by the Authority of the same, That all Persons in this Colony, that are Desirous to be joyn'd together in Marriage, shall make their Application to an Assistant or Justice of the Peace in the Town, where such Persons respectively Dwell, who shall give them a Writing under his Hand and Seal, Declaring their Intention of Marriage, the which shall be set up in some Publick Place of the Town, wherein such Persons respectively Dwell, for the space of fourteen Days ; and that if any Person shall have any lawful Objection to make againtt any Persons so Published, being Married ; He or She shall, and may by leave of any Assistant, or Justice, &c. of such Town, underwrite such Publication, He or She first giving to such Assistant, Sufficient Bond to Refund all Damages that shall accrue thereon. *None to be Married with out due Publication. Publications may be undert writ*

And it is further Enacted, by the Authority aforesaid, That all persons that shall go to be Married in another Town then which they were Published, shall produce to the Officer to whom they apply themselves to be Married, a Certificate of their being duly Published as aforesaid ; and that if any persons shall come into any Town of this Colony to be Married from any other Government, shall produce a Certificate under the Hand of the Authority lawfully Impowered thereto, of such Government where they respectively Dwell, that they have duly Complied with such Laws and Orders as are in such Government in force for Publication.

And be it further Enacted, That if any Affistant, Juftice of the Peace, or Warden in this Colony, fhall prefume to Joyn together in Marriage any perfons that have not been Publifhed as aforefaid, or any perfon whofe Publication hath been lawfully under-writcen, and the Impediment not removed; fuch Officer fo Offending, fhall for the firft Offence Forfeit *Five Pounds* in Money, to the Ufe of the Colony; and for the Second Offence, *Ten Pounds* in Money, to and for the Ufe aforefaid, to be recovered by the General Treafurer, in the General Court of Tryals, upon due Conviction thereof, and for the fame fhall be Sufpended from his Office.

And be it further Enacted by the Authority aforefaid, That whofoever fhall prefume to be Married without duly proceeding as by this Act is required, and thereupon fhall Cohabit together; the perfons fo Offending, being duly Convicted thereof, fhall for fuch Offence, Forfeit *Five Pounds* in Money, to and for the Ufe of the Colony, and fhall be recovered by the General Treafurer, upon Conviction thereof, in the General Court of Tryals, or fhall fuffer Three Months Imprifonment, or be Corporally Punifhed by Whipping, at the Difcretion of the Judges of faid Court, not exceeding Thirty Nine Stripes each.

And be it further Enacted, by the Authority aforefaid, That the abovefaid Act fhall be no ways conftrued, deemed or taken to extend to any perfon that fhall be lawfully Married according to the Laws, Cuftoms, Ufage and Ceremony of the Church of *England,* as by Law Eftablifhed; nor to thofe people called *Quakers,* that fhall duly be Married according to the Act of Toleration allowed them.

And be it further Enacted, That all Marriages fhall be Recorded in the Town where they are Confummated, and the Affistant, Juftice or Warden, fhall return the Names of thofe they Marry, and when Married, into the Town Clerk within Three Months after the Confummation thereof; and fhall Pay to the Town Clerk, *Three-pence* for the Regiftring thereof; and he fhall be paid *Three Shilings* for the fame.

And be it further Enacted by the Authority aforefaid, That all Births and Burials of all Children fhall be Regiftred in the Town Clerks Office in the fame Town where they happen to be Born or Dye, by the Parents of fuch Children as fhall be Born or Dye, as aforefaid, within Two Months Time after the Birth or Burial thereof; for Regiftring of each, the Town Clerk fhall be paid *Four-pence,* by the Parent of fuch Child or Children; and that whofoever fhall Refufe or Neglect fo to do, fhall for every Months Neglect after faid Two Months is Expired, Forfeit *Twelve-pence per* Month, to and for the Ufe of fuch Town; to be recovered upon Conviction thereof, in any Court of Record, by the Treafurer of faid Town.

Laws

L A W S

Made and Paft by the General Affembly of this Her Majefties
Colony of *Rhode-Ifland,* and *Providence-Plantations,* &c. Held at
Newport, the Sixth Day of *May,* 1702.

AN ACT, for Preventing the Inhabitants of this Colony,
from Concealing or Harbouring Vagrants, Runaways, *&c.*

WHERE*AS divers Deferters from Her eMajefties Service, as Vagrant
and Runaway Perfons, often-times come into this Colony, and are
frequently Entertained by the Inhabitants of this Colony, without the*
Knowledge *of the Authority in the fame.*

For the Preventing Whereof for the Future,

BE it Enacted by the General Affembly, and by the eAuthority
of the fame, That if any Perfon or Perfons Inhabiting within this
Colony, fhall Entertain, Harbour or Conceal any Stranger not being
a Known Inhabitant of this Colony, above the fpace of one Week,
without Informing fome one or more of the Affiftants or Juftices of fuch
Town thereof ; the perfon or perfons Offending therein, being duly Convicted
hereof, fhall Forfeit *Five Pounds* in Money, to and for the Ufe of the Town
where fuch Offender Dwells, to be recovered by the Town Treafurer of fuch
Town, together with the Incident Cofts accrueing in the General Court of
Tryals; and if fuch Offender have not Sufficient Eftate to Pay the fame,
that then it fhall and may be in the Power of the Judges of faid Court, to
punifh fuch Offender by Whipping, at their Difcretion, not Exceeding Thirty
Nine Stripes.

*No Inhabi-
tant to En-
tertain De-
ferters, &c.
On the Pe-
nalty of* Five
Pounds.

AN Act, for Eftablifhing and Regulating the Affeffing and
Collecting fuch Rates and Taxes as fhall at any time here-
after be Affeffed and Levied on the Colony, and all fuch
Rates as fhall be Affeffed on the Several Towns in the fame.

BE it Enacted by the General Affembly, and by the eAuthority of the
fame, That from time to time, and at all Times hereafter, as often as
the General Affembly of this Colony fhall Order and Enact any Rates to
be Affeffed & Levied on the Inhabitants of this Colony, the Recorder of the
Colony for the time being, fhall forthwith fend a Copy thereof under the Seal

Q

of

the Colony, to the General Treasurer for the time being, who upon the
The Receiver Receipt thereof shall send an Exact List of each Towns part to the Town
to send a Co- Clerk of each Respective Town, together with a Warrant to each and
py of the d is- every of them, requiring them to Notify the Rate-makers or Assessors of
requiring each Respective Town ; to Assess and Apportion the same, on the In-
Rates to be habitants of said Town, according to the time specified in said Act of
made to the Assembly ; and the Assessors or Rate-makers of each Town, or the Major
General Trea- part of them, shall Ten Days before they Assess or Apportion the same, set
surer. up two Notifications under their Hands, Requiring the Inhabitants of their
Who is to Town, to bring into them in Writing under their Hands, an Exact List of
order the As- their Rateable Estate, by such time as is therein prefixed ; who are hereby
sessors to As- required to give their Engagements thereto ; and the Assessors or Rate-
sess the same. makers are hereby fully Impowred to take the same, in the following
Persons to Engagement.
give in an
Accompt of
their Ratea-
ble Estate, up-
on Engage-
ment.   Y OU A. B. *do on your Solemn Engagement, hereby Declare, that the Account*
The Form of   *and List of your Rateable Estate, by you to us presented, is a True and Just*
the Engage-   *Account of the whole of your Rateable Estate, as you know of, and is in your care*
ment.   *and custody, and this you Declare to be the Truth, and nothing but the Truth, upon*
the Peril of the Penalty of Perjury.

And be it further Enacted, That whosoever shall Refuse or Neglect so to
do, in case he be over-rated, shall have no remedy for the same.

AND be it further Enacted by the Authority aforesaid, That the aforesaid
Assessors or Rate-makers, shall forthwith upon their Assessing and Apportioning
of any Rate or Tax, to them committed to Assess, send and return a true Bill
The Assessors or List thereof to the Town Clerk of such Town, to which they respectively
to send the belong, under their Hands ; and the Town Clerk shall upon his receiving
Rate Bill to thereof, draw an Exact Copy thereof, and send the same to the General
the Town Treasurer under his Hand Indented, and upon Receipt thereof, the General
Clerk. Treasurer shall Issue forth his Warrants, to the several Constables of the
And he a Copy Respective Towns, Commanding every of them in Her Majesties Name to
to the Treasu- Collect and Gather the several Sums, as to them is severally Committed in
rer, who is to Money, by such time as by Law is Required ; and when Gathered and
grant forth Collected, the same to bring, and pay into him, or to his Successors
his Warrants in said Office.
for the Col-
lecting thereof.

AND be it further Enacted, That if any Constable or Constables, shall
refuse or neglect to do the same as aforesaid ; that then and in such Cases,
Upon neglect the General Treasurer shall recover the Sum against such Constable or
of Collecting, Constables, as shall be defective therein, by Action of Debt, at the General
how recovered. Court of Tryals, to be brought at any time before the sitting of such Court,
together with the incident charges accruing ; and the Defendant or Defendants, shall have no Essoign, Protection or Wager of Law allowed him or them.
Any Law, Custom or Usage, to the contrary hereof notwithstanding.

AND the General Treasurer, shall be allowed him *Six-pence per* Pound,
for Receiving and Paying out the same : And Assessors or Rate-makers shall
be Paid   *Shillings* each, for Apportioning thereof, and the
Fees for the Town Clerk for Copying the Rate Bill, according as for other Copies ; and
Bishops, &c. the Constables Fees for Collecting, shall have *Twelve-pence per* Pound, all the
                                                                                                        said

Said Fees to be paid out of each Respective Rate, as it shall be paid into the General Treasury.

And be it further Enacted by the Authority aforesaid, That the Town Clerk of each Respective Town, shall within Ten Days after the Election and Engagement of the Constables of the Town wherein he dwells, send a *The Town* List of the Constables so Chosen and Engaged, unto the General Treasurer *Clerk to re-* of the Colony for the time being ; and that if any Town Clerk shall Neglect *turn the Con-* the same, he shall Forfeit *Forty-Shillings* for every Offence, to and for the Use *to the General* of the Colony, to be Recovered by the General Treasurer for the time being, *Treasurer.* upon Complaint made before any Court of Record in the Colony,

And be it further Enacted by the Authority aforesaid, That all Town *Towns Rates* Rates, that shall be Levied on any Town in the Colony, shall be Assessed *to be Assessed* and Collected in the same manner and form as the Colony Taxes are, and *as the Colony* the Town Treasurer shall have an Action of Debt against any Delinquent, *Rates are.* Constable, or Constables, as the General Treasurer hath ; wherein no Essoign, Protection or Wager of Law shall be allowed the Defendant.

L A W S

Made and Past by the General Assembly of Her Majesties Colony of *Rhode-Island*, and *Providence-Plantations*, &c. Held at *Newport*, the Fourth Day of *January*, 1704.

AN ACT, for Levying of a Duty on Tunage of Shipping.

WHEREAS *the Colony, hath been at a great Charge to Build and Erect a Fort on* Fort-Island, *for the Security of the Shipping and Navagation of the Colony.*

For the better keeping the same in Repair,

BE *it Enacted by the General Assembly, and by the Authority of the same,* That there shall be paid by the Master of every Ship or other Vessel, *Twelve* of above Ten Tons, coming into any Port or Ports in this Colony to *Pence per* Trade or Traffick, which are not wholly Owned by the Inhabitants of *Ton Duty* this Colony ; every Voyage such Ship or Vessel doth make, *Twelve-pence per* Ton, *on Foreign* or one Pound of good New Gun Powder, for every Ton such Ship or Vessel *Shipping* is in Burthen by Register ; to be paid to the Naval Officer of the Town of *Newport*, to be Employed to and for the use of the Fort on *Fort-Island.*

PROVIDED always, and it is the true intent and meaning hereof ; that this Act shall not extend to make any Master or other Vessel, Pay *Twelve-pence per* Ton or one Pound of Gun Powder for any greater part of said Ship or Vessel, than what shall not be owned by any Inhabitant of this Colony. *And be it further Enacted by the Authority aforesaid,* That no Master of

any

any Ship or Veſſel, ſhall Sail from out of the Harbour of *Newport*, without firſt producing to the Gunner of ſaid Fort, a Certificate, from under the Hand of the Governour, or Deputy Governour, that he hath complied with ſuch Orders and Laws, as he is Required to ; whereupon the Gunner of ſaid Fort, ſhall ſuffer the Maſter of ſuch Ship or Veſſel to depart; and that if any Maſter of any Ship or Veſſel, ſhall preſume to Sail or Paſs by the Fort, without proceeding as aforeſaid, that then and in ſuch Caſes the Gunner, ſhall Uſe his utmoſt Endeavour to ſtop ſuch Ship or Veſſel, purſuant to ſuch Inſtructions, as he ſhall receive from the Governour, for the doing of the ſame , who is fully Impowered to Grant ſuch Orders as ſhall be neceſſary there for ; and that if any Ship or Veſſel, ſhall be Damnified, Sunk or Deſtroyed thereby, the Maſter of ſuch Ship or Veſſel, ſhall make good all Damages that ſhall be Suſtained thereby.

AN ACT Prohibiting Negroes and Indians from being abroad at unſeaſonable times of the Night, and for Puniſhing thoſe that ſhall Entertain them contrary hereto.

WHEREAS *divers Thefts and Robberies have been Committed in the Night time by* Negroes *and* Indians, *within this as well as in the Governments adjoining ; For preventing whereof,*

No Negroes or Indians to be abroad after Nine at Night.

BE it Enacted by the General *Aſſembly, and by the Authority of the ſame,* That if any *Negroes* or *Indians,* Freemen or Slaves, ſhall be found Abroad after Nine a Clock at Night, at any time throughout the Year, without a Certificate from their Maſters, or ſome other *Engliſh* Perſon of the Family to the which he, ſhe, or they belong, or ſome lawful Excuſe for the ſame ; that then it ſhall and may be lawful for any Perſon or Perſons to Take, Seiz and Secure the ſame till next Morning, and then bring them before an Aſſiſtant, or Juſtice of the Peace of ſuch Town, who ſhall upon due proof thereof, cauſe ſaid Negro or Negroes, Indian or Indians, to be Publickly Whipt at the Publick Whipping Poſt of ſuch Town where ſuch Offence ſhall be Committed, not exceeding fifteen Stripes, unleſs their incorrigible behaviour deſerve more ; and the Perſons ſo Convicted if Freemen, ſhall pay the Charge of Proſecution, *&c.* and if Slaves, the Owner or Owners thereof, ſhall pay the ſame ; and if the Owner or Owners of any ſuch Slave or Slaves ſhall refuſe ſo to do, that then the Aſſiſtant, or Juſtice, *&c.* ſhall Grant forth a Warrant of Diſtreſs to a Conſtable of ſaid Town, to Diſtrain ſo much of his or their Goods, as will ſatisfie and pay the ſame.

No Houſe-keeper to Entertain any Indians or Negroes. On the Penalty of Five Shillings.

And be it further Enacted by the Authority aforeſaid, That no Houſe-keeper ſhall Entertain any Slave or Servants, either Indian or Negroes, after Nine a Clock at Night, as aforeſaid, without the Owner of ſaid Slave or Servants leave ; and whoſoever ſhall be Convicted of ſuch Offence, before any Aſſiſtant, or Juſtice of the Peace, *&c.* ſhall for every ſuch Offence, forfeit *Five Shillings,* in Money, to and for the uſe of the Town where ſuch Offence ſhall be Committed ; and if the perſon offended, ſhall refuſe to pay the ſame, it ſhall be recovered by the Town Treaſurer of ſuch Town, upon due proof thereof before any Aſſiſtant or Juſtice of the Peace in manner as aforeſaid.

On the Penalty of Whipping.

L A W S

Made and Paft by the General Affembly of Her Majefties Colony of *Rhode-Ifland*, and *Providence-Plantations*, &c. Held at *Providence*, the Twenty Fifth Day of *October*; 1704.

AN ACT Preventing of Damage to be done, by Firing of the Woods in any Town in the Colony.

WHEREAS *great Damage has been done to feveral of the Inhabitants of this Colony; by their Hay, Fencing,* &c. *by Firing of the Woods; at unfeafonable Times of the Year.*

For the Preventing Whereof,

BE it Enacted by the General Affembly, and by the Authority of the fame, That no Perfon whatfoever, fhall fet any Fires, or caufe any Fires to be fet in the Woods, in any part of this Colony, on any time of the Year, fave between the Tenth of *March*, and the Tenth of *May*, Annually; nor on the Firft or Seventh Day of any Week, during faid time, under any pretence whatfoever; and that whofoever fhall be lawfully Convicted of doing the fame, before any two Affiftants, or Juftices of the Peace, &c. of fuch Town where fuch Offence fhall be Committed, either by their own Confeffion, or by the Evidence of Two Witneffes upon Engagement; fhall Forfeit *Thirty Shillings* in Money, to and for the Ufe of fuch Town; and if the Perfon or Perfons fo Convicted, refufe to Pay the fame, that then fuch Affiftants, or Juftices, &c fhall Grant forth a Warrant of Diftrefs, to any Conftable of faid Town, to Diftrain fo much of the Offenders Goods and Chattels, as fhall Satisfy and Pay the fame, to the Ufe aforefaid; and all Incident Charges thereon Accruing.

None to fire the Woods, but between the Tenth of March, and the Tenth of May.

On the penalty of Thirty Shillings.

AND that whofoever fhall fuffer any Damages by reafon of fuch Offence as aforefaid, fhall have an Action of Trafpafs upon the Cafe, againft fuch Offender or Offenders, and fhall Recover his Damages and Cofts accordingly, if under *Forty Shillings* before any Two Affiftants or Juftices of fuch Town where fuch Offence fhall be Committed, and if above *Forty Shillings*, in the General Court of Tryals.

And the Party agrieved thereby, fhall recover his damage.

R AN

AN ACT for the Prefervation of Deer, within this Colony.

WHEREAS many Perfons Yearly, Kill and Deftroy Deer at unfeafonable times, when the Skins and Flefh are of little or no Value, which may be of great Prejudice to the Colony, and hinder their Increafe.

For the Preventing whereof for the Future,

None to kill Deer but between the firft of January, and the laft of June. On the penalty of Twenty Shillings.

BE it Enacted by the General Affembly, and by the Authority of the fame, That no Perfon or Perfons whatfoever within this Colony, fhall from and after the Firft Day of *January* in this prefent Year, unto the laft Day of *June*, in the Year One Thoufand Seven Hundred and Five, and between the faid Firft of *January*, and the laft of *June*, Annually for ever hereafter, Kill and Deftroy any Deer or Fawn, on the Penalty of Forfeiting Twenty Shillings for every Deer or Fawn fo Killed, upon Conviction thereof before any Affiftant, or Juftice of the Peace, &c. of fuch Town where fuch Offence fhall be Committed, the one Half to the Informer, and the other Moiety to and for the Ufe of the Town, to be Levied by a Warrant of Diftrefs, from fuch Affiftant or Juftice, Directed to a Conftable of faid Town.

L A W S

Made and Paft by the General Affembly of Her Majefties Colony of *Rhode-Ifland*, and *Providence-Plantations*, &c. Held at *Newport*, the Second Day of *May*, 1705.

AN ACT for fecuring of Cofts to the Inhabitants and Refidents of and in this Colony, that fhall be Arrefted by any Perfon that are not Inhabitants and Freeholders in the fame.

No Inhabitant of this Colony to be Arrefted, but by a Freeholder of the fame. Unlefs the Plaintiff give Bond.

BE it Enacted by the General Affembly, and by the Authority of the fame, That no Perfon or Perfons whatfoever, that is not an Inhabitant and Freeholder in this Colony, fhall have out of the Recorders Office, any Writ of Arreft, or Summons, againft any Perfon or Perfons Inhabiting or Refiding in the fame, without firft giving in Bond in the Recorders Office, of Twenty Pounds, with Security for to Refund all Cofts that fhall Accrue thereon, upon non profecution of fuch Suit, or if fuch Action fhall be Non-Suit, or caft upon Tryal: Any Law or Cuftom to the contrary hereof notwithftanding.

AN

AN ACT, Eſtabliſhing a Notary Publick, within this Colony.

BE it Enaɛted by the General Aſſembly, and by the Authority of the ſame, That the General Recorder of the Colony for the time being, ſhall be the Notary Publick Notary of this Colony; and he is hereby fully Impowered and Authorized, to Aɛt, Tranſaɛt, Do and Finiſh, all and whatſoever Matters, Cauſes or things,Relating to Drawing of Proteſts,or Proteſting Bills, &c. as are by Law Required, and that he ſhall be Engaged thereto, for the which he ſhall take the following Fees, and no more.

Recorder to be the Notary Publick. Fees for the ſame.

	l	s	d
TO Swearing to Proteſt.	ſo	03	oo
To Drawing Ditto.	oc	03	oo
To Sealing Ditto.	oo	03	oo
To Regiſtring Ditto in the Office	oo	03	oo
To Copy Ditto.	oo	03	oo

L A W S

Made and paſt by the General Aſſembly of Her Majeſties Colony of *Rhode-Iſland* and *Providence-Plantations*. Held at *Providence*, the Thirtieth Day of *Oɛtober*, 1706.

AN ACT for Extending *Eaſt-Greenwich* Townſhip Weſt, to the Colony Weſt Line.

WHEREAS The Townſhip of Eaſt-Greenwich is very ſmall, and there is a Traɛt of Land Lying Weſt of ſaid Townſhip, very Commodious to Enlarge the ſame.

BE it therefore Enaɛted by the General Aſſembly, and by the Authority of the ſame, That the North and South Bound of *Eaſt-Greenwich* Township, being Run due Weſt, from the South Weſt and North Weſt corners of ſaid Townſhip, to the Colony Line, and all the Land therein included, ſhall be, and is hereby Annexed, to be part of the Townſhip of *Eaſt-Greenwich*, and the Inhabitants that are already ſettled thereon, or that ſhall hereafter ſettle thereon, ſhall have the ſame Liberties and Priviledges, as the other Inhabitants of *Eaſt-Greenwich* have and Enjoy.

Eaſt Green-wich to Ex-tend Weſt to the Colonies Line.

R 2   Laws

Made and Paſt by the General Aſſembly of Her Majeſties Colony of *Rhode-Iſland*, and *Providence-Plantations*. Held at *Newport*, the Twenty Fifth Day of *February*, 1706.

AN ACT for Regulating of Tanners, Curriers and Cordwainers.

FOR *PREVENTING of Deceits and Abuſes by Tanners, Curriers, Shoomakers, and Workers up of Leather.*

All Tann'd Leather to be Sealed before Sold.

BE it Enacted by the *General Aſſembly of Her Majeſties Colony of* Rhode-Iſland, *and* Providence-Plantations, *and by the Authority of the ſame,* That no Perſon or Perſons whatſoever, Uſing, or which ſhall Uſe the Myſtery or Faculty of Tanning, ſhall at any time or times hereafter, put to Sale any kind of Leather, which ſhall be Inſufficiently Tanned, or which hath been over Limed or burnt in the Limes, or which ſhall not have been after the Tanning thereof, well and throughly Dryed, or that ſhall not be Sealed, as in and by this Act is hereafter Directed ; upon pain of Forfeiting the whole Side or Peice of Leather ſo offered to Sale ; and no Perſon or Perſons whatſoever, Uſing, or that ſhall hereafter Uſe the Myſtery or Faculty of Tanning, ſhall ſet his or any of their Fatts in Tann-hills, or other places where the Wooze or Leather is put to Tan in the ſame, ſhall or may take any unkind Heats, nor ſhall put any Leather into any Hot or Warm Wooze whatſoever ; on pain of Forfeiting *Twenty Pounds,* for every ſuch Offence.

No Currier to work un-ſeal'd Lea-ther, or un-dried.

How Lea-ther ſhould be Curried.

AND be it further Enacted by the Authority aforeſaid, That no Perſon or Perſons whatſoever, Uſing, or Occupying, or that ſhall hereafter Uſe or Occupy the Myſtery or Faculty of Currying, may, or ſhall Curry any kind of Leather, except it be Sealed as is hereafter Provided ; nor ſhall Curry any Hides, not being throughly dried after his wet ſeaſon, in which wet ſeaſon, he ſhall not Uſe any ſtale Urine, or any other deceitful, ſubtile Mixture of any thing, way or means to Corrupt or Hurt the ſame ; or ſhall Curry any Leather Wet for outer Sole Leather, without any other thing then Hard Tallow, nor with any leſs of that then the Leather will receive, nor ſhall Curry any kind of Leather, meet for upper Leather, and Inward Soles, but with good and ſufficient Stuff, being Freſh not Salt, and throughly Liquor'd, till it will receive no more ; nor ſhall burn or ſcald any Hide or Leather in the Currying, but ſhall work the ſame ſufficiently in all reſpects and points, on Pain of Forfeiting for every ſuch offence or Act done, contrary to the true intent and meaning hereof, every ſuch Hide marr'd or hurt by his evil Work-manſhip or Handling.

And

N, *Cordwain-
er to work up
any Leather
Tann'd, &c.
as aforesaid.
On the penal-
ty of forfeit-
ing the same.*

And be it further Enacted by the Authority aforesaid, That no Person or Persons, Using, or shall hereafter Use or Occupy the Mystery or Faculty of a Shoemaker or Cordwainer, shall work up into Shoes, or other Wares, any Leather that is not Tanned and Curried as aforesaid, or shall Use any Leather made of Horse hides for inner Soles, of any Shoes or Boots, on Pain of Forfeiting of all such Boots, Shoes or other Wares, wrought up of such Insufficient Leather

And for the more Effectual Execution of said Act.

*All Leather
before work'd
is to be Seal'd.*

AND be it further Enacted by the Authority aforesaid, That all Leather that is or shall be Tanned or Curried, shall before the same pass out of the Tanner's or Curriers Yards, Houses, or Places Respectively where it was wrought, be Viewed by Sworn Searchers or Sealers of Leather, by Law directed; to be Annually Chosen in such Towns where there shall be need, who shall have two several Marks or Seals, to be procured by each Town for that purpose, with one of which they shall Seal all such Leather, as they shall find sufficiently Tanned in all respects as aforesaid, and with the other all such Leather as they shall find well and sufficiently Curried, as is before mentioned, and no other.

*All whole
Sides out of
the Curriers
possession, un-
seal'd to be
Seiz'd.*

AND the Shearchers and Sealers, shall and are hereby Authoriz'd and Impower'd, *ex Officio*, to make Search, and View in all respective Places or Houses, Shops, Ware-houses, or other places, within the Limits of their respective Precincts, where they conceive any Leather to be wrought into Shoes, Boots or other Wares, or any Leather offered to be Sold, or offered to be Searched or Sealed, and shall not be Tanned as aforesaid, and well Curried according to the aforecited Act, and the true intent and meaning thereof, or shall find any Leather in whole Sides, out of the Possession of the Currier, not Sealed with the Mark or Seal to be Used for Leather well Tanned or well Curried; in all such Cases, it shall and may be lawful, for the Searchers and Sealers, to Seize all such Leather Insufficient or Unsealed, whether it be wrought up into Wares or not; and if the owner or challenger thereof, shall not submit to the Judgment of the Officer or Officers that Siez'd the same, such Officer or Officers shall retain such Leather in his or their custody, till Tryal thereof be had, as is hereafter directed, and Judgment thereon.

*How to pro-
ceed with
Leather
Seiz'd.*

IN such Cases the Officer or Officers, shall within four Days after said Seizure, Inform some Justice of the Peace in said Town thereof, who shall thereupon appoint four Persons, or more honest skilful Men in Leather, to View the same in the owner or claimers of such Leather's presence, or without him (if having notice thereof he doth not appear) to report to any Justice, the defect which they find in said Leather, which Report the said Justice shall return unto the next General Court of Tryals for the said Colony, for a Conviction in Law on the Fine Imposed; but in Case the Viewers shall Report that they do not find such Leather or Wares so Seized in any respects defective, according to the intent of this Act, the Justice that appointed such Viewers, shall cause the same forthwith to be discharged from the Seizure, made by such Officer or Officers.

*None to resist
the Searchers
& Sealers.
On the penal-
ty of Five*

And be it further Enacted by the Authority aforesaid, That no Person whatsoever, shall or may withstand or resist the Searchers and Sealers in the Execution of their Office, nor in the Searching for any Insufficient Leather or Wares Pounds,

Wares, upon the Forfeiture of *Five Pounds* for every such Offence.

Fees for Seal.ing and Searching. AND the Fee for Searching and Sealing of Leather, shall be *One-penny per* Hide, for any parcel less then Six Hides, and for all other Parcels, if by the Dozen, then *Eight-pence,* which Fees the Tanner or Currier shall Pay on the Sealing thereof from time to time, and shall also pay *Three-pence per* Mile, for every Mile any Searcher or Sealer shall Travel above on Mile.

No Searcher or Sealer to. refuse his Duty on the Penalty of Forty Shillings.. AND no Searcher or Sealer of Leather, shall rfuse within convenient time to do his Office, nor shall allow any Leather or. Wares which are not sufficient, on the Penalty of forfeiting *Forty Shillings,* nor shall take any Bribe, nor exact more than his Fees, on pain of Forfeiting the Sum of *Ten Pounds,* for every such Offence.

How the Fines shall be disposed of. AND be it further Enacted by the Authority aforesaid, That all such Fines, Forfeitures and Penalties, as shall arise or grow due by virtue of this Act, or any Clause therein contained, shall be disposed of in manner following, viz. two third parts thereof, to be paid into the Town Treasury, to and for the Use of said Town, where the Offence shall be committed ; and the other third to the Seizer or Seizers of such insufficient Leather, or to him or them as shall Inform and Sue for the same; to be recovered by Action, Bill, Plaint, or Information, in any General Court of Tryals within the Colony, or before any two Justices of the Peace, when the matter doth not exceed *Forty Shillings.*

And be it further Enacted by the Authority aforesaid, That when and as often as any Leather shall be Seiz'd in the Hands of either Tanner or Currier, and become forfeited by virtue of this Act, through their default, and if belonging to any particular person, the Tanner or Currier shall be liable to make satisfaction to the Owner thereof for the same; to be recovered in any General Court of Tryals, or before any two Justices of the Peace, if the value do not exceed *Forty Shillings.*

AND for the ascertaining of which value, the persons to be appointed as aforesaid, for viewing the defects in Leather, (shall when the same is Seiz'd, for being marr'd and spoyl'd by the Currier or Tanner) through his ill Workmanship or handling, be also appointed to Estimate and judge the value thereof, and make Report of the same, together with the Defects.

Each Town. to Chuse Searchers and Sealers of Leather. And be it further Enacted by the Authority aforesaid, That each Town in the Colony, shall at their Town Elections, Annually Chuse two Sealers and Searchers of Leather, who shall take their Engagement to the performance of their Office, as other Town Officers do.

An A C T, Stating the due Assize of Bread.

BE it *Enacted by the General Assembly, and by the Authority of the same,* That henceforth every Baker, shall have a distinct Mark for his Bread, that he shall Bake and Sell, which he shall Stamp thereon, and shall keep the due Assize hereafter Expressed, on all sorts of Loaf-Bread that he shall Bake, to Weigh by Averdupoize Weight, as is hereafter mentioned, according to the several Prices of Wheat by the Bushel, as is hereafter set down.

Every Baker to stamp his Bread with a distinct mark, and to Sell according to the Rates hereafter mentioned.

The Price of Wheat.		Of Penny White Loaf.		Of Penny Wheaten.		Of Penny Houshold,	
s.	d.	oz.	dr.	oz.	dr.	oz.	dr.
At 3	0	11	4	17	2	23	00
3	6	10	2	15	3	20	04
4	9	02	0	13	7	18	20
4	6	08	3	12	5	16	04
5	7	00	5	11	4	15	03
5	6	07	1	10	5	14	02
6	0	06	4	09	7	13	01
6	6	06	0	09	0	12	00
7	0	05	6	08	5	11	04
7	6	05	2	08	1	10	04
8	5	07	0	04	4	10	00
8	6	04	6	07	1	09	04
9	0	04	4	06	6	09	00

And so proportionably, under the penalty of Forfeiting all such Bread, as shall not be of several Assizes, as is afore-mentioned; to the Use of the Poor of such Town where such Seizure shall be made, and otherwise as is hereafter mentioned.

And be it further Enacted by the Authority aforesaid, That the Town-Council of each respective Town in the Colony, where Bread is Baked for Sale, shall once a Month, Enquire, State and Record the middle Price of Wheat; and cause the same to be made known, by setting of it up in some Publick Place of said Town; and the Bakers shall accordingly Regulate the Weight of their Bread, after the Assizes before-mentioned.

The Town Council to state the price of Wheat once a month.

And be it further Enacted by the Authority aforesaid, That in every Town in the Colony, where Bread is Baken for Sale, there shall be Chosen one Clerk of the Market, or more, as each Town shall find needful, at their Annual Election of Town Officers, who shall duly be Engaged, to the faithful performance of said Office, as other Town Officers are; and such Clerk or Clerks of the Market, shall once a Month, or oftner, as he shall see cause, enter into any Shop, or Place where Bread is Sold, or Baken for Sale, and weigh the same; and all such Bread as they shall find under the Assize afore-mentioned, or nor marked, he or they shall make Seizure of, and two third parts thereof shall deliver unto the Town Treasury, to and for the use of said Town; and the Officer shall have the other third for his pains therein; and the Constable or Constables of such Town, are hereby Required, to aid and assist the Clerk or Clerks of the Market, in his or their Executing, of his or their Office, when and so often as he or they shall be thereunto Required.

A Clerk of the Market to be Annually Chosen.

His Duty.

S 2

Laws

Made and Paſt by the General Aſſembly of Her Majeſties Colony of *Rhode-Iſland*, and *Providence-Plantations.* Held at *Newport*, the Third Day of *May*, 1710.

WHEREAS *this Colony, has Received Orders from Her Sacred Majeſty, Queen* ANNE, *for an Expedition, to be Proſecuted with ſpeed againſt the French and Indian Enemies, which by reaſon of the great Scarcity and want of Silver Money, this Colony without ſome extraordinary means be uſed for the effecting the ſame, would be unable to perform ; For Remedy whereof, and the ſpeedy procuring and Equipping out all things neceſſary for the ſame,*

BE *it therefore Enacted by the General Aſſembly of this Colony, and by the Authority of the ſame,* That there be with all expedition, Printed to the value of *Five Thouſand Pounds* in Bills of Credit on this Colony, as followeth, viz. One Thouſand Pounds in Five Pound Bills, One Thouſand Pound in Three Pound Bills, Five Hundred Pound in Forty Shilling Bills, Five Hundred Pounds in Twenty Shilling Bills, Five Hundred Pounds in Five Shilling Bills, Five Hundred Pounds in Two Shillings and Six-penny Bills, and Five Hundred Pounds in Two Shilling Bills ; which Bills to be Printed as aforeſaid, ſhall be in value equal to current Silver Money of *New-England*, in all Publick Payments, and ſhall have the *Anchor* and *Hope* affixed in the Scutcheon, with ſuch other Impreſſions, as ſhall be thought needful by the Committee, in this Act hereafter Named, which ſhall be in the manner following.

THIS Indented *Bill of* *Due from the Colony of* Rhode-Iſland, *and* Providence-Plantations, *in* New-England, *to the Poſſeſſor thereof, ſhall be in equal value to Money, and ſhall be accordingly accepted by the Treaſurer and Receivers, ſubordinate to him in all Publick Payments, and for any Stock at any time in the Treaſury.* Newport, Auguſt 16th. 1710. *By Order of the General Aſſembly, for the Colony above-ſaid.*

And be it further Enacted by the Authority aforeſaid, That the aforeſaid Bills of Publick Credit ſhall be Signed by Lieutenant Colonel *John Wanton*, Lieutenant *John Odlin*, Major *Nathaniel Sheffield*, Major *Joſeph Jencks*, Mr. *John Coggeſhall*, and Mr. *Job Green*, or by any three of them, who are hereby appointed and impowered to Sign the ſame, and deliver them unto the General Treaſury ; which Bills are, and ſhall be received and paid for the ſame value, and equal to the current Coin paſſed in this Colony, for Goods, or any other thing Bought or Sold in all Payments to be made whatſoever ; Specialties only excepted, for and during the ſpace and time of five years enſuing the Date hereof, if the General Aſſembly ſhall then ſee cauſe to Call them in ; and when called in, the Poſſeſſor of ſuch

Bills

Bills fhall 'be Reimburs'd the Sum mentioned in fuch Bill .or Bills, in Current Money of faid Colony, by the General Treafurer hereof ; and the fame fhall be Levied and Collected by Act of Affembly, and duly Apportioned on the Inhabitants of each Town in the Colony.

L A W S

Made and Paft by the General Affembly of Her Majefties Colony of *Rhode-Ifland*, and *Providence-Plantations*, &c. Held at *Providence*, the Twenty Fifth Day of *October*, 1710.

AN ACT, for Preventing Counterfeiting of the Bills of Credit Emitted, or that fhall be Emitted by any of the Governments of *New-England*, and to prevent Dfaceing of the fame, &c.

BE it Enacted by the General Affembly, and by the Authority of the fame, That whofoever fhall Forge, Counterfeit or Utter, any Bill or Bills, (knowing the fame to be falfe and counterfeit) of the Tenor, or in Imitation, of any of the Bills of Credit, Emitted by this Colony, the Province of the *Maffachufetts-Bay*, the Colony of *Connecticut*, or the Province of *New-Hampfhire* by Law Eftablifhed therein ; or that fhall Counfel, Advife or Procure the fame in any ways;by Forging,Counterfeiting,Imprinting orSigning any fuch falfe Bills, or make or Ingrave any Plate or other Inftrument for that purpofe ; or that fhallAlter or Increafe anyFigure or Sum in any Bills of CreditEmitted, or that fhall be hereafter Emitted, by this or any other Governments as afore-faid,' or that fhall Forge or Counterfeit, any Name, Hand, Stamp or Mark, that now is or hereafter fhall be made or fet thereon ; the Perfon or Perfons fo Offending therein, fhall Suffer the Pains of having their Ears Cropt, being Whip'd or Fined at Difcretion, and Imprifoned as the nature of the Offence Requires, by the Judges of fuch Court, where fuch Offence fhall be Tryed, and fhall pay double Damage, to the Perfon -or Perfons Defrauded and Cheated by fuch Falfe Bills ; and in Cafe fuch Offender or Offenders, have not Eftate fufficient to defray the charge of their Profecution, Imprifonment, and double Damages as aforefaid ; that then and in fuch Cafes, the Offender or Offenders therein, fhall be fet to work or Sold for any term of Years, for fatisfaction of the fame, at the Difcretion of the Judges of fuch Court, where fuch Offence fhall be Tryed.

The Make. or Paffer of Bills, &c. fhall be punifhed by Whipping, Pillory, &c. And the per- fon aggrieved thereby fhall recover double damages.

T AN

AN ACT, for Impreſſing and Emitting one *Thouſand Pounds* in Publick Bills of Credit on this Colony.

One Thou-
ſand Pounds
Imprinted in
Bills of Cre-
dit.

BE it Enaƈƚed by the General *Aſſembly, and by the Authority of the ſame,* That there be forthwith Imprinted and Raiſed, one *Thouſand Pounds* of Publick Bills of Credit on this Colony, in the ſame Manner and Form, that the Five *Thouſand Pounds* of Credit formerly Emitted by this Colony were, and they ſhall be Signed by the ſame Committee, paſs in all Payments whatſoever, as the other Bills aforeſaid, already Emitted by this Colony do.

L A W S

Made and paſt by the General Aſſembly of Her Majeſties Colony of *Rhode-Iſland,* & *Providence-Plantations,* &c. Held at *Newport,* the Twenty Seventh Day of *November,* 1710.

FOR*ASMUCH at the Bills of Credit already Emitted by this Colony, are not ſufficient to ſatisfy the Debts, Created by this Colony, in the late Expedition undertaken againſt* Annappolis-Royal, *in purſuance to Her Majeſties Command, whereby many Perſons are very great ſufferers, and ſeveral like to be Ruined thereby, and there not being ſufficient Silver in the Colony, to anſwer the ſame,*

One Thou-
ſand Pounds
of Bills of
Credit Im-
printed.

BE it *therefore Enaƈƚed by the General Aſſembly, and by the Authority thereof,* That there be forthwith Imprinted and Raiſed; One *Thouſand Pounds* in Publick Bills of Credit on this Colony, and that they be Signed by the former Committee, and paſs in all Publick Payments, as the former Bills of Credit do and have done,

L A VV S

Made and Paſt by the General Aſſembly of Her Majeſties Colony of *Rhode-Iſland,*and *Providence-Plantations,* &c. Held at *Newport,* the Twenty Eighth Day of *June,* 1711.

AN ACT for Settling Coſts at the General Courts of Tryals.

He that reco-
vers the laſt

BE it Enaƈƚed by the *General Aſſembly, and by the Authority of the ſame,* That whoever ſhall Recover the Laſt and Final Judgment of any Matter,

Matter, Caufe or thing, that fhall be Heard and Tryed, at the General *Judgment, to* Court of Tryals, fhall Recover, Have and Receive all Cofts that fhall be *the Cofts in* Taxed, during the rending of any fuch Suit. Any former Cuftom or Ufage *faid Cafe.* to the Contrary hereof notwithftanding.

AN ACT, for the raifing of Six *Thoufand Pounds*, in Bills of Credit.

BE it Enacted by the General Affembly, and by the Authority of the fame, That there be forthwith Imprinted and Raifed, the Sum of Six Thoufand *Pounds* of Publick Bills of Credit on this Colony, by the former Committee *Six Thou-* that Signed and Finifhed the former Bills. They are hereby fully Impowred *fand Pounds* to Make, Sign, and Finifh the fame, in the fame Form as the former Bills *Emitted in* were;whichBills when Signed and Finifhed,the faidCommittee fhall deliver into *dit by this* the General Treafury, to and for the Ufe of this Colony ; and fhall pafs in all *Colony.* Publick Payments as the Bills of Credit already Emitted by this Colony do.

L A W S

Made and Paft by the General Affembly of Her Majefties Colony of *Rhode-Ifland* and *Providence-Plantations*, &c. Held at *Warwick*, the Fourteenth Day of *November*, 1711.

AN ACT, for Imprinting and raifing Three *Hundred Pounds* in Bills of Credit on the Colony.

BE it Enacted by the General Affembly, and by the Authority of the fame, *Three Hun-* That there be forthwith Imprinted and Raifed, the Sum of Three *dred Pounds Hundred Pounds* of Bills of Credit on this Colony,in the fame manner *Credit Emit-* and form, as the former Bills of Credit were, the which Bills fhall be Signed *ted.* by the faid Committee ; and fhall pafs in payments, as the current Coin in this Colony doth, Specialties only Excepted.

L A W S

Made and Paſt by the General Aſſembly of Her Majeſties Colony
of *Rhode-Iſland* and *Providence-Plantations*, &c. Held at
Newport, the Twenty Seventh Day of *February*, 1711.

AN ACT for laying a Duty on Negro Slaves that ſhall be
Imported into this Colony.

WHEREAS the. *bringing of Negroes into this Colony, diſcourages the*
Importing of White Servants herein, and may in time prove Prejudicial
to the Inhabitants, if not timely diſcouraged.

BE it *therefore Enacted by the General Aſſembly, and by the Authority of*
the ſame. That every Maſter of any Ship or Veſſel, Merchants or
others, that ſhall Import or bring into this Colony, any Negro Slave or
Slaves, of what age ſoever, ſhall enter their Number, Names and Sex,
in the Naval Office ; and the Maſter ſhall Inſert the ſame in the Manifeſt of
his Lading, and ſhall pay to the Naval Officer in *Newport*, Three Pounds per
Head, to and for the Uſe of the Colony, for every Negro Slave, Male or
Female, ſo Imported or brought in ; and it any Maſter or Merchant, ſhall
refuſe or neglect to pay the ſame, by the ſpace of Ten Days, after ſuch Slave
or Slaves ſhall be Landed in this Colony ; that then the Naval Officer on
knowledge thereof, ſhall Recover the ſame by Action of Debt, in the
General Court of Tryals.

And be it further Enacted. That if any Maſter of any Ship, or other
Merchant or others, ſhall Refuſe or Neglect to make Entry as aforeſaid,
of all Negroes Imported in ſuch Ship or Veſſel, or ſhall be Convicted of not
Entering the full Number of ſuch Slaves as ſhall be Imported ; He or
They ſo Offending, ſhall Forfeit and Pay the Sum of *Six Pounds per* Head,
for every one that he ſhall Refuſe or Neglect to make Entry of ; one Moiety
thereof, to and for the Uſe of the Colony, and the other Moiety to
him or them that ſhall Inform and Sue for the ſame.

And be it further Enacted by the Authority aforeſaid, That whoſoever ſhall
bring into this Colony, any Negro Slave or Slaves from any of Her Majeſties
Governments adjoyning, either by Water or Land, ſhall in like manner
Enter their Number, Names and Sex in the aboveſaid Office, under the like
Penalty as aboveſaid, to be Recovered as aforeſaid : and ſhall Pay into the
Naval Office, the like Sum of *Three Pounds per* Head, for every ſuch Slave
ſo brought in, within the time of Ten Days as above ſpecified, and for
default of Payment thereof, to be Recovered by the Naval Officer, in
manner as aforeſaid.

Pro-

(marginal notes:)
All Negro Slaves Imported into the Colony, to be Entred in the Naval Office.

And pay Three Pounds each.

Whoſoever neglects the ſame, ſhall Pay Six Pound per Head, for every one ſo omitted.

PROVIDED always, that if any Perfon whoſoever is not Reſident in this Colony, and ſhall only paſs through the ſame with a Waiting Man or Men, &c. and ſhall not Reſide herein for above the ſpace of Six Months, then ſuch Waiting Man or Men, &c. ſhall be free from the abovelaid Duty, ſuch Perſons giving their ſolemn Oath, that they are not for Sale. *This Act not to Extend to Negroes Imported directly from Africa.*

AND it is further Provided, That no clauſe or clauſes in the aforeſaid Act, ſhall be Conſtrained, Deemed or taken to Extend, to any Maſter or Maſters of Ships or other Veſſels, that ſhall Import Negroes in this Colony, directly from the Coaſt of *Africa.*

Fees for the Naval Officer.

	l.	*s:*	*d.*
EVery Slave Imported, to be paid out of the Impoſt.	00	05	00
Entering Manifeſt, to be paid by the Maſter.	00	01	00

Naval Officers Fees for the ſame.

An ACT, to Prevent the Spreading of Infectious Sickneſs.

WHEREAS *Contagious Diſtempers have been ſeveral times brought into this Colony, by the Maſters of Ships, and other Veſſels, coming into the Several Ports of this Colony, from Places that are Infected therewith.*

For the Preventing whereof for the Future,

BE it Enacted by the General Aſſembly, and by the Authority of the ſame, That no Maſter or Commander of any Ship or other Veſſel, that ſhall come into any Port or Harbour of this Colony, and ſhall in their Paſſage hereto, have any Perſon or Perſons Sick on Ship-board, with the Small Pox, or any other Contagious Diſeaſe, or ſhall come from any other Port or Place where any Contagious Diſtemper is brief or prevalent, ſhall not bring to Anchor their Ship or Veſſel, in any of the Ports of this Government, within the diſtance of one Mile of any Publick Ferry, Pier or Landing place ; or if any Veſſel or Veſſels that are at Anchor therein, ſhall Land nor ſuffer any Perſon or Perſons, on Board ſuch Ship or Veſſel to be Landed, nor ſuffer any Perſons to come on Board ſuch Ship or Veſſel, without a Licence firſt had from the Governour of this Colony for the time being, if they ſhall Anchor in the Harbour of *Newport,* or in his Abſence from one or more Juſtices of Peace of ſaid Town, and if they ſhall Anchor in any other Harbour of this Colony, a Licence ſhall be firſt had and Obtained from ſome one or more Juſtices of the Peace of ſuch Town, under the Penalty of Forfeiting *One Hundred Pounds,* Good and lawful Money of this Colony, to and for the Uſe of the Colony, to be Recovered by the General Treaſurer of the Colony, in the General Courts of Tryals of this Colony, by Bill, Plaint or Information, &c. and where the Offender or Offenders herein, ſhall have no Eſſoin, Protection or Wager of Law allowed.

No perſon having any ſick perſon on Board, or that come from any Place Infected with any contagious Sickneſs, to Anchor within one mile of any Landing-place. Without a Licence On the penalty of One Hundred Pounds.

AND be it further Enacted by the Authority aforeſaid, That if upon the Arrival of any ſuch Ship, or other Veſſel as aforeſaid, in any Harbour of this

V

this

*Whofoever
fo ll and
without Li-
cence. fhall
be fent on
Board again,
and fhall
Forfeit
Twenty
Pounds.*

this Colony, as aforefaid, any Paffenger on Board, or any Mariner thereto belonging, fhall and do come on Shore or Land from fuch Veffel, without a a Licence firft had and obtained as aforefaid, that then, and in fuch Cafes, it fhall and may be lawful for any Juftice of the Peace of fuch Town, where fuch perfon and perfons fhall Land, to Require and Command, and fend fuch perfon and perfons fo offending, on Board fuch Veffel again, or to Confine them afhore to any fuch Place, as to him fhall feem convenient, for to prevent the fpreading of any Infection ; and the perfon or perfons fo offending, fhall anfwer, fatisfy and pay all Charges that fhall arife thereon; and fhall Forfeit *Twenty Pounds*, good and lawful Money of faid Colony, to and for the Ufe of the Colony, to be recovered as aforefaid.

And if the Offender or Offenders have not Eftate fufficient to fatisfy and pay the fame ; that they fhall be fet to Work, by the direction, and at the difcretion of the Judges of fuch Court where fuch Caufe fhall be Tryed, until the fame be fully fatisfied and paid.

And for the better putting this Act in Execution.

How the Naval Officer is to proceed upon Information.

Be it Enacted by the Authority aforefaid, That the Naval Officer fhall keep this Act publickly fet up in his Office, for the view of all Matters of Ships, and other Veffels that fhall Enter with him ; and the faid Naval Officer is hereby Impowered upon any Information unto him given of any Ship or Veffel Arriving in this Harbour, that hath any Infectious Diftemper Aboard, to fend on Board of fuch Ship or Veffel, a Doctor, to examine the fame, as need fhall require, and return thereof to the Governour, or in his abfence, to fome of the Affiftants, or Juftices of the Peace of the Town of *Newport* to make report, that due care may be taken therein ; and the Matter of fuch Ship or Veffel, fhall pay all charges arifing thereon ; and if he refufe to pay the fame, it fhall be Recovered by the Naval Officer in any Court of Record within this Colony.

If any fick perfon happen to be Landed, a Juftice. &c. to remove fuch perfon, as he thinks fit.

And be it further Enacted by the Authority aforefaid, That if notwithftanding the above-faid Precautions to prevent any Infectious Diftemper from being brought into this Colony, that if any perfon or perfons, Paffengers, Mariners, or Slaves fhall be Landed from on Board any Ship, or other Veffel, and fhall after being Landed, be taken Sick with the Small-pox, or any other Infectious Diftemper ; that then and in fuch cafe, it fhall and may be lawful, for any one Affiftant, or Juftice of the Peace of any fuch Town where fuch Caufe fhall happen, to remove fuch fick and diftempered perfon and perfons to fuch convenient Place, as fhall to them appear to be neceffary, to prevent the fpreading thereof ; and the perfon or perfons fo removed, it fee to pay the Charge thereof, and fhall be Recovered in any Court of Record within this Colony, by the perfon or perfons that fhall disburfe the fame ; and if the perfons fo removed be Slaves, then the Owners thereof fhall pay the fame ; and if the Slaves are Configned to any perfon within the Government, then fuch perfon to whom Configned, fhall pay the charge of the fame, to be recovered as aforefaid.

AN

AN ACT, for Quieting Possessions, and avoiding Suits at Law.

WHEREAS *at the first Settling of this Colony, and for sundry Years afterwards, Lands were of little or no Value, and Skilful Men in the Law were much wanted, whereby many Deeds, Grants and Conveyances were weakly made, which may Occasion Great Contests in Law, if not timely prevented.*

BE *it therefore Enacted by the General Assembly, and by the Authority of the same,* That all Grants, Charters, Profits, Rights and Priviledges, heretofore *Ancient* Granted and Given by the General Assembly of this Colony, unto any Town, *Grants ci* Corporation, Community and Proprie.y, and to any other Person or Persons, *Firmed.* shall be, and they hereby are Ratified and Confirmed to be Good and Effectual to all Intents and Purposes in the Law, for the Granting and Conveying all such Lands, Tenements, Charters, Corporations, Priviledges as is therein Mentioned, to the Persons therein Mentioned, and their Heirs and Assigns for ever.

And be it further Enacted by the Authority aforesaid, That where any Person or Persons, or others, from whom he or they derive their Titles, either *Twenty yea* by Themselves, Tenants, Leases, Hath, Have or shall by the space of Twenty *Possession to* Years, be in the Uninterrupted, Quiet, Peaceable and Actual Seisin and Possession *make a Ti* of any Land or Hereditaments within this Colony, for and during the said time, Claiming the same as his, her or their proper, sole and Rightful Estate in Fee Simple, such Actual Seisin and Possession, shall be allowed to give and make a Good and Rightful Title to such person or persons, their Heirs and Assigns for ever; and this Act being Pleaded in Bar to any Action that shall hereafter be brought for such Lands, Tenements or Hereditaments, and being duly proved, shall be allowed to be Good, Valid and Effectual, in the Law for Barring the same.

PROVIDED, that nothing in this Act shall be Construed, Deemed or Taken, to Extend to prejudice the Rights & Claims, of such Persons under Age, *Feme Cove* Non Compos Mentis, Feme Coverts, Imprisoned or beyond Seas, they bringing *Feme Cove* their Suit there for, within the space of Ten Years, next after such *&c. except* Impediment is Removed.

AN ACT, for Granting Administrations to the Wives of Persons Three Years absent, and unheard of.

WHEREAS *many Merchants and Mariners, going to Sea on Voyages, are often absent many Years and unheard of, and leaving no Power of Attorney for the Receiving of Debts, Rents and Profits of their Estates, whereby their Wives and Families may suffer.*

For

For the Preventing whereof for the Future,

BE it Enacted by the General Assembly, and by the Authority of the same, That whosoever hath been departed or shall depart out of this Government on a Voyage to Sea or otherways, and hath left an Estate in this Government, and be unheard of for the space of Three Years, next immediately succeeding such departure, and leave no Power of Attorney with his Wife, to Receive his Debts, Rents and Profits of such Estate, which he hath within this Government ; that then and in such Cases, the Town Council of such Town, where such departed Person last dwelt, upon due Application to them made, by the Wife of such departed Person, are hereby fully Impowered and Authoriz'd, to Grant Administration. to the Wife of such departed Person, Enabling and Impowering Her to Sue for, Recover the Debts, Rents and Profits of the Estate of such Her departed Husband,for the Comfortable Subsistance of Her Self and Children,if any She have,until such time as Her departed Husband shall Return home, or send sufficient Power of Attorney for the same ; or until he shall be Adjudged and Deem'd Dead in Law, and then such Her Administration shall cease and determine.

If a person be three years absent and unheard of. Administration to be granted to the Wife.

L A W S

Made and Past by the General Assembly of Her Majesties Colony of *Rhode Island* and *Providence-Plantations,* &c. Held at *Newport,* the Sixth Day of *May,* 1713.

WHEREAS Ninigret the Indian Sachem,in the Narraganset Country, on the Twenty Eighth Day of March, 1709. *did, by an Instrument under his Hand and Seal, Covenant and Agree with the Governour and Company of this Colony, that they should have the oversight and care of his Lands, &c. and that he would not Sell, or Hire out any of his Lands, without their consent, approbation, under the Penalty of Forfeiting such Lands by him Sold and Hired ; and notwithstanding which several evil minded Persons for the Lucre of Gain, have Craftily and Designedly Cheated the said Sachem of some of his Lands, and of the Profits of his other Lands, so that he has not Sufficient to maintain Himself and People upon.*

BE it therefore Enacted by the General Assembly, and by the Authority of the same, That all Deeds of Sale, Deeds of Mortgage and Leases of any of said *Ninigret*'s Lands,which have been by him made and Granted, since the said Twenty Eighth of *March,* One Thousand Seven Hundred and Nine, to this present Sessions of Assembly, be and they are hereby declared.to be Null and Void, and of no Force, Validity and Effect in the Law, to any such Use or Purpose whatsoever.

All Grants, Leases, &c. made by Ninigret, since March, 1709. to be void.

And

And for the Preventing of Clandestine Proceedings for the Future.

BE it further Enacted by the Authority aforesaid, That no Person whatsoever, shall Buy, Purchase or Hire any Lands of the said *Ninigret* Sachom, either by Deed of Sale or Mortgage, or Lease, unless they first Have and Obtain, the Assent of the Governour and Company, of this Colony for the time being, under the Penalty of Forfeiting Twenty Shillings per Acre, for every Acre that shall be so Bought, Purchased or Hired, to and for the Use of the Colony; to be Recovered by the General Treasurer, in the General Courts of Tryals, where no Essoin, Protection or Wager of Law shall be allowed; and all such Feoffment, Sales, Mortgages and Leases, are hereby declared to be Void, Null and of none Effect in the Law. *No person to Buy or Hire of Ninigret, on the penalty of Twenty Shillings per Acre.*

AND be it further Enacted by the Authority aforesaid, That no Recorder or Town Clerk in this Colony, shall Register or make Record of any such Deed of Sale, Mortgage or Lease, under the Penalty of *Fifty Pounds*, to be Foseited to and for the Use of the Colony, to be Recovered as aforesaid, for every such Deed of Sale, Mortgage or Lease, that shall be by him Recorded. *He that Records any such Grant or Lease, forfeits Fifty Pounds.*

L A W S

Made and Past by the General Assembly of Her Majesties Colony of *Rhode-Island*. and *Providence-Plantations*. Held at *Newport*, the Twenty Fourth Day of *February*, 1713.

AN ACT for Preventing Pedlers from Selling of Goods in this Colony.

BE it Enacted by the General Assembly, and by the Authority of the same, That from and after Forty Dayes, of the Publication of this Act, no Pedler shall open his Pack, and Sell or Expose to Sale any sort of Dry Goods, within any Town of this Colony, under the Penalty of Forfeiting for every such Offence Forty Shillings, to and for the Use of such Town, where such Offence shall be Committed; to be Recovered by the Town Treasurer of such Town, upon Conviction thereof, by the Evidence of Two Witnesses upon Oath or Engagement, before any Two Assistants or Justices of the Peace of such Town. *No Pedler to Sell within this Colony, under the penalty of Forty Shillings.*

X Laws

L A W S

Made and Paſt by the General Aſſembly of Her Majeſties Colony of *Rhode-Iſland*, and *Providence-Plantations*, &c. Held at *Newport*, the Fifteenth Day of *June*, 1714.

AN ACT, for Eſtabliſhing a Gunner at Fort-*Ann*.

One Gunner to be main-tain'd at Fort-Anne.

BE it Enacted by the General Aſſembly, and by the *Authority of the ſame*, That there ſhall be one Gunner, kept and maintained in Fort-*Ann*, who ſhall be allowed *Twenty Pounds per Annum*, for his Peforming and Exerciſing the Duty of a Gunner therein, and that it ſhall and may be in the Power of the Governour of this Colony, to appoint the Gunner, ſuch as he ſhall Judge to be beſt Qualified and Experienced in the Art of Gunnery, &c.

L A W S

Made and Paſt by the General Aſſembly of His Majeſties Colony of *Rhode-Iſland*, and *Providence-Plantations*, &c. Held at *Providence*, the Twenty Seventh Day of *October*, 1714.

AN ACT, to Prevent Slaves from Running away from their Maſters, &c.

WHEREAS *ſeveral Negro and Molatto Slaves, have Ran-away from their Maſters and Miſtreſſes, under pretence of being Employed in their ſervice, and have been Tranſported over the Ferries out of this Colony, and ſuffered to paſs through the ſeveral Towns, under the aforeſaid pretence, to the great Damage and Charge of their Owners, and many times to the loſs of their Slaves.*

No perſon to Tranſport any Slave over a Ferry, or out of the Colony, without a Certificate. On the penalty of Twenty Shillings, &c.

BE it therefore Enacted by the General Aſſembly, and by the *Authority of the ſame*, That no Ferry-man, or Boat-man whatſoever, within this Colony, ſhall Carry, Convey or Tranſport, any Slave or Slaves as aforeſaid, over any Ferry, or out of the Colony, without a Certificate under the Hand of their reſpective Maſter or Miſtreſs, or ſome Perſon in Commiſſion for the Peace, on the Penalty of *Twenty Shillings*, to be Forfeited to and for the Uſe of the Colony, to be Recovered upon Conviction thereof, before any Two

Aſſiſtants

Affiftants or Juftices of the Peace, of fuch Town where fuch Offence fhall be
Committed, and fhall Pay all Cofts and Charges that fhall arife, on his or *At Minifters*
their Carrying or Tranfporting any Slave or Slaves as aforefaid to the Owner *of Juftice to*
thereof, to be Recovered by the Perfon agrieved thereby, if not Exceeding *take up all*
Forty Shillings, before any Two Juftices of the Peace, &c. and if above Forty- *Negro*
Shillings at the General Court of Tryals, by Action of Trafpafs upon the Cafe. *Slaves.*
And all His Majefties Minifters of Juftice, and all other his Subjects in this
Colony, knowing of any Slave or Slaves Travelling through the Townfhip
wherein they Dwell, without a Certificate as aforefaid, they are hereby
Required to caufe fuch Slave or Slaves to be taken up, Examined and Secured,
fo as the Owners of fuch Slave or Slaves may be Notified thereof, and
have their Slave or Slaves again, Paying the reafonable Charges arifing thereon.

L A W S

Made and Paft by the General Affembly of His Majeflies Colony
of *Rhode Ifland* and *Providence-Plantations,* &c. Held at
Kings-Town, the Twenty Third Day of *February,* 1714.

AN ACT, for the Regiftring Deeds and Conveyances.

FOR *the Prevention of Clandeftine and Uncertain Sales of Houfes and Lands,*
and to the intent that it may be the better known what Right Titles or In-
tereft Perfons have in or to fuch Eftates as they offer to Sale.

BE *it Enacted and Declared by the Prefent Affembly, and by the Au-* *Conveyances*
thority of the fame, That henceforth all Deeds and Conveyances of a- *to be Sign'd*
ny Houfes or Lands within this Colony, Sign'd and Seal'd by the *and Seal'd,*
Party or Parties granting the fame, having good and lawful Right or *Acknowledged* *and Recorded.*
Authority thereto, and acknowledge by fuch Granter or Granters, before any
Affiftant or Juftice of the Peace in the Colony, and Recorded at length in
the Regiftry of the Town where fuch Houfes and Lands do Lye, within
the fpace of fix Months, from the Date of fuch Conveyance, every fuch
Conveyance fhall be Valid, without any other Act or Ceremony what-
foever.

AND that from and after three Months next after Publication of this Act,
no Bargain, Sale, Mortgage, or other Conveyance of Houfes or Land made
and Executed within this Colony, fhall be good and effectual to hold fuch
Houfes and Lands againft any other perfon or perfons ; but the Granter or
Granters, or their Heirs only, unlefs the Deed or Deeds thereof be Acknowledged and Recorded in manner as is Exprefs'd.

X 2 Pro-

PROVIDED nevertheless, that when and so often as it shall happen any Granter to Live in Parts beyond the Seas, or to be Removed out of this Co-lony, or to be Dead before any such Conveyance by him or them made, be acknowledged as aforesaid; in every such Case, the proof of such Deed or Conveyance made by the Oaths of the Witnesses thereto Subscribed, before any Court of Record within this Colony, it shall be equivalent to the Par-ty's Acknowledgment thereof.

If the Grantee, &c. before Acknowledgment be proved by the Witnesses.

And be it further Enacted by the Authority aforesaid, That if any Grantor or Vendor of any Houses or Lands, shall refuse to acknowledge as is aforesaid, any Grant, Bargain, Sale or Mortgage by him, her, or them Signed and Sealed, and being thereto Required by the Grantee or Vendee, his, her, or their Heirs or Assigns. It shall and may be lawful for any Assistant, or Justice of the Peace, within the Town where such Grantee or Vendee Lives, upon Complaint made, to send for the Party so refusing; and if he, she, or they persist in such refusal, to Commit him, her, or them to Prison, without Bail or Mainprize, until he, she, or they shall acknowledge the same; unless he, she, or they shall Appeal to the next General Court of Tryals; in that Case it being first made appear, and proved to be the Act and Deed of the Party refusing to acknowledge the same, by the Oath of one or more Wit-nesses thereto Subscribed : And such Grantee or Vendee filing a Copy of his Deed or Mortgage so proved in the Town Clerk's Office, in the Town wherein the Land doth Lye, shall thereby secure his Title in the mean time; and the same shall be accounted sufficient caution to every other person and persons, against purchasing the Estate in such Deed mentioned to be Granted.

If the Grantor refuse to acknowledge the same, to be Committed to Goal.

PROVIDED that nothing in this Act shall be construed deemed or extend-ed to bar the Widow of any Vendor or Mortgager of Lands or Tenements, from her Dower or Right in, or to such Lands or Tenements, who did not legally join with her Husband in such Sale or Mortgage, or otherwise lawful bar, or exclude her self from such her Dower Right.

No Widow to be barr'd of her Dower by this Act.

And be it further Enacted by the Authority aforesaid, That any Mortgage of Lands or Tenements, his or her Heirs, Executors or Administrators, having received full satisfaction of all, and every such Sum and Sums of Money, as are really due to him, by him such Mortgage, shall at the Request of the Mortgager, his Heirs, Executors or Administrators, acknowledge and cause satisfaction and payment to be Entred in the Margent of the Record of such Mortgage, in the Town Clerk's Office, where the Land lies, and shall Sign the same, which shall for ever hereafter discharge, defeat and release such Mortgage, and perpetually bar all Actions to be brought thereupon, in any Court of Record.

Mortgages to Discharge their Mortgages by Record when paid.

AND if any such Mortgages, his, her, or their Heirs, Executors or Ad-ministrators, shall not within ten days next after Request in that behalf made; and tender of his, her, or their reasonable Charges, repair to the Town Clerk's Office, and there make and sign such Acknowledgment as aforesaid, or otherwise Sign and Seal a Discharge, and Release and Quit Claim to the Estate therein mentioned to be granted, and acknowledge the same, before any one Assistant, or Justice of the Peace of this Colo-ny; he, she, or they so refusing to do, shall be liable to make good all

and if they refuse to pay the same, to pay all Damages accruing.

Damages

Damages that shall accrue, for want of such a Discharge or Release, to *To pay all* be Recovered by any Action or Suit in any Court of Record, and in case *Damages ac-* Judgment pass against the Party so Sued, he, she or they so Cast, shall pay *cruing.* unto the adverse Party, treble Costs arising upon such Suit.

L A W S

Made and Past by the General Assembly of His Majesties Colony of *Rhode Island* and *Providence-Plantations*, &c. Held at *Newport*, the Fourth Day of *May*, 1715.

An A C T, For the convenient Laying out of High-ways and Roads in the several Towns within this Colony, where wanted.

B E it Enacted by the General Assembly, and by the Authority of the same, That the Proprietors of all, and every Town in this Colony, shall with *Town Council* all convenient speed, take care to Lay out convenient High-ways, and Roads *to lay out* from Town to Town, and to Market and Mill, &c. within three Months of *High ways* the Publication hereof; and in case the said Proprietors shall refuse, or neg- *by a Jury.* lect so to do, it shall, and may be lawful for the Town-Council of each respec- tive Town where (such Defect shall be) to order and appoint a Jury of Twelve, or more, lawful and Judicious men, who have no particular interest, in laying out the same in such Towns where such Defect is, as shall be found *The Jury to* most beneficial, for the interest of His Majesty, and the Benefit of the Sub- *be Engaged* ject, the which Jury shall be first duly Engaged to the true, faithful and su- perbial performance thereof;

And be it further Enacted by the Authority aforesaid, That in case it shall be found most convenient to lay out any Road or Highway through any particu- lar persons Land or Property, or part thereof; (who is not under any Obli- gation to allow the same ;) that then the said Jury shall agree with the *And agree* Owner or Proprietor thereof, what reasonable allowance shall be made for the *with the* same. *Proprietors* *for the Land.*

But if the Owner or Proprietor of such Land shall refuse to agree with such Jury ; then the said Jury is ordered and Impowered to Estimate and Value *If they refuse* the Price of such Land as shall be laid out as aforesaid, as near as they can, to *to agree, then* the best of their knowledge ; which Estimation so made, shall be allowed *to value the* good against such Owner or Proprietor, as refused to agree as aforesaid, and *Land, which* shall be accordingly paid to such Owner or Proprietor by such Town, out of *by the Town.* their Town Treasury and also all other incident Charges accruing on the performance of the same. Any Law Custom or Usage to the contrary hereof notwithstanding.

AN ACT, Appointing and Stating Two Juries, to attend the
General Courts of Tryals, and General Goal Delivery.

FORASMUCH as the many *Actional and Criminal Cafes, that of late Years
come upon Tryal, before the General Court of Tryals, and General Goal Delivery,
and but one Petit Jury to attend faid Courts ; which Prolongs the Sitting of fuch
Courts very much, which is a great Ill-conveniency to the Judges, and a great Charge
to fuch Perfons as have Actions depending there, before they can be heard
and difpatched.*

*Two Juries to
attend the Ge-
neral Court of
Tryals.*
BE it therefore Enacted by the **General Affembly**, and by the **Authority** of the
fame, That for the Expediting and Difpatch of Bufinefs for the Future,
there fhall be two Petit Juries Elected and Appointed, to attend the Refpective
General Courts of Tryals, and General Goal Delivery in this Colony, and the
faid Juries fhall be Improved as the Judges of faid Courts, fhall fee caufe in all
Actional or Criminal Cafes.

*Each Town
Quota of
Jury-men:*
And be it further Enacted by the Authority aforefaid, That each & every Town in
the Colony, fhall Elect and fend to the aforefaid General Courts of Tryals, and
General Goal Delivery, the feveral Numbers of lawful honeft Petit Jury-men,
as it is hereafter Expreffed, (That is to fay) *Newport* Ten, *Providence* Four,
Portfmouth Four, *Warwick* Two, *Wefterly* Two, *New-fhoreham* Two, *Kingftown*
Two, *Eaft-Greenwich* Two, and *Jameftown* One ; which Jury fhall be Elected by
each Refpective Town, according to their Ufual Cuftom ; and the faid
Jury-men fo Elected, fhall attend the Refpective Courts, for which Chofen.

*A Jury-mans
Fine upon
neglect of
Appearance.*
AND be it further Enacted by the Authority aforefaid, That if any Jury-
man Chofen and Elected as aforefaid, fhall Refufe and Neglect to make his
Perfonal Appearance at fuch Court, on the firft Day of the fitting of fuch Court,
fhall Pay as a Fine, *Thirteen Shillings*, and *Four-pence*, for fuch his defect, unlefs
the Judges of fuch Court fhall think fit to Remit the fame.

*The Recorder
to return all
Delinquents
to the Sheriff,
who is to Col-
lect the Fines.
Fines how
difpofed of.*
AND it is further Enacted by the Authority aforefaid, That the General Recorder
fhall from time to time, keep a fair Record of all fuch Jury-men, as fhall not
appear at the Refpective Courts, and fo many of them as fhall not have their
Fines Remitted as aforefaid, he fhall at the breaking up of fuch Court return
a Lift of their Names to the Sheriff, who is hereby Required before the next
Court, to take and receive the faid Refpective Fines ; and in Cafe any of the
faid Perfons fhall Refufe to Pay faid Fine on Demand, the Sheriff fhall then make
Diftraint upon the Perfonal Eftate of the Perfon fo Refufing or Neglecting, to
the Value of fuch Fine, and the Charges thereupon accruing, or like to accrue,
which Goods Diftrained are to be difpofed of, in manner as other Diftreffes,
and by the Laws of this Colony, for the fatisfying fuch Fine and Charges,
and the Overplus if any, to be returned to the Perfon Diftrained on ; the one
Moiety of fuch Fines to be and remain to the Sheriff, for his fervice therein,
and the other Moiety to be difpofed of by the Court where fuch default was
made, for defraying the Incident Charges of faid Court, and Account of
all Fines fo Received or Levied by the Sheriff, with his proceedings thereupon,
fhall be by him duly rendred to the next fucceeding Court, together with the
moiety of fuch Fines unto faid Court belonging.

Laws

L A VV S

Made and Paſt by the General Aſſembly of His Majeſties Colony
of *Rhode-Iſland* and *Providence-Plantations*, Held at *Newport*
by Adjournment, *July* the Fifth, 1715.

AN ACT for Emitting *Thirty Thouſand Pounds* in Publick
Bills of Credit.

An Act for Emitting Thirty Thouſand Pounds in Bills of Credit.

WHEREAS it hath Pleaſed GOD, to ſuffer the French and Indians, *our*
late Enemies, to Maintain, a long, Bloody and Expenſive War *a-*
gainſt His Majeſties Subjects in theſe parts of the Northern America ; *in which*
Calamity of War, this Colony hath been no ſmall ſharer, a Great part thereof Lying
Expoſed to the Inſults and Depredations of the Enemy both by Sea and Land, which
to defend this His Majeſties Colony, hath from time to time ; for this many
Years paſt been put to great Charge and Expence, which together with the Extraordinary
Additional Charge that accrued by Her late Majeſties Commands, to Aſſiſt in ſundry
Expeditions, for the Reducing of Port-Royal *and* Canada, *the Defraying the Charge*
whereof proved ſo great a Burthen, that it hath Reduced the Mony of this Colony,
and other Mediums of Exchange unto a very low Ebb, that thereby Trade is ſenſibly
Decayed, the Farmers thereby Diſcouraged, Husband-men and others Reduced to
great Want, and all ſorts of Buſineſs Languiſhing, few having wherewith to Pay
their Arrears, and many not wherewithal to ſuſtain their daily wants, by reaſon the
Silver and Gold in the firſt place, neceſſary to defray the Incident and Occaſional
Charges hath been Exhauſted ; thoſe few Bills of Publick Credit put forth by this Go-
vernment falling far ſhort of diſcharging the Colonies Arrears, hath left us little or no
Medium of Exchange ; and whereas the Annual, Neceſſary and unavoidable Charge
of the Colony makes a conſiderable Account, and that His Majeſties Fort, called Fort-
Anne is gone much to Decay, and almoſt every thing therein out of Repair, and
that all Sorts of Ammunition and Stores are Wanting, to furniſh the ſame for De-
fence ; eſpecially at a time when War ſeems to threaten us. And alſo His Majeſties
Goal in the Metroplis of this Government, is calling for Speedy and Conſiderable
Repairs and Enlargement, and many other Publick Emergencies, which cannot be
Omitted, Requiring conſiderable Sums of Money, which to Effect there is no poſſibility
in View, ſaving that of Emitting Publick Bills of Credit of this His Majeſties
Colony, to accompliſh the ends aforeſaid, and to Reduce the Arrears thereof
unto a Ballance, always depending on our Dread Sovereign's Countenance and Tole-
ration therein, unto whoſe Royal Commands this Colony, as in Duty bound will at
all times readily Submit.

All which being duly Conſidered.

BE it therefore Enacted by the General Aſſembly of this His Majeſties Colony
of Rhode-Iſland, and by the Authority of the ſame ; and it is hereby
Enacted, That the Sum of *Thirty Thouſand Pounds* in Bills of Publick Credit,

Thirty Thouſand Pounds to be emitted.

Y 2

*Trustees ap-
pointed for
the same.*

of the same Tenor with those already put forth by this His Majesties Colony, be forthwith made, and put into the Hands of six Trustees, hereafter named and appointed in this present Act, with full power to act therein ; which Trustees, or any three of them, are hereby Impowered, to Sign said Bills, and them to ' deliver unto the Persons Chosen for Committees of the several and respective Towns in this Colony ; the said Trustees taking Receipts from the said Committees, for such - Sums as shall be by them received, as the proportion of such Town , which said Bills, being by such Committee receiv'd the same, is to be Let out to the Inhabitants of their Respective Towns in this Colony, in Good and Sufficient Land

*And to be
lived out at
five per Cent.
upon Land
Security, for
ten years.*

or other real Security within the saidTowns,at *Five Pounds per Cent per Annum*, in Sums not exceeding *Five Hundred Pounds*, nor under *Fifty Pounds* to any one Person, and that for the space of Ten Years. Always PROVIDED, That all such Persons that shall take said Bills upon such Security, shall at the Expiration of Five Years from the Date, of their Deed of Mortgage or other assurance renew the same, or give any further, and other better Security for the continuation of any such Sum by them borrowed for the remaining five

*Bonds to be
given for In-
terest.*

years ; if by the Trustees, then for the time being, such person shall be thereunto Required, and that persons so borrowing the said Bills, shall before receiving of the same, give five Bonds payable to the General Treasurer of this Colony for the time being, to the use of this Colony, for the orderly and duly payment of the first five years Interest : And if any such person, at the Expiration of the five years, shall see cause to pay down the Principal,

*The Mortgages
taken, to be
Recorded.*

and Discharge the Interest in like Publick Bills of Credit, or current Money of said Colony ; upon his or their so doing, such Mortgage or Security shall be released and delivered up, and the Lands, or other real Estate so Mortgaged or Engaged, discharged therefrom. And the said Trustees and Committees for the several Towns, are hereby required, carefully to inspect into the true value of such Estates as shall be offer'd to Mortgage, and that they be of double the value of the Sums Lent thereupon ; and whether the Title of the person desiring to Mortgage his Lands, &c. appears to be good by the Town Records, where such Land or real Estate lies, and that no Encumbrance be thereupon, which appearing good and satisfactory, such Mortgages to be taken by the Committee of the several Towns as aforesaid, and forthwith at the Charge of the Mortgager, be put upon the Records of such Town where such Estate lies ; and the said Deeds of Mortgage after-

*To be made
to the Trustees,
&c. for the
Colonys use.*

wards with all convenient speed, together with the Bonds for payment of the Interest, by Lodging in the Custody of the Trustees for the time being, for the use of this Colony, they giving Receipts for the same, to the Committee of the several respective Towns, upon delivery of the same, the said Trustees to be always accountable unto the General Assembly of this His Majesties Colony for the time being, for all such Mortgages and Bonds, together with the Profits thereof, the which they shall surrender up to the General Assembly of this Colony, when by them they shall be thereunto Required ; And that all Mortgages made, or to be made as a Security for the Bills so borrowed to be to the first Trustees, and such others as shall from time to time be appointed by the General Assembly of this Colony.

*The first Trus-
tees appoint-
ed.*

And be it further Enacted by the General Assembly, and by the Authority of the same, That Lieutenant Colonel *John Wanton*, Captain *Job Almy*,

Major

Major *Nathaniel Codddington*, Captain *Benjamin Ellery*, Major *James Brown*, and Mr. *Robert Gardner*, be, and they hereby are appointed and Chosen to be the Six first Truftees, and them, or any three of them, fhall Sign all fuch Bills as fhall be made as aforefaid ; and the aforefaid Six Truftees are hereby appointed to be the Committee for the Town of *Newport*, to Let out, and take Security for their proportion of faid Publick Bills of Credit afore-deferibed in this Act. And the Honourable *Jofeph Jencks*, Efq; Deputy Governour, and Captain *Richard Waterman*, be a Committee for the Town of *Providence*, to Lett out their proportion of faid Bills, and that Mr. *Thomas Cornell*, and Mr. *George Cornell*, be a Committee for the Town of *Portfmouth*, to Execute faid Truft ; and Major *Randal Houldon*, and Major *Job Green*, be a Committee to Execute the faid Truft for the Town of *Warwick* ; Captain *John Babcock*, and Captain *Jofeph Stanton*, be a Committee to Execute faid Truft, for the Town of *Wefterly* ; Captain *Simon Ray*, and Captain *John Sands*, be a Committee to Execute faid Truft, for the Town of *New-Shoreham* ; Captain *John Eldred*, and Mr. *Stephen Hafzard*, be a Committee to Execute faid Truft for the Town of *Kingftown*, Major *Thomas Fry*, and Mr. *Thomas Spencer*, be a Committee to Execute faid Truft for the Town of *Eaft-Greenwich* ; and that Mr. *John Hull*, and Captain *Nicholas Carr*, be a Committee to Execute faid Truft for the Town of *James-Town*. All the aforefaid Committees fhall be under Oath for their due and faithful performance of the Truft repofed in them, in the Premifes aforefaid, and fhall be allowed and paid for their Service therein, *TenShillings* on every *Hundred Pounds* by them Lett out, to be divided amongft them, as followeth, (*viz.*) two thirds of the whole amount unto the firft fix Truftees afore-named, together with a proportionable part of the third part alotted to be divided with the other Committees, for their care and trouble in Receiving and Signing, and Letting the Town of *Newport*'s proportionable part of faid Bills ; and delivering the remainder to the Committees of the feveral Towns in proportion to fuch Money, as fhall be by them Lett out.

Committees appointed to Lett at each Towns Quota.

And be it further Enacted by the Authority aforefaid, That the Publick Bills of Credit to be Emitted by this Colony, fhall be made and finifhed according to the feveral Sums and Values hereafter mentioned, *viz.* Of Five Pound Bills, Ten Thoufand, Four Hundred and Five Pounds ; of Three Pound Bills, fix thoufand, two hundred and forty three Pounds ; of Forty Shilling Bills, four thoufand, one hundred and fixty two Pounds ; of Twenty Shilling Bills, two thoufand and eighty one Pounds ; of Ten Shilling Bills, two thoufand, five hundred and fix Pounds ; of Five Shilling Bills, one thoufand two hundred and fifty three Pounds ; of Four Shilling and Six-penny Bills, one thoufand three hundred and fifty Pounds ; of Three Shilling Lills, nine hundred Pounds ; of Two Shilling and Six-penny Bills, feven hundred and fifty pounds ; and of One Shilling Bills, three hundred Pounds ; being in the whole, Thirty Thoufand Pounds ; which Bills fhall not be Pafted, Covered or Lin'd on the back-fide, on any pretence whatfoever. And the faid Truftees are as foon as poffible to Sign the aforefaid quantity of Bills, and to make them of divers forms and diftinctions, as much as poffible may be, to prevent Counterfeiting ; and the Charges of the fame to be reimburs'd out of the General Treafury of this Colony.

The quantity and Denominations of the feveral forts, of Bills.

Z

And

And be it further Enacted by the Authority aforesaid, That if the Inhabitants of any Town in the Colony, do not within three Months, after their Committee has received their proportion of the aforesaid Bills, take it up and improve it according to the intent and purport of this Act, that they may Lett it out to any persons in the Colony, upon good Security as aforesaid, or return it to the Grand Committee, whose Receipts shall be their Discharge.

AND be it further Enacted by the Authority aforesaid, That One Thousand Pound out of the Interest of Thirty Thousand Pounds to be Lett out, be Annually improved for the Sinking of One Thousand Pounds of our old Bills of Credit formerly Emitted by the Colony, until the whole be Consumed, and the aforesaid Grand Committee are hereby Impowered to Exchange the Sum of One Thousand Pounds annually of our own Bills of Credit, in order to be burnt, until they be wholly sunk as aforesaid, and the remaining part of the Interest of the aforesaid Thirty Thousand Pounds, shall be annually Disposed of for the Interest of the Government, as the Assembly shall from time to time order and direct.

One Thousand Pound of old Bills to be Annually Sunk with the Interest of the New.

AND be it further Enacted by the Authority aforesaid, That the General Treasurer of this Colony for the time being, shall have the same benefit and liberty to Arrest each respective Obligor, as the General Treasurer hath against each respective Constable, upon default of paying the General Tax or Rate to him Committed.

The General Treasurer's Power of Arresting the Obligors.

AN ACT, Prohibiting the Importation, or bringing into this Colony, any Servants or Slaves.

WHEREAS *Divers Conspiracies, Insurrections, Rapes, Thefts, and Execrable Crimes have been lately perpetrated in this, and the Neighbouring Governments by Indian Slaves, and the daily increase of them in this Government, discourage the Importing of White Servants from Great-Britrain, &c. into the same, which if not immediately Remedied, may prove very Pernicious and Destructive to the Colony.*

BE it therefore Enacted by this Assembly, and by the Authority of the same, That from and after (Three Months next ensuing) the Publication of this Act, all Indians Male, or Female, of what age soever, Imported into this Colony by Sea or Land, from any part or place whatsoever, to be disposed of, Sold or lett within this Colony, shall be Forfeited to this Colony, to and for the Use and support of the same; Unless the Person or Persons Importing or bringing in such Indian or Indians, shall give Security at the Secretary's Office of *Fifty Pounds per* Head, to Transport and Carry out the same again, within the space of one Month next after their coming in, not to be return'd back to this Colony.

All Indian Slaves Imported into the Colony, to be Forfeited, unless Bond be given for their Transportation.

AND every Master of any Ship or other Vessel, Merchant or Person whatsoever Importing or bringing into this Colony, by Sea or Land, any

Indian

Indian or Indians Male, or Female, within the space of Twenty-four Hours, *All Masters* next after their arrival or coming in, shall Report or Enter their Names, *to report the* Number and Sex, and give Security in the Secretarys Office as aforesaid, on *of the Slaves* pain of Forfeiting to the Colony, the sum of *Fifty Pounds per Head*, to and *by them Im-* for the Use of the Colony; to be Sued, for and Recovered in any of His *ported. into* Majesties Courts of Record, by Action, Bill, Plaint, Suit or Information. And *the Secreta-* the Fee to be paid for such Entry and Bond as aforesaid, shall be *Two Shillings* On *penalty of* and *Six-pence* and no more. Any Act or Acts, Clause or Clauses of Acts to the *Fitty Pounds* contrary hereof notwithstanding. *per Head.*

Secretary's Fee.

L A W S

Made and Past by the General Assembly of His Majesties Colony of *Rhode-Island*, and *Providence-Plantations*, &c. Held at *Warwick*, the Twenty Sixth Day of *October*, 1715.

AN ACT, for Raising and Emitting *Ten Thousand* Pounds in Publick Bills of Credit on this Colony.

BE it *Enacted by the General Assembly, and by the Authority of the same*, Ten Thou- That there be forthwith Imprinted and Signed, the Sum of *Ten Thousand* sand Pounds Pounds in Bills of Credit in this Colony, by the former Committee who *Emitted.* Signed the *Thirty Thousand* Pounds Emitted by this Colony, and by them *And hired* to be delivered to the Committees of the several Towns in proportion as *out.* aforesaid, to be hired out upon good Security, as the *Three Thousand* Pounds aforesaid is, the said Bills to pass in all Publick Payments as the other Bills are and do pass.

AND be it further Enacted by the Authority aforesaid, That every Person or Persons whatsoever within this Colony, that have hired any Bills of Credit of this Colony, and by their Obligations are Obliged to pay in the same specie agian, shall be discharged from their said Obligations, they paying the same in Current Mony of *New-England.*

Z 2 An

L A W S

Made   and Paſt by the General Aſſembly of His Majeſties Colony
of   *Rhode-Iſland*, and *Providence-Plantations* Held at   *New-port*, the Second Day of *May*, 1716.

AN ACT, Regulating the Maintainance of Miniſters within this
Colony.

WHEREAS in the Fifteenth Year of the Reign of His Gracious Majeſty, Charles
the Second, there was a Charter Granted to this His Majeſties Colony, in which
contained many Gracious Priviledges, for the Incouragement and Comfort of the
Inhabitants thereof ; amongſt others that of free liberty of Conſcience in Religious
Concernment, being of the moſt Principal, it being a Moral Priviledge due to every
Chriſtian, as by His ſaid Majeſty is obſerved, that true They rightly grounded
upon Goſpel principles, will give the beſt and greateſt Security to Sovereignty, and will lay
in the Hearts of Men, the ſtrongeſt Obligations to true Loyalty. And this
preſent Aſſembly being ſenſible by long Experience, that the aforeſaid Priviledge by the
Good Providence of GOD, having been continued to us, has been an outward means of
continuing a Good and Amicable Agreement amongſt the Inhabitants of this Colony ;
and for the better continuance and ſuppore thereof, as well as for the timely preventing
of any and every Church, Congregation and Society of People, now Inhabiting, or which
ſhall hereafter Inhabit within any part of the Juriſdiction of the ſame, from Endeavour-
ing for Preheminence or Superiority one over the other, by making Uſe of the Civil
Power, for the Enforcing of a Maintainance for their Reſpective Miniſters.

No Miniſter
to be main-
tained other-
wiſe, than by
free Contribu-
tion.

BE it Enacted by this Preſent Aſſembly, and by the Authority of the ſame, That
what Maintainance or Sallery, may be thought needful or neceſſary by a-
ny of the Churches, Congregations or Society of People now Inhabiting, or
that hereafter ſhall and may Inhabit within the ſame, be raiſed by free Con-
tribution, and no other ways.

Laws

L A W S

Made and Paſt by the General Aſſembly of His Majeſties Colony of *Rhode Iſland* and *Providence-Plantations*. &c. Held at *Providence*, the Thirty Firſt Day of *October*, 1716

AN ACT, for the better ſettling the Payment of Officers Fees, at the General Courts of Tryals.

BE it Enacted by the General Aſſembly, and by the Authority of the ſame, *He that ob-*
taining Judg-
ment, to pay
Coſts.
That all Perſons whatſoever, whether Plantiff or Defendant, that
ſhall at the General Court of Tryals, Recover or Obtain Judgment
of ſaid General Court of Tryals, he, ſhe or they ſo Recovering or Obtaining Judgment, ſhall Pay to the Recorder all Officers Fees due in ſaid Caſe,
before He, She, or They, ſhall have His or Their Bill of Coſts Taxed; any
Act or Acts, Clauſe or Clauſes or Acts to the contrary hereof, in any ways
notwithſtanding.

L A VV S

Made and Paſt by the General Aſſembly of His Maieſties Colony of *Rhode-Iſland* and *Providence-Plantations*, Held at *Newport*. by Adiournment. *June* the Eighteenth, 1717.

AN ACT for the Explanation of, and further Enlargement of an Act Paſt by the General Aſſembly of this Colony, begun and Held at *Newport* by Adjournment, the Twenty Seventh Day of *February* 1711, 12. For Granting of Adminiſtration to the Wives of Perſons Three years abſent, and not heard of.

WHEREAS the aforeſaid Act of Aſſembly, hath by Experience been found
very beneficial and Uſeful to the Wives of ſuch Seafaring Perſons and
others, as have departed out of this Colony, and not heard of in Three Years after
Departure, without leaving of a good and ſufficient Power of Attorney, with any
Perſon or Perſons, the Due Recovering and Managements of their Eſtates both
Real and Perſonal in their abſence ; but the ſaid Act not being ſo Full and Extenſive
as hath ſince been found neceſſary in ſuch like Caſes, for the further Enlargement and
Explanation thereof, and in Addition thereunto.

IT is further Enacted by the General Aſſembly of this Colony, and by the Autho-
rity of the ſame, That in caſe any perſon being an Inhabitant of this
A a Colony,

*If a perfon
be abfent,
three years
unheard of,
his Wife, or
other Relati-
ons fhall have
Adminiftrati-
en granted.*

Colony, hath, or fhall depart. out of the fame, being Entitled unto, or
leaving any Eftate, either Real or Perfonal, within the Limits thereof unto fuch Perfons belonging or appertaining, and hath not, or fhall not at
his Departure leave a good and fufficient Power or Letter of Attorney,
with fome perfon or perfons for the due care, recovering, management,
and orderly Difpofal of the fame ; or in cafe fuch Attorney or Attorneys
by him left fhall Die, whereby the faid Power fhall be determined; and after
his Departure, hath not, or fhall not be heard of and from, within the fpace
of three years then next immediately fucceeding fuch his Departure ; that
then, and in fuch cafe, it fhail and may be lawful, upon the due application of
the Wife or Children, or other Relations or Friends of fuch perfons fo Departed, unto the Town-Council of fuch Town in the faid Colony, where
fuch Perfons was laft an Inhabitant, or did Dwell ; For the faid Town-Council, who are hereby Impowered, upon due and fatisfactory proof thereof to
them made, to Grant, Authorize and Impower the Wife of fuch perfon, if
any he hath ; or in cafe he hath none, then fuch perfon or perfons as they
fhall think meet and proper for and in the name, and to the ufe, benefit and
behoof of fuch Departed Perfon to enter into, Demand, Sue for, Recover,
Poffefs and Improve all fuch Lands and Houfes, or other Real Eftate whatfoever, as at the Departure of fuch perfon unto him of right did any ways belong or appertain ; and alfo all fuch perfonal Eftate whatfoever, confifting either in Leafes, Rents, Goods, Chattels, Debts, or otherwife, as at the time of
fuch Departure, fhall be left by him to Ask, Sue for, Recover, Receive
aud Difcharge as well and effectually in Law, as it fuch Departed perfon had
himfelf left a good and fufficient Power of Attorney to fuch Ends and
Purpofes.

*The Ordinary
to take fuffi-
cient Bond,
for their
faithful Ad-
miniftration.*

PROVIDED always, and it is the true intent and meaning of this Act,
That each refpective Town-Council fhall upon their Granting fuch Power
and Authority as aforefaid, take good and fufficient Security by Bond, to
be given joyntly and feverally by two Freeholders of this Colony, together
with the perfon or perfons unto whom they fhall Grant fuch Power as aforefaid unto the faid Town-Council, and to their Succeffors, for his and their
true and faithful acting and doing therein, according to the power thereby
given for the benefit and ufe of fuch Departed Perfon ; and to render unto
him a juft and true Accompt at his Return to this Colony, or to any perfon
or perfons by him Impowered, to demand the fame, when lawfully thereunto
Required ; and that in cafe fuch Departed Perfon fhall after fuch his Departure be by reafon of his long abfence, or other due proof, deemed and adjudged Dead in Law before his Return to this Colony, then to render unto
the Heirs, Executors, Adminiftrators or Affigns of fuch Departed Perfon fuch
Eftate, both real and perfonal, as by Law fhall become their, or either of
their juft Dues and Rights refpectively to have and enjoy.

*The Admini-
ftrators to
maintain by
confent of the
Ordinary, fuch
perfons as the
Departed
perfon was
obliged to.*

AND be it further Enacted by the Authority aforefaid, That in cafe fuch
Departed Perfon fhall leave any Child, or Children, or other Relation or
Perfon, the Charge of whole Education and Maintainance by Law fhall be
Incumbent or Obligatory upon him ; that then, and in fuch cafe, the perfon
or perfons fo Authorized and Impowered by the Town-Council as aforefaid,
fhall and may with the confent and approbation of fuch Town-Council, lay
out, and Expend out of the Eftate of fuch Perfon Departed as aforefaid, for
the

the Maintainance and Education of fuch Child or Children, or other Relation; the Charge of whofe Maintainance or Education was Incumbent or
Obligatory upon fuch Departed perfon, fuch Sum or Sums of Money as fhall
be by fuch Town-Council thought needful and convenient, which fhall be
allowed him in any Accompt afterward to be Adjufted.

AN ACT, Enabling and Appointing Overfeers to Leafe out the
Lands of *Ninigret* the Sachem in the *Narraganfett* Country.

WHEREAS Ninigret *Sachem, in the* Narraganfett *Country, in the Colony
of* Rhode-Ifland, *&c. Hath Petitioned this Affembly, to appoint three
Overfeers to Overfee and Rent out his Lands, to prevent his being Defrauded therein,
and has alfo defired this Affembly, to Difpoffefs all thofe that fhall refufe to Hire of
his Overfeers as fhall be appointed by the Governour and Company of faid Colony, for
the time being; and alfo in cafe he fhall have need to Sell any of his Lands, that he
may by the faid Governour and Company, for the time being, be affifted therein.* For
the Complying with which Petition, and for the better fecuring the faid Sachems Lands and Profits.

BE *it Enafted by the General Affembly, and by the Authority of the fame,* Overfeers *ap-
That* Col. *William Wanton,* Major *Thomas Fry,* and Captain *Jofeph* pointed to
Stanton be, and they hereby are appointed Overfeers, to Overfee and Leafe Leafe out
out the faid Sachems Lands, as fhall to them feem moft conducive for the Ninigret's
faid Sachems Intereft. And they, or any two of them are hereby Impower- Lands.
ed to Difpoffefs all and every perfon that now is, or hereafter fhall be in the
poffeffion of any of the faid Sachems Lands, and fhall refufe to agree, com-
ply and hire faid Lands, at fuch Rents and Services as by them, or the major
part of them fhall be found moft beneficial for the faid Sachems Intereft,
they not Granting any Leafe for any longer Term than feven years, the faid
Sachem to pay the Charge thereof, and the faid Overfeers to render an Accompt of, and furrender up their Truft to the General Affembly, when
thereunto Required.

A a 2   Laws

L A W S

Made and Paſt by the General Aſſembly of His Majeſties Colony of *Rhode-Iſland*, and *Providence-Plantations*. Begun and Held at *Warwick*, the Thirtieth Day of *October*, 1717.

AN ACT for Explaining an Act, Paſt by the General Aſſembly of this Colony ſitting at *Newport*,the Thirty-firſt Day of *October*, 1677. For Granting Re-hearings from one General Court of Tryals to another, and for the better ſupport and defraying the Charges of the Judges of ſuch Courts.

WHEREAS the *aforeſaid Act for the granting of Rehearings in Actional Caſes, being in General termes (to wit) that the Plaintiff and Defendant, ſhall each of them have one Rehearing if deſired, without any Limitation or Expla-nation ; ſo that Rehearings have been frequently Inſiſted upon by the Defendant,upon a Nihil dicit, Default Bonds Obligatory and ſo forth ; and many have been Granted upon the aforeſaid Act in ſuch Caſes as aforeſaid, which tends to the General Obſtruct ion of Juſtice, keeping of Creditors out of their Juſt dues,*

For the better Regulation whereof,

BE it *Enacted by the General Aſſembly, and by the Authority of the ſame,* That from and after the Publication of this Act. no Rehearing ſhall be Granted upon any *Nihil dicit*,ariſing for want of anſwers,being duly Filed in the Recorders Office,nor upon any wilful Defaults,neither upon Bond Obligatory duly proved, unleſs the Defendant, ſhall by good and ſatisfactory Evidence, prove to the Court either before or upon Rendering Judgement, that ſuch *Nihil dicit* or default, was Occaſioned by Sickneſs, Stormy-weather, or other ſuch Providential Obſtruction of the Defendant or his Attorney, as ſhall be by the Judges of ſuch Courts allowed of, nor ſhall a Rehearing be Granted upon any Judgment obtained upon a Bond Obligatory duly proved, unleſs the Defendant give in good and ſufficient Security, to the ſatisfaction of the Judges of ſuch Court, to pay double Coſts and Damages to the Plaintiff, in Caſe he ſhall not obtain a Reverſal of ſaid Judgment, on ſuch Rehearing by him to be proſecuted.

No re-hearing upon Nihil dicit, &c.

AND be it *further Enacted by the Authority aforeſaid,* That upon Granting every Rehearing, the party deſiring the ſame, ſhall pay to the Clerk of ſuch Court, the Sum of *Seven Shillings* and *Six-pence,* Current Mony. Any Act or Acts Clauſe or Clauſes of Acts to the contrary hereof notwithſtanding.

The Party re-hearing to Pay Seven Shillings & Six-pence.

LAWS

Made and Past by the General Assembly of His Majesties
Colony of *Rhode-Island,* and *Providence-Plantations,* in *New-
England,* begun and Held at *Newport,* the Seventh Day of *May,*
1718. and Continued by Adjournments to the Ninth Day of
September following.

AN ACT, to prevent *Indians* being Sued for Debt.

WHEREAS *several Persons in this Colony, out of Wicked Covetous and
Greedy designs, often draw* Indians *into their Debt, and take unjust advantages
of their inordinate Love of Rum, and other Strong Liquors, by Selling the same to
them, or otherwise to take advantages by Selling them other Goods at Extravagant Rates
upon Trust, whereby said* Indians *have been Impoverished, to the dishonour of this
Government.*

For the preventing thereof for the Future,

BE *it Enacted by the General Assembly of this Colony, and it is hereby Enacted,*
That from and after the Publication of this Act, no Process shall be
Granted, nor Suit be Received or Lye before any Justice or Justices of
the Peace, Assistants or Courts of Tryals in this Colony, against any Indian
or Indians for Debt, to be made or Contracted by such Indian or Indians, at
any time or times after the Publication hereof; and that no Indian shall be
Bound an Apprentice or Servant to any of His Majesties Subjects, without the
Consent, Allowance and Approbation of Two Justices of Peace of this Colony,
and for good cosideration there for, and Testifyed to, under the Hands of such
Justices ; any Law, Custom or Usage to the contrary, in any wise notwithstanding.

*No Indian
be trusted up
any account
whatsoever.
Whosoever
Trusts an In-
dian loses
his Debt ,
No Indian
to be a Ser-
vant, but for
a good consi-
deration.*

WHEREAS *the Body of Laws for Settling and Regulating of the Military
Forces within this Colony, are increased to so Great Number by reason of the
many Wars, which from time to time this Colony hath so engaged in against* French,
Indians *and other Enemies, which hath rendred many of them Useless, and may be for
the Future Prejudicial, if not Repealed.*

BE *it therefore Enacted by the General Assembly of this Colony, and by the
Authority of the same, and it is hereby Enacted,* That all Acts heretofore
made, Relating to the Militia, or appointing Officers of the same, Be
hereby and Absolutely Repealed and Declared Null and Void, and that for
the future the following Order, Regulation and Rules Relating to the same,
be Kept and Observed by all Persons in this Colony.

First, it is Enacted and appointed, that all Male Perſons Reſiding for the ſpace of Three Months within this Colony from the Age ofSixteen,to the Age

All perſons to Train, from Sixteen to Fifty. Theſe only excepted.

ofSixty Years, ſhall bear Arms in their Reſpective Train-bands or Companies whereto by Law they ſhall belong, Excepting only all Perſonsthat ſhall have Served in the Place of General Officers, Juſtices of the Peace or other Commiſſion Officers, one Miniſter or Teacher of each reſpective Congregation in each reſpective Town, all Sworn Practitioners in Chirurgery and Phyſick, all Apothecaries and School-maſters, and alſo one Miller to each Griſt Mill, one Ferry-man to each ſtated Ferry, one Goaler to each of His Majeſties Goals in the Colony,and all thoſe that have loſt one of their Eyes,or diſabled by Lameneſs, and allPerſons that are under Oath or Engagement to any Office.

Captain General, and Lieutenant General appointed.

AND it is hereby Declared and Enacted,That the Governour of this Colony the time being, ſhall be the Captain General and Commander in Chief, of and over all the Military Forces within this Colony, and the Deputy Governour for the time being ſhall be Lieutenant General of the ſame.

The Militia divided into Companies.

AND be it further Enacted by the Authority aforeſaid, That for the better Ordering and Training up the Inhabitants of this Colony, that the ſeveral Companies or Train'd-bands,ſhall remain in the Stations and Bounds and Diviſion by the which they have been heretofore Divided Known & Diſtinguiſhed, until ſome further or New Diviſion or Bounds be Stated Appointed or Limited by lawful Authority.

That is to ſay, Three Companies in the Town of *Newport*, Three Companies in the Town of *Providence*, one Company in the Town of *Portſmouth*, one Company in the Town of *Warwick*, Two Companies in the Town of *Weſterly*, one Company in the Town of *New-ſhoreham*,Two Companies in the Town of *Kingſtown*, one Company in the Town of *Eaſt-Greenwich*, and one Company in the Town of *James-Town.*

And into a Regiments. Each Regiment to be Led by one Colonel, Lieutenant Colonel and Major to be appointed by the Aſſembly. Each Company to have one Captain, Lieutenant & Enſign to be appointed by the Aſſembly. The Governours power to appoint Officers, if they Die.

AND be it further Enacted by the Authority aforeſaid, That the Militia of this Government be, and it is hereby Divided into Two Regiments. That is to ſay, The Militia of *Rhode-Iſland*, *New-Shoreham*, alias *Bleck-Iſland*, *Conanicut*, *Prudence* and *Patience-Iſland* be one Regiment, and ſhall be the Firſt and Eldeſt Regiment ; and the Militia on the *Main-Land* in this Colony, ſhall be one other Regiment, and ſhall be the ſecond and youngeſt Regiment ; each of which Regiments ſhall be Govern'd, Guided and Led by one Colonel, one Lieutenant Colonel,and one Major,which ſhall be Annualy Choſen for each Regiment by the General Aſſembly of this Colony, during their Sitting on the Firſt *Wedneſday* of *May* annually ; and that each Company or Trained Band in each of the aforeſaid Regiments, ſhall be Guided, Conducted and Led by one Captain, one Lieutenant, and one Enſign ; the which ſhall annually be Elected and Choſen by the General Aſſembly of this Colony, during their Seſſions on the Firſt *Wedneſday* of *May* annually ; all which Military Officers ſo Choſen as aforeſaid, ſhall be Commiſſionated by the Governour of the Colony for the time being, under the Seal of the Colony : And if any Colonel, Lieutenant Colonel, Major, or other Commiſſion Officer Choſen as aforeſaid, ſhall refuſe to Serve in ſuch Office, to the which he ſhall be Choſen, or ſhall happen to Die ; that then and in ſuch caſes, it ſhall and may be lawful for the Governour, or in his abſence, for the Deputy Governour, by and with the conſent of the General Council, at any time when the General

neral Affembly fhall not be Sitting to chufe and appoint fo many other Officers to Serve in the room and ftead of thofe that fhall refufe or Die as aforefaid, until the firft Wedaefday of *May* next enfuing fuch choice and appointment ; the which Officers fo Chofen, fhall be Commiffionated as above-faid ;
and before any Military Officer fhall Enter upon the Execution of his Office,
he fhall take the following Oath or Engagement.

The Form of the Engagement of Military Officers.

YOU A. B. *Being by the General Affembly of His Majefties Colony of
Rhode-Ifland, and Providence-Plantations, Chofen and Elected unto the
Place and Office of* of *Do folemnly Engage true Allegiance unto
His Majefty, King George, His Heirs and Succeffors to bear, & alfo good Fidelity to
this His Majefties Colony, and the Authority therein Eftablifhed, according to
our Charter. And you do alfo further Engage, well and truly to Execute the
Office of to the which you are Elected according to your Commiffion, and to
perform and obferve the Laws made and provided for the fupport, and well or-
dering of the Militia, without partiality ; and that you will obferve and follow fuch
Orders and Inftructions as you fhall from time to time receive from your Superiours.
And this Engagement you make and give upon the Peril of the Penalty of Perjury.*

*The Engage-
ment of Mi-
litary Officers.*

AND be it further Enacted by the Authority aforefaid, That it fhall and
may be in the power of a Captain, Lieutenant and Enfign, of each refpective Company, to nominate and appoint a Clerk, and all other Inferiour
Officers as fhall be requifite, for the management of their refpective Company ; the which Clerk fo chofen, fhall be under Oath or Engagement,
for the performance of his faid Office, and the Captain of each Company
is hereby Impowered and Required, to adminifter the fame ; the which
Oath fhall be in the Form following.

*The Captain,
&c. of each
Company to
appoint Infe-
riour Officers.*

YOU A. B. *Do folemnly Engage well and truly to perform and Execute the Office of Clerk of the Company, or Train-Band, under the Command of C. D.
to the utmoft of your skill and ability, without partiality, according to the Laws of
this Colony, as Relate to your Office.*

*The Clerk's
Engagement.*

AND be it further Enacted by the Authority aforefaid, That every Lifted
Soldier of the faid Militia, fhall be always provided with one good Musket,
or Fuzee, the Barrel whereof not to be lefs than three foot and an half in
length, to the fatisfaction of the Commiffion Officers of the Company ; alfo
one pound of good Gunpowder, thirty Bullets, fit for his Gun, fix good
Flints, fit for Service ; one good Sword, or Baionet, a Cartouch Box, ready
fitted with Cartriges of Gunpowder and Bullets, on the penalty of Three
Shillings, for each time he fhall be found not provided as aforefaid ; the
which fhall be Diftrained by the Clerk of the Company, by Warrant from
the Captain of faid Company, and Six-pence more for fuch Diftraint, upon
the Goods and Chattels of fuch defective perfon, to and for the ufe of fuch
Company.

*The Accoutre-
ment of the
Militia. Who-
foever neglects
the fame, fhall
pay Three
Shillings.
To be taken
by Diftraint.*

AND be it further Enacted by the Authority aforefaid, That the Captain of
each refpective Company or Train-band or in his abfence, the next Superiour
Officer, fhall lawfully Warn and Call together the Company under his Command

*The Captain,
&c. to call
together his
Company.*

mand, and Exercife them in Martial Difcipline, two Days in each Year in
time of Peace and Four in War ; which Days fhall be at his own appointment,
the firft of which Warnings fhall be by a Warrant directed to the Corporals, to
Notifie them to appear compleatly Accoutred as aforefaid, and other Days
according to his own Difcretion.

The number of days.

AND be it further Enacted by the Authority aforefaid, That every Enlifted
Perfon, that fhall Refufe or Neglect to make his Perfonal appearence Accoutred as aforefaid, on fuch Training Days as he fhall be Legally Warned to,
fhall for every fuch Default pay to the Clerk of the Company, *Three Shillings*
in Mony, within one Months time after fuch default, or make his lawful excufe
to the Captain, or in his abfence to the next Superiour Officer for the fame,
it any he have,& if fuch defaulter fhall Refufe fo to do,that then the Captain,
or in his abfence the nextSuperior Officer fhall Grant forth his Warrant to the
Clerk of the Band, to take and diftrain fo much of the Perfonal Eftate of fuch
delinquent Perfon, or fuch as fhall have them in Tuition, as near as conve-
niently may be will pay his Fine or Fines, together with *Six-pence* more for
each Fine diftrained for the Clerks Fees ; and fuch Eftate that fhall be taken
by diftrefs,fhall be duly Apprized by Two Free-holders of faid Company,under
Engagement at the head of faid Company, and the Captain is hereby Impowred to Adminifter the fame, and the overplus if any there be, to be
returned to the owner thereof, and if he fhall refufe to receive the fame, then
the Clerk fhall give him Credit for the fame, which fhall be accounted for
out of his next Fine that fhall become due ; and all fuch Fines taken as aforefaid, fhall be laid out to and for the Ufe of fuch Company, by order of the
Commiffion Officers thereof, for the defraying their Incident Charge.

Three Shil-lings Fine for neglect of depending. How taken. The overplus to be retained. How the fines fhall be difpofed of.

AND be it further Enacted by the Authority aforefaid, That in Cafe fuch
Perfons as fhall be delinquent as aforefaid, fhall have no Perfonal Eftate to be
found to fatisfy fuch Fines as aforefaid, that then the Captain of fuch Company, fhall fet fuch delinquent Perfon to work,in mending the Highways of fuch
Town, not exceeding one Day for each Fine; and if fuch defective perfon
fhall refufe to do the fame, then the Captain, &c. fhall commit fuch Offenders to Prifon, twenty-four Hours, or wait further to take his Eftate by Diftraint.

How to pro-ceed with perfons that have no vifible Eftate.

AND be it further Enacted by the Authority aforefaid, That if any Clerk
or other Inferiour Officer of the Band, fhall refufe to obey his Superiour Officers Warrant when to him Directed, fhall forfeit for every fuch Offence, *Ten
Shillings*, to and for the ufe of fuch Company, to be taken by Diftrefs in manner as aforefaid.

The penalty on the Inferi-our Officers refufing to obey his Su-periour.

AND be it further Enacted by the Authority aforefaid, That all fuch Perfons before in this Act excus'd from Training, yet fhall notwithftanding be provided
with the fame Arms, Ammunition, &c. as by this Act is required of fuch as are
obliged to Train,& that once every year, or oftener,as theChief Officers ofany
Company fhall fee needful,there fhall be either by fuch Officers,or others by
them appointed, a Survey and Examinination made, whether fuch Perfons are
provided as by this Act is Required ; and all fuch Perfons as fhall be found
unprovided with fuch Arms as before Required, fhall pay the Fine of *Five-
Shillings* for each default, to be Levied by Diftrefs and Sale of the Defaulters
Goods,as in other Cafes.

All perfons to be provided with Arms, &c. On the penalty of Five Shil-lings for eve-ry default.

AND

AND be it further Enacted by the Authority aforesaid, That upon any Alarm in time of War, or other emineent danger of any Assault or Invasion, all Male Persons, both Listed Soldiers and others in this Colony, of and between the Age of Sixteen Years and Sixty, shall upon notice of the same, forthwith Repair to the Colours and Ensigns of such Company, within whose Precincts they Inhabit or dwell, provided with Arms & Ammunition required of Trained Soldiers upon Training Days, and in Cafe any Perfon shall not appear as aforesaid, such Defaulter shall Pay the Fine of *Five Shillings*, to be Levied by order of the Chief Officers of such Company, by Diftrefs and Sale of such Defaulters Goods as in other Cafes.

A perfon from Sixteen to Sixty, to appear upon Alarm. On the penalty of Five Shillings.

AND it is further Enacted by the Authority aforesaid, That it shall and may be in the Power of the Governour and Deputy Governour of this Colony for the time being, or either of them, to Assemble and call together each of the Regiments of the Militia in this Colony, or any part of them or either of them at any time, as they shall think needful or necessary for the same; and if any Enlisted Soldier being duly warned to appear at any such time as shall be appointed, shall neglect the same, he shall Forfeit and Pay as a Fine, *Five Shillings* in money, to be taken and difpofed of for the Use of the Company, where such defect shall be, as other Fines are.

AND be it further Enacted by the Authority aforefaid, That if the Captian, or in his abfence the next Superior Officer of any Company or Train'd-band, shall neglect legally to Warn and Call together his Company under his Command, two Days in every Year in time of Peace, and four in time of War, he shall for every Day by him omitted or neglected, Forfeit and Pay as a Fine to and for the Use of faid Company, *Forty Shillings* in Money; and if such Officer to neglecting shall Refufe to Pay the fame, for the fpace of one Month next after such his default, that then and in such Cafes the Colonel, or in his abfence the Lieutenat Colonel of the Regiment where such omiffiion or neglect shall happen to be, shall Grant foth his Warrant to the Clerk of the Band where such omiffion or neglect has been, to diftrain fo much of the Eftate of such defaulter to be difpofed of as aforefaid.

Every Captain &c. to Call his Company together twice in the year. On the penalty of Forty Shillings.

AND be it further Enacted by the Authority aforefaid, That in Cafe any Captain, or in his abfence, the next Superiour Officer of any Company or Trained Band, shall neglect to give forth his Warrant to the Clerk of the Band to Colect and Gather such Fine or Fines as shall be due, he shall Forfeit and Pay to and for the Use of such Company, all such Fines as shall be to them due, the which shall be taken by diftraint, by Warrant as abovefaid.

If the Captain of the Company neglects to give forth his Warrant for the Gathering of the Fines, he shall pay the fame.

AND be it further Enacted by the Authority aforefaid, That if any Enlifted Soldier, shall upon any Training or Mufter Days, Refufe to Obey his Refpective Officers, or otherways misbehave himfelf, that then it shall be in the Power of the Captain & Commiffioners of each Refpective Company, to Punish such Offender, by laying him neck and heels, or Riding the Wooden-Horfe, or Fine him at Difcretion, not exceeding *Five Shillings*.

On Training Days the Captain to punifh by fine, or otherways, fuch as offend.

AND it is further Enacted by the Authority aforefaid, That the Colonel of each of the aforefaid Regiments, shall by and with the Advice or Order of the Captain General, or Lieutenant General, Call together the Refpective Regiments

C c

A General Muster to be but once in five years.

giment under his Command, to a General Muster, to Review and Exercise the same once in five years, and not oftener; and the Commission, and other Inferiour Officers and Private Centinels of each respective Company, are hereby Commanded and Required, to yield all due Obedience to their respective Field Officers upon a General Muster, or upon any other Training and Muster Day, as Private Centinels are Required to do to their other Commission Officers, upon the Penalty of incurring the like pains and forfeitures as afore provided.

A*ND WHEREAS it appears needful for His Majesties Service, and the Defence of this Colony, that there should be a Body of Horse Raised, for the more speedy opposing or prosecuting of any Enemy.*

B*E it therefore Enacted by the Authority aforesaid,* That all proper means be used, and Encouragement given by the Governour, Deputy Governour, and General Officers of this Colony, for the Raising of three Troops of

Three Troops of Horse to be Raised.

Horse, each Troop not to consist of more than Sixty Persons, including Officers, one of which Troops is to be Raised out of the Regiment upon the Islands, and the other two Troops to be Raised out of the Regiment upon the Main-Land: And that when there shall be to the Number of Twenty Eight Persons Enlisted in any of said Troops, that then upon due application

To consist of sixty men each.

to the General Assembly, there shall be by them Nominated and Appointed such Officers for the Commanding, Ordering and Disciplining of such Troop, as to said Assembly shall appear proper and needful for the ends aforesaid; which Officers shall be Engaged and Commissionated as the Officers of the Foot Companies are: And that every Trooper shall be always provided with

Trooper's Accoutrements.

one good serviceable Horse, of fourteen hands high, one good Saddle, Bitt-Bridle, Holsters, Breast-plate and Crouper, one Carbine, one pair of good Pistols, one Sword, one pound of Gunpowder, thirty useable Bullets, twelve good Flints, one good pair of Boots and Spurs, upon the Penalty of *Two Shillings* for every default in every of the aforesaid Accoutrements; and that the Field Officers of each Regiment, shall appoint the Cloathing of every of the Troops of the same

A*ND be it further Enacted by the Authority aforesaid,* That the Captain, or in his absence the next Superiour Officer, shall Warn the Troop un-

How many days to Muster in a year. Upon Non-appearance to be fined Five Shillings.

der his Command to Muster two several Days in every year in time of Peace, and four in time of War, at his own appointment, as the Foot Companies are; Every Trooper upon default of Non-appearance of such Muster, when legally Warned thereunto, shall pay as a Fine, to and for the use of such Troop, *Five Shillings* in Money, to be taken by Distress in like manner as the Fines in the Foot Companies are; and for every default of Appearance on an Alarm, every Trooper shall pay a Fine of *Ten Shillings,* to be taken and disposed of in manner as aforesaid.

A*ND be it further Enacted by the Authority aforesaid,* If the Captain, or in his absence the next Commanding Officer shall neglect to Muster and

Penalty on the Captain, &c. that neglects their Duty.

Exercise his Troop two several Dayes in each year, &c. he shall be under the like Fines as the Commission Officers of the Foot Company are; to be Recovered and Disposed of in the like manner

And

AND be it further Enacted by the Authority aforesaid, That the Commissi-on Officers of each Troop, shall have the same power to punish or fine such Troopers as shall refuse to obey their Commands on their Muster Days, or shall otherways misbehave themselves as the Captain of the Foot Companies have. And that the Clerk of each Troop shall pay *Ten Shillings* for every de-fect of his, in neglecting to observe such Warrant as from his Superiour Offi-cers shall be to him directed. *Penalty on the Clerk.*

The Form of the Commission for Colonel

By the Honourable *A B.* Esq; Governour of His Majesties Colony, of *Rhode Island,* and *Providence-Plantations* in *New-England.*

To *C. D.* Gent. Greeting.

YOU *C. D. Being by the General Assembly of this Colony, Elected and Chosen to the Post and Office of Colonel of the Regiment of Militia on the Islands in this Colony, are hereby in His Majesties Name,* George, *by the Grace of* GOD, *over* Great Britain, France *and* Ireland, *King, Defender of the Faith,* &c. *Authorized, Impowered and Commissionated to Exercise the Of-fice of Colonel of the said Regiment, and to Command, Guide and Conduct the same, or any particular Company or Companies thereof ; and in case of any Invasion or Assault of a Common Enemy, to infest and disturb this His Majes-ties Plantations ; You are to Alarm and Gather together under your Command, or any part thereof, as you shall deem sufficient, and with them to the utmost of your skill and ability, you are to Resist, Expulse, Expel, Kill and Destroy the same, in order to preserve the Interest of His Majesty, and His Good Subjects in these Parts: You are also to follow such further Instructions and Directions as shall from time to time be further given forth either from the General Assembly, the Governour and General Council : And for your so doing, this Commission shall be your sufficient Warrant and Discharge.* *A Colonels Commission.*

And the like Form of Commission shall serve for all other Com-mission Officers, *Mutatis Mutandis.*

AND be it further Enacted by the Authority aforesaid, That all the Com-mission Officers of the Militia, shall be and remain in their Respective Posts, until the General Assembly at their Sitting on the first Wednesday of *May* next, shall appoint Commission Officers for the same.

AND be it further Enacted by the Authority aforesaid, That the Governour and Deputy Governour, Members of the General Council, with the Field Officers and Commission Officers of each Regiment, and the Justices of the Peace that live within the same, or the Major part of them, shall be a Council of War, for each of said Regiments, both in Peace and War, to settle all Watches and Wards, and to put in Force and Execute the Law Martial as need may Require, and Generally to Say, Do and Act all and whatsoever Things shall be needful, necessary or proper for a Council of War to do. *Who shall be a Council for each Regiment.*

C c 2   *And*

In time of any Invasion, &c. the Governour, or Deputy Governour to Commissionate and Equip out sufficient Force to repel the same.

AND be it further Enacted by the Authority aforesaid, For the securing of this Colony, and the Navigation thereof against Privateers, in time of War, and Pyrates in time of Peace, which may infest the same; that the Governour of this Colony for the time being, or in his absence, or by his leave and permission, the Deputy Governour of the same, shall, and may in time of War, or any other emergent Occasion, Impower and Commissionate such person or persons, as he shall deem and adjudge to be Loyal, Couragious, and capable to Command such Ship or Ships, or other Vessels (as by and with the advice of so many of the Council, and Field Officers, as may be had at such time be thought needful for, as to Repel, or take any Privateer or Pirate, as shall infest this Colony; and also to take up and Impress such Ship or Ships, or other Vessels, as shall be deemed needful for the same; and to equip and fit the same for the Sea, and with Arms, Ammunition and Provisions, and such other necessary Stores as shall be requisite, out of the Colonies Magazine, if sufficient there be ; otherwise to Seiz and Impress such Stores and Ammunition as shall serve for the same ; and also to Enlist or Impress such and so many Seamen and others, as shall be needful and requisite to Man out such Vessels as shall be taken up or Impressed as aforesaid ; such Vessel or Vessels so fitted out, not to Cruise any longer at one time, than ten days, the Danger of the Seas only excepted.

And for the Encouragement of Seamen and others to Enlist themselves voluntarily on such Occasions.

All that's taken to belong to the Captain.

Be it further Enacted by the Authority aforesaid, That all such Ships or other Vessels that shall be taken from the Enemy, during such Cruise, together with their Loading and Appurtenances, shall be, and remain to the Captors, His Majesties Dues, and the Charge of the Out-fett only excepted ; and in case that nothing shall be taken from the Enemy during such Cruise ; the Charge thereof shall be born by the Colony.

AN ACT for Relieving such as shall be Maimed in the Colonies Service, and the Widow, Parents or Relations of such as shall be Kill'd in the Colonies Service, and shall not be able to Subsist and Maintain themselves.

Whosoever shall be disabled in the Colonies Service, to be maintain'd at their Charge.

BE it Enacted by the General Assembly of this Colony, and by the Authority of the same, That if any Officer, Soldier or Sailor, that shall be imployed by this Colony, against HIS MAJESTIES Enemies, in defence of this Colony or otherwise, shall be Maimed and Disabled by loss of Limb or Limbs, or otherwise from getting a livelihood for himself and Family, or other Relations that have dependance on him for Maintainance ; that then and in such Cases, such Maimed Person, shall have his Wounds carefully looked after and healed at the Colonies charge, and shall have an Annual Pension allowed him out of the General Treasury, sufficient to maintain himself and Family, or other Relations whose Maintainance is incumbent on him.

AND be it further Enacted by the Authority aforesaid, That if any Person or Persons shall be Slain in this Colonies Service as aforesaid, and have the charge

charge of Maintaining a Wife, Children, Parents or other Relations, that then and in such Cases, such Wife, Children, Parents or other Relations ; the Charge of whose Maintainance was Incumbent on such Person Slain as aforesaid, shall be Subscribed and Maintained by the Colony, by a Yearly Pension, to be allowed them out of the General Treasury, as by the General Assembly shall be deemed sufficient for the same, until such Wife, Children, Parents or other Relations, shall happen to Die or be able to Sublist and Maintain themselves.

And for the better putting this Act in Execution.

BE it further Enacted by the *Authority aforesaid*, That the Town Council of each Respective Town in this Colony, shall have the care and oversight of such Persons as Reside in their Respective Towns, as are Intituled to any Pension as aforesaid, and from time to time to Receive the same, and therewith supply such Persons as they shall stand in need thereof.

AN ACT for the better Regulation of Attachments in Civil Actions.

WHEREAS *by the Custom of this Colony of late Years it hath been allowed, that the Sheriff or his Deputies Attaching of Goods of small Value, and not anfwerable to the debt or damage Sued for by the Plaintiff, to be a good service of such Writt in Cafe of the Defendants abfence, which hath been a cause that there hath not been that diligence used for the Arrefting the Defendants Person as ought to be.*

BE it therefore Enacted by the General *Affembly of this Colony, and by the Authority of the fame,* That for the future upon any Writ delivered the Sheriff in a Civil Action, he shall by himfelf, or his Deputy, Ufe his beft Diligence to Arreft the Body of the Defendant, or Defendants, and shall not Attach the Defendants Goods or Chattels, unlefs such Goods and Chattels so Attached be of fufficient Value to anfwer the damages laid in such Writ ; Excepting only where the Plaintiff or his Attorney shall on the back of such Writ order the fame under the Hand of such Plaintiff, or his Attorny ; But in Cafe the Plaintiff, or his Attorney, shall fo order the same, such fervice shall be fufficient to bring the cause to a Tryal.

AN ACT, For Diftribution and Settling of Inteftates Eftate.

WHEREAS *it hath been found by Experience in this Colony, to be very wrongful and injurious to the Publick Good, as well as Private Intereft of the younger Children of Perfons Dying Inteftate, That the whole Real Eftate of such Perfon Dying Inteftate, should Defcend to his Eldeft Son, and thereby the other Children, whose Labours have been very ufeful and advantageous to their Parents, in Reducing and Improving such Real Eftate, should be left Deftitute.*

And

Adminiftrators to Exhibit Inventories to the Ordinary.

BE it therefore Enacted by the General Affembly of this Colony, and by the Authority of the fame. And it is hereby Enacted, That from and after the Publication of this Act, when any perfon fhall Die Inteftate, his Eftate both Real and Perfonal, fhall be under the care and management of fuch Adminiftrator, as fhall be legally appointed in this Colony; who fhall Exhibit an Inventory of the fame unto the Town-Council that granted fuch Letter of Adminiftration, and the Appraifement of fuch Eftate fhall be by three or more good and fufficient Freeholders upon Oath to be appointed by faid

How divided.

Town-Council; which Appraifement and Inventory being duly Exhibited and allowed by the Town-Council; the faid Eftate fhall after Debts, laft Sickness, and Funeral Charges of fuch Inteftate paid, be divided by order of fuch Town-Council amongft the Widow, Children, and their Reprefenta-

The Eldeft Son a double Portion.

tives, or others next of Kin of the Inteftate, in manner and form following; That is to fay, one third part of the perfonal Eftate to the Wife of the Inteftate for ever; as alfo one third part of the real Eftate for her Dower, during her Life, where fuch Wife fhall not be otherwife Endowed by faid Inteftate before Marriage; and alfo the reft of the Refidue and Remainder of

All the reft equal.

both the real and perfonal Eftate amongft the Children of fuch Inteftate, or their legal Reprefentatives as followeth, viz. to the Eldeft Son, or in cafe of his Death, to his legal Reprefentatives a double Portion or fhare, and to each of the other Children; or in cafe of any of their Death, to fuch Child's legal Reprefentatives, one equal part or fhare of faid Eftate, faving only that where any Child fhall have had or Received from the Inteftate any Portion or Settlement in the life-time of the Inteftate, fuch Portion or Settlement fhall be valued as it was worth at the time of fuch Settlement; and fuch Child fhall only have fo much more of the Inteftates Eftate, as may make the faid Portion or Settlement before had or made, equal with the reft of the Children, and in cafe the Eldeft Son fhall Die in the Life-time of the Inteftate, leaving no Children, nor Grand-Children; that then fuch double Portion fhall go to the next Eldeft Son of the Inteftate, or his Legal Reprefenattives, And where the Inteftate fhall Die, leaving no Sons nor their Legal Reprefentatives, that then fuch Eftate fhall be equally divided amongft the Daughters of fuch Inteftate, or their legal Reprefentatives, they to Inherit the fame as Co-partners.

In what cafe the Ordinary may order the Eldeft Son all the Lands, &c. he paying the other Children their proportionable parts.

PROVIDED neverthelefs that where any Eftate in Houfes or Lands, cannot be divided amongft all the Children or their Legal Reprefentatives, without great perjudice to, or fpoiling the whole, and being fo Reprefented and made to appear unto the Town Council, the faid Town Council may order the whole or any part to the Eldeft Son, he Paying to the other Children their Equal and Proportionable parts or fhares according to the Apprizement thereof, and in Cafe the Eldeft Son fhall Refufe, then to fuch next Eldeft Son fuccefïively as fhall accept the fame, he Paying to the other Children their proportionable parts. as aforefaid.

If any Inteftate leave no Children, the Wife to have half the perfonal, and one thad of the real Eftate.

AND be it futher Enacted by the Authority aforefaid, That when any Perfon fhall Die Inteftate, leaving no Children nor their Legal Reprefentatives, That then one Moiety or half part of the Perfonal Eftate of fuch Inteftate, fhall be Allotted to the Wife of the Inteftate for ever, and one Third part of the Real Eftate for Term of her Life, and the Refidue and Remainder of both the

the Real & Perfonal Eftatefhall be equally divided amongft fuch of the next of
Kin of the Inteftate, within equal Degree, or their Legal Reprefentatives, as *The Remain*
fhall put in their Claims thereunto before fuch Town Council, within the *des to be e-*
times herein after limited, *viz.* all fuch Perfons as at the time of the Death of *equally di-*
the Inteftate, fhall be Inhabiting or Refiding within the Limits of this Colony, *vided.*
the Province of the *Maſſachuſetts-Bay*, Province of *New-Hampſhire* or Colony *Claims if in*
of *Connecticut*, to put in his or her, or their Claim or Claims, within one Year *land, to be*
next after fuch Adminiftration Granted; and all other Perfons Inhabiting *brought in*
in other parts, within three Years next after fuch Adminiftraion Granted, and *one years*
in default thereof, fuch Perfon or Perfons fhall be utterly Barred and Excluded *time, other-*
for ever after, from Claiming or Challenging any Right or Intereft in the fame, *wiſe in three*
or any part thereof.

AND be it further Enacted, That in Cafe there fhall be no Wife of the
Inteftate Surviving him, that then all fuch Eftate of the Inteftate both Real
and Perfonal, fhall be Divided amongft the Children of the Inteftate in manner as aforefaid ; and if no Children, then amongft the next of Kin of fuch
Inteftate in equal Degree, and their Reprefentatives in manner as aforefaid.

AND be it further Enacted by the Authority aforeſaid, That every Perfon
to whom any fhare or part fhall be allowed, fhall give Bond with two good
and fufficient Sureties to the Adminiftrator before the Town Council, to Refund and Pay back to fuch Adminiftrator, his or her Rateable and Proportionable part of any Debt or Debts, that fhall afterwards appear to be Due and
Owing, from the Eftate of fuch Inteftate to any perfon or perfons whatfoever,
as alfo the Charges accuring thereon, by any Suit or Suits in Law or Equity.

And be it further Enacted, That after the Death of the Wife or Widow of
fuch Inteftate, her Thirds or Dower of the Real Eftate fhall be divided
amongft the Children, or next of Kin of the Inteftate, as by this Act
fhall at fuch time have a right to the fame.

Provided always, and be it further Enacted, That it fhall be lawful for any per- *Appeals to*
fon or perfons agrieved at any Sentence or Judgment of any Town-Council, *the General*
for any Matters contain'd in this Act, to appeal from fuch Sentence or Judg- *Council.*
ment, to the Governour and General Council of this Colony, for a final Judgment thereon ; fuch perfons giving in Bond, with fufficient Sureties, to profecute the fame with effect ; and in the mean time, all Procefs on the Sentence or Judgment of fuch Town-Council to be fufpended. Any thing herein contained to the contrary notwithftanding.

AND be it further Enacted by the Authority aforeſaid, That when any per- *The Eſtate of*
fon being Seiz'd in Fee in his own fole and proper right of any Lands, Tene- *any Inteſtate*
ments or Hereditaments Lying within the Limits of this Colony, and fhall *leaving no*
Die Inteftate, leaving no Wife or Children, nor other perfon or perfons of *Heirs Eſ-*
Kin to him, that can lawfully claim fuch Eftate, as Heir or Heirs at Law ; *cheat to the*
that then and in fuch cafe, fuch Eftate fhall efcheat and go to the Town *Town.*
where fuch Land Lies, for the ufe, and benefit of fuch Town ; and in cafe
fuch perfon fhall leave any Perfonal Eftate, fuch Eftate fhall go and accrue to
fuch Town where fuch perfon Died, or laft Inhabited within this Colony ;
And the Town-Council of fuch Town, fhall take due care of the fame, for
the benefit of fuch Town. **Dd 2** But

Except such Lands as are held in Common, shall go to the Common-romers.

But in cafe fuch perfon fhall Dye Seiz'd of any Lands, or right in Lands lying in common with other perfons, and undivided, that then fuch Lands, or his right in fuch Lands fhall go and accrue to fuch other Perfons and their Heirs, as were at the time of his Death, Tenants in common with him in the fame.

AN ACT, For taking Depofitions out of Court.

FORASMUCH *as the taking Depofitions of Witneffes in Civil Caufes, is often neceffary, by reafon of the uncertainty of the Life, Health and continued Refidence of fuch Witnefs, until the Sitting of the Court, to Try fuch Caufes ; and that the Depofitions of Witnefs be rightly and truly taken, according to their intent and meaning, and Tranfmitted to the Court.*

Evidences to be taken before a Juftice, &c.

BE it therefore Enacted by the General Affembly of this Colony, and by the Authority of the fame, That it fhall and may be lawful for either Plaintiff or Defendant in any Civil Action Commenced for or againft him at any Court in this Colony, to take out a Summons from any Affiftant. or Juftice of the Peace of the Neighbourhood for fuch Witnefs or Witneffes to appear before him, to give in his or their Evidence of what he or they know in the Cafe

If the perfon notifie the adverfe party to be there.

then depending ; provided that a Notification be firft taken out from faid Juftice, to the adverfe Party, if dwelling within ten Miles of the Place, and unto him Read, to be prefent if to be found at the place of his or their ufual Habitation ; or if not to be found, a Copy thereof being left there for him or them a reafonable time before the Examination of fuch Witnefs or Witneffes, every fuch Witnefs to be carefully Examined and Charged by fuch Juftice to Declare the whole Truth, and nothing but the Truth, between faid Parties, which Depofition fo taken, and wrote by the Juftice, or other perfon by his appointment ; and being attefted by fuch Juftice, is to be delivered to the Party, at whofe defire the fame was taken. a Copy thereof to be delivered to the adverfe Party, if by him or them then defired, and paying for the fame ; which Charges fhall be allowed to the Party that fhall obtain Judgment in the Bill of Cofts, neither of the Parties, nor their Attorneys to draw any fuch Evidence.

A N ACT for Difcouraging, Vexatious and Unjuft Suits in Law

WHEREAS, *it hath been found that Suits and Actions at Law, have been much Increafed of late Years, by the Vexatious and Letigious Difpofitoins of either Plantiffs or Defendants, in either Suing for what is not their due, or Unjuftly witholding the fame from others, and are much Encouraged thereto by reafon the Ufual Cofts to the Parties Obtaining Judgment is not enfwerable to what may reafonably be allowed.*

For

For the Difcouraging the fame for the future.

BE it therefore Enacted by the. General Affembly of this Colony, and by the Authority of the fame, and it is hereby Enacted, That when and fo often as either Plantiff or Defendant, in any Action or Suit in Law or Equity, fhall obtain the judgement of any Court of this Colony, for him, her or them, that there fhall be allowed and Taxed in the Bill of Cofts, *Two Shillings* and *Six-pence*, for every Ten Miles diftance from the Place of fuch Perfons ; and each of the Witneffes Habitations to the Court where fuch Caufe fhall be Tryed, and *Two Shillings* per Day for fuch Perfon or Perfons, and each of his, her or their Witneffes, for their Attendance on faid Court.

Two Shillings and Six pence allowed for every ten Miles Travelling to Court. Two Shillings Diem for Attendance.

PROVIDED always, that in Cafe the Evidence of any fuch Witneffes fo attending, fhall appear to fuch Court to be frivlous and not material to prove the Iffue in the Caufe, it fhall be in the Power and at the Difcretion of the Court to allow him nothing, for fuch their Travel and Attendance in fuch Bill of Cofts, and the Perfons who Summoned them, fhall Pay their Cofts for Coming, Attendance, &c.

AN ACT, Directing Proceedings in Actions and Suits, wherein either the Recorder or Sheriff are Parties.

BE it Enacted by the General Affembly of this His Majefties Colony, and by the Authority of the fame, That when and fo often henceforward, as the Recorder of this Colony for the time being, fhall be a Party in any Action or Suit, either as Plantiff or Defendant ; the Writ or Writs both Original and Judicial, fhall be Signed and Sealed(as the Law in fuch Cafes Requires) by the General Attorney of this Colony, and that in all Actions or Suits wherein the Sheriff of this Colony for the time being fhall be a Party,the Writs both Original and Judicial, fhall be directed to the Town Sergeant of the Town, for the time being, where the Defendant in fuch Action or Suit, fhall be an Inhabitant to Execute the fame.

The General Attorney to Sign all Procefs where the Recorder is party. All Writs where the Sheriff is a party, fhall be directed to the Town Sergeant.

AN ACT, for the better Regulating of the Collectors and Naval Officers Fees within this Colony.

FORASMUCH as the General Affembly of this Colony held at Warwick, on the Twenty-fifth Day of October, 1710. Paft an Act for the Regulating and Stating the Collectors and Naval Officers Fees within this Colony ; which Act being found not to be fo Extenfive as was intended, Therefore the fame is hereby Declared Null and Void, and of none Effect.

AND be it Enacted by this General Affembly, and by the Authority thereof it is Enacted, That thefe Fees hereafter mentioned, fhall be the ftated Table of Fees for the Collector and Naval Officer within this Colony, and that the

E e

Collector

The Collector and Naval Officer to take no greater Fees than is herein stated, on the penalty of Twenty Shillings, & paying all Damages.

Collector and Naval Officer, they, or either of them, or any Deputy under either of them, shall not take any other or greater Fees then is therein mentioned, on the Penalty of Forfetting *Twenty Shillings* to the Colony for every Offence, to be recovered before any on Affiftant or Juftice of the Peace, upon Complaint made of fuch, where fuch Offence fhall be Committed, together with the Cofts accruing, and the party agrieved thereby, fhall Recover his damages; if under *Forty Shillings*, before any Affiftant or Juftice of the Peace, of the Town where fuch Offence fhall be Committed; and if above *Forty Shillings*, at the General Court of Tryals.

A Table of Fees for the Collectors Office, for Veffels Trading to *Europe*, or to the *Weft-Indies*.

Collectors Fees.

	l	s	d
ENtering Inwards.	00	02	00
Permit to Unload	00	01	00
Entring Outward.	00	01	06
Permit to Load.	00	01	00
Clearing Outward.	00	02	06
Bill of Store,	00	01	00
Certificate for *Europeam* Goods.	00	01	06
Signing the Regifter.	00	03	00

A Table of Fees for Coafters.

	l	s	d
ENtering Inwards.	00	00	06
Permit to Unload.	00	00	04
Entering Outward.	00	00	04
Permit to Load.	00	00	04
Clearing Outwards	00	00	06
Certificate for *Europæan* Goods.	00	01	00
Bill of Store.	00	00	06
Permit to unload a fmall quantiy, the Veffel not Entered.	00	00	08
Endorfing the Regifler if Requefted.	00	01	06

A Table of Fees for the Naval Officer.

Naval Officers Fees.

	l	s	d
TO the Governour for Signing the Regifter.	00	06	00
To the Naval Officer for Writing the Rigefter.	00	03	00
Entering Sloops, Coafters.	00	00	06
Clearing Ditto.	00	00	06
Entering Ships or Sloops Foreign.	00	01	00
If they give Bond.	00	03	00
Clearing Ships or Sloops Foreign.	00	03	00
Cocquet for European Goods, Each.	00	01	00
Bill of Store.	00	01	00
Bond.	00	01	00
All Certificats from Great Brittain to fhew Bond given.	00	03	00

An

AN ACT For Calling in the Three Pound Bills of Credit Emitted by this Colony in the years One Thousand, Seven Hundred and Ten, and One Thousand, Seven Hundred and Eleven.

FOR AS MUCH as the *Three Pound Bills of Credit on this Colony, Emitted in the Years aforesaid, have been Counterfeited, whereby great Damages have happened to several persons, which may discourage the Currency of said Bills, if not prevented.*

BE it therefore Enacted by this *Present Assembly, and by the Authority of the same,* It is Enacted, That the Possessors of Three Pound Bills of Credit of this Colony, Emitted in the years aforesaid, Do bring into the General Treasury of this His Majesties Colony, all the aforesaid Bills, before or upon the First Day of *May,* in the year of our Lord, One Thousand, Seven Hundred and Nineteen, where all the said Bills shall be Changed with other Bills of Publick Credit ; and all of the aforesaid Three Pound Bills of Credit that shall not be brought into the General Treasury by the aforesaid First Day of *May,* One Thousand, Seven Hundred and Nineteen, Be, and hereby are Prohibited to pass from man to man, or have any further Currency. Any Act or Acts, Clause or Clauses of Acts to the contrary hereof notwithstanding.

Three Pound Bills to be paid into the Treasury, by the first of May, 1719.

AN ACT, For the Relief of poor Prisoners.

FOR AS MUCH as *many insolvent Debtors have been thrown into Goal upon Execution by their Creditors; and have laid long languishing, to the destroying of themselves and Families.*

BE it therefore Enacted by this *General Assembly, and by the Authority of the same,* That whosoever shall keep or continue an insolvent Debtor in Prison any longer time than he shall be able to subsist himself, shall find for such Prisoner, Work sufficient to subsist himself, during his Confinement, or shall pay unto such Prisoner, *Six-pence per* Day during the same ; and that if such Creditor shall refuse to pay the same, that then upon Complaint thereof made to any Assistant, or Justice of the Peace, and Conviction thereof, such Assistant or Justice shall grant forth a Warrant of Distress, to distrain so much of such Offenders Estate as shall satisfie and pay the same.

Insolvent Debtors to be allowed Six-pence per Diem by the Creditor.

AN ACT, For the more speedy Tryal of such Negro and Indian Slaves as shall be found Purloining and Stealing, &c.

BE it Enacted by the *General Assembly of this Colony, and by the Authority of the same it is Enacted,* That all Negro and Indian Slaves that shall be found Purloining, Stealing or Thieving, shall be Tryed,

Negroes and Indians to be Tryed for Theft & the Town where the Fact is committed.
An Appeal allowed to the General Court of Tryals, & Gaol Delivery.

ed, Adjudged for the fame, in the Town where fuch Offence fhall be Committed ; And the Affiftants Juftices of the Peace, and Wardens of fuch Town ,for any two of them are hereby fully Impowered to Hear, Try and Adjudge the fame , and upon Conviction hereof, Definitive fentence to give, as fully and effectually by Whipping, Banifhing, &c. as the General Courts of Tryals, and General Goal Delivery, within this His Majefties Colony have been Authorized, Ufed or Accuftomed to do.

Saving always the liberty of an Appeal to the General Court of Tryals, and General Goal Delivery,if the Owner of fuch Slave or Slaves fhall defirethe fame,and give Bond to profecute fuch Appeal as in other Cafes Any Act orActs, Claufe or Claufes of Acts to the contrary hereof in any wife notwithftanding.

AN ACT, Regulating the Recorders and Sheriffs Fees, Cafes that come before the General Affembly.

Be it Enacted by the General Affembly, and by the Authority of the fame, It is Enacted, That the General Recorder and Sheriff of this Colony, fhall have and take the like Fees in all Cafes as come before the General Affembly, as they are allowed to have and take in Caufes brought to the General Court of Tryals.

General

THE TABLE.

THE TABLE.